THE LEGEND OF NAUGHTY

CLEOPATRA,

EGYPT'S LAST
AND MOST GLORIOUS QUEEN,

AS RELATED BY HERSELF AND OTHERS,
CHIEF AMONG THEM ROME'S MARK ANTONY;

WITH DIGRESSIONS
BOTH FRIVOLOUS AND MEANINGFUL

TOM ANDERSSON

CONTENTS

A GENERAL PROLOGUE
OF PROUD NATIONS

What Is Ancient Egypt All About?

Egypt, Egypt, wonderful Egypt! Gift of the Nile, land of the pharaohs and land of the golden light, center of the three-parted world, most astonishing ancient civilization and fulfiller fulfilling that which cannot be fulfilled!

Cats, jackals, crocodiles — represent!

Such pyramids that are typical pyramids, bent pyramids, step pyramids, and mastaba pyramids are at Giza, Saqqara, Abusir, Lisht, Dahshur, Meidum and such temples that are true and real temples are at Karnak, Luxor, Esna, Edfu, Tanis, Kom Ombo.

Such is the wealth and wonder of Egypt that these are only a few of the 11,839 archaeological sites and points of interest those seduced by the study of the beloved realm can visit and explore.

In an illustration now lost to us, a mouse and a hyena look up from their game of *senet* to watch travelers sail past on their carpets high above.

And did you know that the Egyptians have 153 different words for sand?

TOM ANDERSSON

What Is Ancient Rome All About?

The Roman History furnishes more examples of virtue and
magnanimity, or greatness of mind, than any other.
–Lord Chesterfield

They were men enough to face the darkness. [...] Land in a
swamp, march through the woods, and in some inland post
feel the savagery, the utter savagery ...
–Joseph Conrad

Seen fit and chosen by the Fates to bring order into the chaos of the
world, the Roman people have done exactly that. We are famous for
our virtue in arms and war — and rightfully so, having established
a proven track record of most victorious campaigns. Yet we have
also played an indispensable role in moving civilian matters forward. The unrivalled network of roads connecting all our provinces
is just one of our impressive achievements in that area. Three further specific *exempla* shall tell of our manifold commitment to the
betterment of mankind:

I. Roman vintners share their knowledge with farmers in
    Transalpine Gaul and teach them proper wine-making. So many
    fields otherwise left barren or used to lesser ends have now been
    transformed into highly productive vineyards that 20.3% of all
    the wine drunk in Rome is imported from this province.

II. Our mission to protect the country of Bithynia is a multi-chap-
    ter success story in the making. The first chapter — now con-
    cluded — was the removal of their tyrant and king, in no small
    part thanks to Roman guidance and tactical support. Working
    alongside Bithyni volunteers, our officials are currently imple-
    menting appropriate systems and processes so that the nation's
    democracy and election laws equate to SPQR standards. As
    progress has been swift, we are confidently looking forward

to taking on yet more responsibilities in our partnership with these promising people.

III. In addition to numerous other operational commitments, the men stationed at Camp Priapus — also in Asia Minor — are tasked with taking all the steps necessary to ensure the continued survival of a local all-female warrior tribe that would perish without their assistance.

All in all, there are currently no fewer than sixty-five such pan-Mediterranean projects that complement the day-to-day management of the world's affairs. As the actions of many of our friends are not preceded by thought of any kind, we remain steadfast in our resolve to lead them by way of good government. This means providing expert insight on administrative, legal, or military questions; training and coordinating routine procedures; putting in place appropriate safety measures and risk management capabilities; and identifying a province's priority needs. Within this framework, we will continue to proactively engage with challenges and work on issues important to Romans and barbarians alike.

The satisfaction of a job well done!

BOOK ONE

A Confusion of Characters

Soldiers Two

A Roman scout and a Roman infantryman – both on guard duty at an undisclosed location in a remote part of the Empire — are about to speak.

"Shall we?"

"Sure."

"Her beauty is more than that of a mortal woman."

"Who?"

"Cleopatra."

"Goat droppings!"

"My friend, you would lie with her as well!"

"Goat droppings I say to that! Goat droppings!"

"She must number at least an eight — are the grapes too high for you, my friend?"

"No grapes! Goat droppings!" The infantryman spits on the ground. "Not even a four, that evil witch!"

Correction of pop culture visuals: the average Roman soldier is *not* a mouth-watering hunk. Nor, for that matter, is he given to making sardonic quips to imply that he is somehow unmoved by the challenges of his lot. Rather think along the lines of scruffy Eurotrash, yet well-trained and battle-hardened and not — under any circumstance — to be underestimated.

Who Is Cleopatra?

Cleopatra VII Thea Philopator Thea Neotera — Cleo for short — is the last queen of Egypt and one of reality's biggest stars.

Men Are from Rome,
Women Are from Egypt

At Alexandria, the plot proper gets under way as we see Antony and Cleopatra walking through her palace gardens, her retinue — Charmian, Iras, others — following at a respectful distance. Darkest poison green is the color of Cleopatra's dress, a long, pared down, simple affair, with only very little gold woven into it; the bar is set low, but Antony's resplendent uniform falls short in comparison.

"Pray, Lord Antony, unfold to me once more why you love me?"

"How can words do justice to a love like ours, my dear?"

"Don't you love Rome more than me?"

Antony stops and holds the mistress of Egypt by her shoulders, as tenderly as an Antony — Roman, military man, ruler of one third of the world — can hold the woman he loves. "Cleopatra, my summer and winter, have I given you reason to doubt me?"

She does not return the embrace, but stares at him, unblinking.

"Every hour you are with your soldiers and messengers is a love-token for Rome; every communication with the capital, good or ill, is a love-token for Rome; and the big fat love-token *du jour* is that little conspiracy between you and Octavius to get rid of Lepidus."

"Wait a minute! How did you know that?"

"A little bird told me."

Antony collects himself and, trying to humor Cleopatra, asks her what love-token for Cleopatra could make up all his love-tokens for Rome.

She moves on. "Your hand in marriage."

"That's ... complicated. You know that. My position in Rome ... it's like one of these realpolitik things."

"Isn't it always?" And these are her final words, as she abandons Antony on the walkway, between the mermeb and the blue plants.

Who Is Antony?

Mark Antony is a Roman of greatest military distinction and was once thought to be Julius Caesar's obvious successor. He divides his time between Rome and Egypt.

Who Is Octavius?

Gaius Octavius, the future Emperor Augustus, but for now only the fellow triumvir of Antony and Lepidus, is the adopted son of Julius Caesar — as decreed in his will. Conscious of the power of his great-uncle's name as a brand, Gaius Octavius henceforth refers to himself as Caesar. We shall be obstinate and for clarity's sake stay with his original name. Imperator Gaius Octavius Julius Caesar Divi Filius Augustus et cetera et cetera lives and works in the Roman Empire.

And Who Is Lepidus?

Does one even have to ask? Good old Lepidus!

Fulvia

In her general's tent in a forested area about thirty miles from Rome, Fulvia shares her thoughts with her second-in-command Erissa.

"And once I'm done putting this house in order, I'm going to go and get my boy back! And a stern talking-to is the least he can expect!"

The first part of Fulvia's plan seems to be very much on target, as her fight for the control over the Italian Peninsula has been gaining serious momentum and given Octavius a bit of a headache.

The captain of the night watch appears with news. "Mistress, our guards have spotted a small group of enemy soldiers making their way through the forest. We doubt they number more than eight."

"Where?"

"They are following the trail along the lower ridge and have just passed our position. They do not seem to know we are here."

Erissa has a question: "What about other troop movements?"

"None we could detect. And, as you well know, Octavius has had most of his units fall back to the capital."

Erissa is not satisfied. "This doesn't make sense. When Octavius' troops are that far from camp, they usually have backup."

Fulvia has come to her own conclusion. "So they're lost! Easy pickings, I say!"

Erissa urges caution: "Mistress, right now most of our troops are on missions and the few we have here are on guard duty. If we wait until daybreak —"

"They'll be long gone!" Fulvia faces the captain of the night watch again. "Only a small group, right?"

"Yes, mistress."

"Just the usual cowards and weaklings. I'll take care of them myself!"

Still not sure what to make of this irregularity, Erissa asks "What if ... ?" — to no avail, as Fulvia has already grabbed her gear and left.

The result: two dead, four critically wounded, and an open-mouthed Erissa coming up on a Fulvia about to finish her work. But now it is Fulvia's turn to sink to the ground as a loud swishing sound announces the hail of a thousand arrows loosened by one of Octavius' best long-range archery assault teams.

Octavius, having gone over battle reports and thoroughly studied Fulvia's psychological profile, determined that she was a fearsome fighter and a charismatic leader, but not much of a general. The events Octavius engineered to eliminate her were thus first of all a non-event, to deny Fulvia battle so as to make her want to fight even more; secondly, to draw her out in the open by offering her bait in the form of some of his more expendable troops; and thirdly, to crush

Fulvia by overwhelming force from a safe distance. Checkmate in three moves.

Who Was Fulvia?

Fulvia was Antony's lawful wife and a real piece of work.

The Falcon Cannot Hear
the Falconer, Part 1

Coincidence or not? Charmian and Iras, Cleopatra's ladies-in-waiting, spot an acquaintance at the palace bar. Drinks in hand, they make a beeline for his table.

"Say, aren't you the soothsayer?" Without waiting for an answer, they pull up chairs around the man, who is somewhat disoriented by being cornered and bracketed like this.

"I am the first royal seer of Egypt, the one who shares the knowledge of the gods; I am the adept of Ptah, whose seat endures; I am the personal prophet of Cleopatra VII, who lets me speak freely; of the temple of Benent, I am the fourth superior honor in —"

Iras interrupts. "And isn't this the most boring drink, like, ever?"

Charmian disagrees. "Let's not be hasty. It is water with ... other water ... with yet ... other water."

"With just a *hint* of H_2O."

"Maybe a bit shaken, but certainly not stirred."

"And a slice of lemon — what extravagance!"

The soothsayer sighs. "How do I get rid of you?"

"By telling us our fortunes."

"We won't leave before that!"

"What shall we wear for the bilateral reception?"

"Your interest in fashion will wane as more pressing matters come to your attention."

"Hmmm ... so who shall rub up against me tonight?" Now that Charmian has said this, they both seem to lose some of their cattiness as they begin dreaming of new male prey.

It is the soothsayer's turn to cross and queer the others. "Your fate, Charmian, is inextricably bound to our queen's, as is yours, Iras; indeed all our fates are one as what befalls the ruling house and the people of Egypt cannot be divided. We are sick in fortune, be dismayed in this our woeful age. Our lot is not to live, but merely exist, in a world dark unto us. Wild desert beasts will roam our streets and no one will know what to do. Things happened. Things happened, mostly far away and generations ago. Crossroad events that could have gone one way or another. Too many of them have not been in Egypt's favor, leading to a past that leaves us with no future. The elephants failed and now wit, beauty, splendor, learning, even magic are all no defense. The fox can only trick the wolves for a while."

Charmian bursts out laughing. "What was *that*?"

Iras knows. "I have always suspected you of being a bit of a nut, Soothsayer, but disaster porn? Shame on you, old man!"

Just so You Know

The Romanization of Egyptian names personal and Egyptian names geographical follows the McClusky-Droppeldörfer system.

The Falcon Cannot Hear the Falconer, Part 2

"E-no-bar-bus!" Antony's ADC, en route between meetings, is their next victim. He's already kicking himself for not having seen them coming.

"Girls, I'm kind of busy."

"You Romans are *always* kind of busy."

"Guess what the soothsayer told us!"

From experience, Enobarbus knows that there is only one way to deal with Cleopatra's companions, which is most certainly not to indulge them in their moods. "What kind of naifs are you that you even listen to such a charlatan? Reality is neither a fairy tale nor a Newtonian clockwork universe. The uncertainty principle rules and any belief in the validity of divination is due to dumb luck or, more likely, confirmation bias. That you, grown-ups, fall for a basic fallacy like this is the height of immaturity. Your character, or lack thereof, determines your future. And now you will *definitely* have to excuse me." Having sufficiently deflated their enthusiasm, he makes an exit right, leaving Iras and Charmian to their own devices.

"Grum-py!"

"What is it with men these days?"

Iras has to concur. "They're just not what they used to be."

Charmian now tries to look forward, not backward. "Those new Roman guys better be hot."

Pride and Prejudice

"China sucks! India sucks! Egypt sucks! Europe is numero fucking uno!" Did Johann Wolfgang von Goethe, the German literary genius, really say that? Of course not! He said: "Chinese, Indian, Egyptian antiquities are always mere curiosities; it is very well done to acquaint yourself and the world with them; as far as moral and aesthetic education are concerned, however, they are of little use to us."

In all fairness, though, it must be remarked that the study of ancient Egypt is one of the world's *youngest* sciences. Extenuating circumstances and stuff.

Well, What Worst?

Enobarbus finally finds Antony in the Nekhbet Lounge. Antony — loose, tipsy, uncrushed — waves him over with a smile. "Enobarbus! Where have you been?"

"In the Sekhmet Lounge, in the solitary company of my briefcase, going over various papers, waiting for your arrival."

"The Sekhmet Lounge ... hmm, must have been some kind of mix-up. But sit!"

"I see you have already made yourself quite comfortable," comments Enobarbus, referring to the troupe of female acrobats and jugglers entertaining Antony.

"Yeah, it's a nice show."

"Maybe also because they are in the nude?"

"That's totally a possibility."

"My lord, I'm afraid we have some business to discuss."

"Mm-hm."

"Confidential business. *State* business."

"Right, right." With a sigh, Antony dismisses the artists. He takes another sip from his drink and turns to face Enobarbus. "So, what's up?"

"Sir, I am very sorry to tell you that I have nothing but bad news for you."

"Can't be *that* bad. I mean, Egypt has been *fun*."

"I'm not so sure if our sojourn here will have been worth it in the end."

"Now, now, Enobarbus, life should not be about waiting for the other shoe to drop."

"If you say so, sir."

"Do you want to try one of these fabulous cocktails? All I have to do is to pull this rope ... thingy ... contraption, that's the word ... and they'll have it over ASAP."

"I'm fine, sir. Thank you, sir."

"So, what do you have to tell me?"

"The Parthian Empire —"

"Oh, those guys!"

"The Parthian Empire has taken control of Syria, Lydia, and much of Ionia. General Labienus, the leader of their campaign, has also been making inroads in further provinces and derailed several non-combatant evacuation operations, capturing or killing Roman troops in the process. There is also refugee movement on such a scale that we have had to establish and provision five large reception centres in the region; I should note that they may run out of essentials sooner rather than later. In short, we are dealing with massive insecurity along our eastern borders."

"Okay ... that's not good." Antony has now lost some of his joviality.

Enobarbus moves on to the next point. "Italy is also in turmoil."

"There's more?!"

"For quite some time, there has been unrest because of land-ownership issues. Local populations have not been willing to yield areas pledged to veterans from our war against Brutus and Cassius."

Antony remembers. "Ah yes, we kind of promised them that. Go on."

"Hoping to topple Octavius, whose position had been weakened due to the internal disorder of which I spoke, your wife started and led an insurrection in your name. However, her movement, which had initially been able to score some significant victories, soon fell apart after Octavius managed to eliminate her."

"Imagine that! The bitch is dead!" Fulvia has recently been rather much to take. Antony pulls the rope in order to celebrate.

"My condolences, sir."

"It's, like, a good thing that she's gone, isn't it?"

"If you had supported Fulvia in her endeavor and joined her in battle, you might very well be master of the world, sir."

Antony's mood has turned sour again. "And now, what am I?"

"The object of a concerted propaganda effort by Octavius and his associates."

"Well, haters gonna hate."

"Sir, I consider it my duty to tell you in no uncertain terms that this is no idle slander, but a calculated play to erode your power base at home. Both your marriage to Fulvia and your ... *relation* to Cleopatra have given them convenient cause to paint you in a less than flattering light." Enobarbus gives Antony some newspaper clippings from the capital's papers. Antony's mood takes another hit as he studies the highlighted sections: "The choice of Fulvia as mate was nothing but repressed homosexuality. She was man to man, man to woman, and man to Antony." "Mark Antony is living the high life in Alexandria while Roman soldiers are dying in combat." "ANTONY SLUT'S TOY BOY AT 52!"

Enobarbus resents having to mention the most stinging critique, but hopes this might anger Antony enough to drive him to action. "They are also reprinting Cicero's *Philippics*."

"Enobarbus, I think you have done enough for today." Antony's voice has become toneless. "You're dismissed."

As Enobarbus takes his leave, the cocktails arrive. Antony just looks at them. He has some thinking to do.

What Is Parthia?

Parthia is the male "Other" as opposed to the female "Other" that is Egypt.

Decisions, Decisions

Her is non hoom, her nis but wildernesse:
Forth, pilgrim, forth! Forth, beste, out of thy stal!
–Geoffrey Chaucer, "Balade de Bon Conseyl"

Antony strides into the spa — boy, this palace has everything! — to tell Cleopatra why he has to leave for Rome. He is wearing a uniform that ... — but who cares what he is wearing as Cleopatra comes into view, partially obscured by the ladies applying perfumed ointments to her, dressing her hair, kneading her back, beautifying her hands, beautifying her feet, taking care of *all* of her.

"My dear queen!"

"Hmmm?"

"I have come to let you know what I purpose."

"Hmmm? 'Purpose'? Is that you, Antony?"

"I have to attend to business in Rome, as —"

"Really? No pampering at the spa for you? Some side-by-side relaxation?"

"There are some issues I have to sort out. As much as I'd like to stay, —"

"You're leaving?"

Antony's resolve is not quite what he thought it would be. He tries not to show it and presses on. "As I said, in spite of our very pleasant time here together, I have to —"

"You don't have to do anything. You're Antony."

"Well, if you put it like that. Still, I —"

"You've been here for barely a year."

"Yes, but there's some really serious stuff in Parthia and Rome going down, so —"

"You haven't come to rub my feet? As you like to do?"

"I'm sorry. I have to take care of a lot of other things back home."

"Isn't this home to you? Am *I* not 'home' to you?" Careful, Antony!

"Of course, in a manner of speaking ..." Oh, no.

"In a manner of speaking?!" Cleopatra is no longer dreamy. Cleopatra is angry. She sits up, only making it worse. Antony is used to verbal sparring and also enjoys looking at women's breasts, but combining the two is a skill he has yet to master. But no matter, as he has already lost.

"Tell me, my dear Antony, who trusted the bat? The birds or the beasts?"

"What?"

"The bat first sided with the birds ... then with the beasts ... then with the birds ... then with the beasts ... until neither sided with the bat."

"What's that got to do with anything?"

"Leave if you think you have to, Antony. *Enjoy* your time in Rome."

A Question for Pundits

Is the triumvirate still a win-win-win idea?

Bad Tattoo Bad

Cleopatra lets go of one of her female attendants when she discovers that the girl has gotten a tattoo. "How utterly tacky and hopelessly lower middle class of you."

"But I am of one of my nome's most prestigious families and of noble lineage."

"Not in my book you are, anymore. And how, in the name of the gods, could I be expected to govern all that is Egypt if I had to keep lecturing my inner circle on basic points of style? Now scram."

A Lesson for Lepidus

An austere luxury of marble — Octavius' office in Rome, that is. Another meeting of the triumvirs. Present and accounted for: Octavius, accompanied — as always — by his most trusted lieutenant Agrippa, and Lepidus.

Octavius acts distraught. "Oh Antony, where are you?"

"He is at present in Egypt, at Queen Cleopatra's court," Lepidus offers helpfully.

"As if we didn't know. But what does he do there besides Cleopatra?"

"Good Octavius, I have a letter from Enobarbus from which I shall read to you: 'Most worthy Lepidus, you have my personal assurance that Antony and his staff are fully engaged with governmental issues and also follow all Parthian matters very closely.'"

Octavius snorts in derision. "'Antony and his staff' ... — Agrippa, tell him."

"Enobarbus is indeed a man of work and merit and a capable officer. However, his loyalty to Antony leads him to cover up his master's faults."

"Such as?" asks Lepidus.

"Such as his prolonged negligence of duties. In Alexandria, Antony fraternizes with lower ranks, sots away his evenings, loses himself all-too-often in the warm embraces of the female, and generally turns nights into days."

"Methinks, good Agrippa, that you lay charges that are just in themselves, but too heavy for an Antony. Granted, his love for his fellow men is not measured; even so, it is too much of a virtue, not a vice. And —"

"And his debauchery is an excess of virtue as well?" interjects Agrippa.

"Simply an excess — which he makes up for by letting Roman scholars study Egypt for possible profit; who knows what useful lessons we could learn from that ancient culture?"

It is time for Octavius to take back the reins and school the man. "Lepidus, Lepidus, Lepidus. Egypt is ancient indeed, but what is its success? In all those millennia that civilization, as some people call it, has failed to build an empire of note or otherwise impress the world; instead, the Egyptians have nothing to show for their efforts but a few oversized piles of rock scattered throughout their desert — is that time well spent? I would think not. And as for their religion — what kind of people is so lacking that they have to elevate their animals into gods? Take my word, Lepidus, that research project is yet another case of Antony's wasting resources that could have been put to better use."

"But —"

"No buts. Considering the timeframe given to them to excel, they have failed miserably, as has Antony. It is their luck that Rome is taking such an active interest in their progress and well-being."

"Maybe I shouldn't have said anything."

"Very true. Remember that before speaking so recklessly on Antony's behalf, here or in public. Now, Lepidus, when one triumvir forgets what it means to be a Roman, the others must remember it all the more."

"Of course, of course."

"Can we rely on you to remember what it means to be a Roman?"

"You can, good Octavius."

"That's all we needed to hear."

Seneca Was a Roman

"Vivere militare est." That's what he said. Seneca, that is. "Life is military service." Seneca. Totally Roman dude.

Military or "Hierarchy" Individuals

What we need for the role of Agrippa is an actor who specializes in playing military or "hierarchy" individuals.

What Do They All Look Like?

You have seen the statues.

Bathing

In Alexandria, dusk is turning into night as Cleopatra disrobes and sheds her luxurious garments and slides into her bath of milk she has had prepared — not a bath of milk only, mind you; a bath of milk and a few other select ingredients the true identities of which are frankly none of your concern. A treatise on the exquisite sensual pleasures a female pharaoh can experience while bathing — on her own — is withheld for the very same reason. But Cleopatra is feeling less sensual than pensive, bittersweet, melancholic, tired, restless, unsatisfied. And not just because of the absence of Antony and his leathery hmmm-sigh-yummy-hmmm.

She needs her space. Strong protests from the court were over-ruled, and everybody, even Iras and Charmian, was dismissed until morning, the bringer of the sponge the last to be expelled from her immediate field.

Cleopatra *does* need to reintegrate as her evening is not the charmed "tale of a tub" one might imagine, notwithstanding sur-roundings to soften — and then soften some more — the heart of the most jaded and cynical bitch anywhere; rather, it is a "fragmentary" that consists of observations of a few meagre rain clouds up above, thoughts of court and state matters that Cleopatra is not quite able to banish, an awareness of the slowly cooling liquid enfolding her, and memories of how Cleopatra's younger sister Arsinoe was simply too stubborn to know her place — all thankfully interspersed with moments of dozing and just-comfortably-being. Happiness is such a delicate proposition.

"The Former Age": A Poem by Geoffrey Chaucer, Put into Our English

A blissful life, peaceable and sweet,
led the people in the former age.
They were content with the fruits they had,
the fruits that the fields gave them by and by;
they were not of a sick appetite.
Strange to them was the mill, and the grindstone, too;
in the forests they were nursed by the trees,
with acorns and nuts dropped when the time was right,
and they drank cold water from the wells.

Yet was the ground not wounded with the plough,
but corn up-sprung, unsown of man's hand,

the which they ate as if enough was too much.
No man yet knew the furrows of his land,
no man yet knew the fire of the flint,
secret still was the malefaction of the vine;
no man yet in a mortar spices ground
to sauce up his daily bread.

What should it have availed to war?
There lay no profit, there were no riches,
there were no coins either true or false;
But cursed was the time, I dare well say,
that men first did their sweaty business,
to dig up metal, lurking in the dark,
and to seek out gems in the rivers.
Alas, then came about all the hunger
that brought us to our present state.

Palace-chambers? Mansions? Forts?
Towers, round or square?
This blissed folk slept in woods soft and sweet
on grass and leaves in perfect tranquility.
No down of feathers was theirs,
but they dreamed their dreams in peace.
Their hearts were all one, free of spite,
one and all for all and one.

Lepidus Takes Off — A Letter

Goodest Octavius,

I am terribly, terribly sorry I cannot come to our upcoming meeting or any further meeting for the foreseeable future. I am suffering from the most troublesome tummy ache and am in consequence much indisposed. My personal physician Gaetanos has assured me and I assure you also, good Octavius, that the culprit could not have been the amphorae of Falernian wines that you put into my hands so generously and kindly and which I have very much enjoyed and for which I thank you once more, good & noble Octavius, but quite likely those Egyptian strawberries Antony had sent me from Egypt and which might have been improperly packed or shipped, one or the other or both.

In addition, my personal physician Gaetanos who is renowned also in Greece and as many say ranks with the first of his profession ordered rather than recommended that I take medical leave effective immediately and to take up residence once more in the province of Africa Nova where as you remember I served our country in the capacity of governor of the province. On the good authority of my personal physician Gaetanos my tummy ache and a few other minor but persistent and in their own way quite aggravating ailments I have also had the misfortune to have been laboring under should abate to the point of full recovery or at least lessen in degree in the Numidian climate that had proved to be a tonic to various conditions of mine during my first stay in that locale.

I must dreadfully apologize for having to make myself scarce like this, so suddenly and without even being able to bid adieu in person. It has been an honor to work alongside you, good Octavius, and under your tutelage; I shall always most fondly remember your reasonings upon statecraft, especially upon the role of normative contexts, instructive and perceptive without fail. But in my work as a triumvir I have also had the privilege to learn that the greatness of our task cannot bear the luxury of undue ambiguity and as I am — alas! — uncertain of again being able to attend to my duties in the manner demanded by this lofty position, I ask you for your understanding and to please accept my resignation from the triumvirate.

Toodeloo!

Lepidus

Roman Genesis

In the beginning was the she-wolf and the she-wolf gave suck to Romulus and Remus. And Romulus got the stronger and Remus had to give way. And Romulus learned that the wolf's milk was good and that Romulus was good also. And Romulus gathered unto himself men of his understanding. And they went unto the Sabines and united with them and caused their women to be with child and that felt good indeed. And the women bore fruit and their crop were the first of Rome and that was more than good. For it is they who built the baths, the barracks, the streets, the bridges, the temples, the theaters, the markets, the hills, the gardens, and — excelsissimus excelsissimorum! — the *Senate*.

And the Senate saw that Rome was good, but that the rest of the earth was without form, dwelling in darkness: undeveloped prestate societies, barbaric chiefdoms, failed states — peoples of false gods and beastly living, without reason or justice. And Rome felt compelled to dispel the darkness that was upon the lands and to assume the reins of government far and wide. And the sons of Rome put themselves into cohorts and legions and decided to go forth and bring order to the world, from Pannonia to the dunes of Mauretania, from Perea to the shores of the Oceanus Hibernicus, from Cyrene to the island of Taurica. And it was so. And that was good.

And in all its domains, Rome bestowed rules; and to rules, added mercy; and to mercy, brotherly kindness; and to brotherly kindness, wisdom; and to wisdom, temperance; and to temperance, patience; and to patience, diligence; and to diligence, discipline. And the children of Rome, given such riches and blessings, never suffered misfortune again for the rest of their days.

Octavius and Agrippa
Discuss Lepidus

It is Agrippa, out of all people, who has a compliment for the runaway. "Say what you will about Lepidus, he is a smart kind of stupid." "He chose an appropriate course of action. His house and estate?" "Secured." "Good."

Who Is Agrippa, Really?

Marcus Vipsanius Agrippa is a thinker, doer, warrior, supporter, strategist, and a man of great quality and judgment. He is a reality-savvy Octavius insider known for his "hard" approach both to physical existence and to the fantasies of others. His method is not to see problems as problems, but to put forward workable solutions and to make short work of longstanding challenges. Although Agrippa's focus is on the Roman Empire, he is also interested in various design disciplines and has taught at the art department of the Sora Military Academy. Some of his recent projects include uniforms for the Navy X/X "black" 35 BC collection, a new logo for Novum Castrum security, and several wall-sized mosaics commissioned by Maecenas. Agrippa has held forth at Pyrgi and SPQ&A as well as at other prestigious institutions and events. At the time of writing, he serves as Senior Strategic Advisor to Octavius and as Chairman of the Board of Directors of the Mare Nostrum Group.

Hmmm

Rumor has it that Octavius met Agrippa in a men-only pottery class — or was it a Roman military history retreat after all?

BOOK TWO

Estranged

A Frank Exchange of Views

In order to discuss a number of issues that have accumulated during a certain triumvir's dallying in the east, Antony and Octavius are to meet at a country retreat once owned by Lepidus. Conveniently located in a place the exact geocoordinates of which are not available for reasons of imperial security, the primary mansion and the buildings adjacent to it form a structure typical of a luxe Roman-style settlement of the time. The stark interiors are in contrast to the lush gardens outside; the only artworks in evidence are some Greek vases and terracotta objects — few in number, but so expensive as to be close to invaluable.

"Hey Octavius, how's it going?" — Antony, of course.

"Antony. We have much to discuss."

"Well, let's get to it then."

Antony and Octavius sit down at the conference table — tumblers, jugs of water, tablets and styluses, and little bowls of nuts are the predictable materials — and Agrippa and his counterpart Enobarbus follow suit.

Antony has decided not to complain about the unsatisfactory feast and instead concentrates on the business at hand. "So, what's up?"

"I have not a few grievances."

"Well, that's too bad. But understandable. I don't know what is worse, the dumb pigheaded farmers who don't want to support our troops here or those Parthians skulking about in the east."

"You are."

"Me?!"

Octavius would not be Octavius if he didn't know to delegate the bulk of his argument to his subordinate. "Agrippa?"

"While Octavius certainly appreciates Antony's now meeting him in such free and friendly conference, Antony's past misdeeds need to be addressed. Acting on behalf of Antony and in gross violation of previous accords, his late wife Fulvia, along with his brother

Lucius, not only stirred up Roman citizens against the rightful rule of Octavius as triumvir, but also led armed units against him in the name of their kinsman. Moreover, Antony himself has repeatedly failed to honor the terms of the second triumvirate and Octavius as his comrade: no public stance in support of Octavius and against the insurgents was taken, emissaries sent to the court of Alexandria were ignored or rebuffed in the curtest manner thinkable, and the provision of reserve troops and military materials as well as the shipment of grain and other foodstuff as laid out and agreed upon in Articles 14, 15, 16, and 17 subsections a, b, and d have not been forthcoming or only in a haphazard and fitful manner, even upon express request. Shall I go on?"

Since Antony fails to reply and seems to be lost in thought, Enobarbus responds in his place.

"Speaking for Antony, I most forcefully disavow any culpability concerning recent events in the homeland. It is not upon Antony to enforce compliance with the aforementioned treaty or other Roman laws in the case of an unruly private citizen such as Fulvia if said citizen resides in another triumvir's domain; in addition, to become party to the conflict in such a manner would have conveyed a lack of trust in Octavius' ability to keep his own house in order. And, as we all know, Fulvia and Lucius were acting on their own initiative; Antony's having been the word of war is anything but conclusive evidence of any endorsement or other type of involvement on his part. As for the issue of the supposed mistreatment of Octavian messengers, I can only restate what I have communicated to your office, in more than one memorandum. When in Egypt, we have to — up to a point — do as the Egyptians do and follow the local court protocol; it should really come as no surprise that failure to do so leads to swift ejection from the royal grounds. Finally, it is simply not feasible to maintain our ongoing commitment to Egypt without certain infractions; strictly adhering to SPQR rules and arrangements would lead to massive upheaval, if not catastrophe. There are several reasons why troop contingents could not be met: first of all, considering the extent of the eastern part of the Empire and the manpower needed to control it, there are not that many legions to begin with; secondly and more specifically with our presence in

Egypt in mind, it would be unwise to squander the hard-won expertise of our desert regiments by uprooting them to milder climates; and most recently, Antony had to make a command decision to send troops to the Syrian theater to help stave off the worst of the attacks by the Parthians — would you rather have them whistling to the air in Etruria or Spain?"

Although the question was meant rhetorically and Agrippa knows so, he feels bound to defend himself. "There is much work to be done in the west!"

"Which is why, undoubtedly, troop rotation out of Gaul has proven to be so problematic. But let me refute the last of your accusations."

"Enobarbus, it's okay." He has been interrupted again, but this time by Antony.

"Sir?"

"It's okay. I screwed up. I screwed up and I'm sorry."

Now nobody is interrupting anybody, but everybody is trying to make sense of Antony's sudden confession.

At last, Octavius finds the words to express his astonishment: "Well, I'll say … What do we do now?"

Digging Egypt

At the edge of our terrain we find Stavros, once more going over the notes he took during the morning shift. Just as young as the rest of the team, he is nonetheless thoroughness-dedication-virtue of Thoth personified.

No one has ever looked more beautiful playing in the dirt than our beloved Francesca, a blonde research assistant we had somehow managed to wrangle from the Lower Egypt division of the Egyptian Museum (yes, *the* Egyptian Museum in Cairo), Hathor be thanked a thousand thanks.

Mary-Ellen, our girl next door (B.A. and M.A. from Northwestern, Ph.D.-in-progress from UPenn), strikes a pose as she once more renews and protects our field of joy like Nekhbet and Wadjet shelter the Two Lands and the Lady of the Two Lands.

Archaeology-as-therapy and archaeology-as-service-in-the-temple are practiced by Léna, Martine, and Bernard as they are with the Great Goddess Isis and the Great Goddess Isis is with them.

We have also been joined by Jürgen and Ulrike, a husband-and-wife team of civil engineers, as nothing invokes serendipity and Bes like an interdisciplinary approach.

Conflict Resolution by Means of the Fairer Sex

We, the triumvirs, in the spirit of intra-Roman reconciliation, reaffirm our bond and brotherhood, and agree to the following package of measures:

I. Octavius is to give his sister Octavia to Antony to marry.

II. Octavia is to bear Antony several children, at least one of which a boy, within the quadrennium.

III. In addition to and conjunction with the administration of the eastern provinces, Antony officially assumes direct responsibility for the Egyptian account.

IV. While Lepidus is on sick leave, his personal assets and effects are supervised by Agrippa.

V. While Lepidus is on sick leave, the administration of his territory devolves to the Senate.

VI. The triumvirs will endeavor to regard all grievances hitherto incurred between them as null.

All these agreements shall be binding and supplementary to our prior accords.

Done at Rome, on the Anniversary of the Republic

Signed: [signatures of Antony, Octavius]

Witnessed: [signatures of Enobarbus, Agrippa]

What Kind of Woman Is Octavia?

You'll find out soon enough.

Prospect of Restored Stability As the *Puer Aeternus* Finally Grows Up

The *Roman Gazette* has learned that the verily august triumvir Octavius has been successful in bringing the loose cannon by the name of Antony back into the fold of Roman partnership and respectability. Speaking on condition of anonymity, high-ranking government officials, while also giving partial credit to Agrippa for seeing through this masterstroke of rapprochement, openly question the veracity of Antony's version of events in which, as hard to believe as the tales of his own bravado he has been prone to put in circulation, it was Antony who had extended the olive branch.

In either case, the end result is the same. On an exquisitely landscaped country estate in Brundisium, in a remarkably short amount of time, Rome's foremost men managed to create what future generations may come to call a Pax Augusta. Sources in attendance tell that though they would hesitate to describe Lepidus as anything other than erratic, dubious in his sartorial choices, and an imbecile, he was unusually alert and a host as gracious as his faults permitted.

The technical minutiae of this new consensus are secondary; what is of primary importance is Antony's oath to pivot from Cleopatra to Octaviana, Octavius' only daughter. Says Ra-Ptahhotep II, an Egypt-born foreign affairs specialist with the East Roman Politics and Society Assembly and the spokesman for the Romans for a Free Egypt: "Much as I have hitherto deplored Rome's lack of a robust response to the totalitarian ills that plague my country of origin, much as I rue that the head of state of one of Rome's most vital trading partners is the product of numerous generations of royal inbreeding who has been known to fondle herself in public, much as I am hard put to empathize with an aging Antony whose unkempt mane and often unfortunate facial expressions only serve to emphasize his anarchistic actions, as an African-Roman and a concerned observer of the region I am gladdened that the triumvir of the east has at last matured sufficiently to do the right thing for himself, for Egypt, and the world at large."

Perhaps Cleopatra will now learn that Egyptian exceptionalism has an expiry date, perhaps Cleopatra will now learn that there is such a thing as a deliberative political process, perhaps Cleopatra will now learn that she has to lean in and commit to the real work of fostering human rights and democracy. No more of our men demeaning themselves as canines at her feet. Welcome to the new world of Roman foreign policy of the late 1st century BC.

What's So Funny?

A few weeks later, in a funny little turret of the regent's palace in the Parthian capital of Parthianopolis, the very same *Roman Gazette* article is read out loud at the breakfast table by a funny-looking chap to two other funny-looking chaps, dressed all funny in their slippers and turbans and other funny gear like funny little ceremonial daggers. As the reading goes on, the listeners start giggling, making funny faces, generally getting worse and worse in spite of trying not to give way, and, when the text nears its conclusion, one of the funny-looking chaps — plotch! — collapses on the cushy floor, right away — plotch! — followed by the second of the funny-looking chaps, tears running down their chubby little cheeks.

The Engagement Party

Antony has been reminded that if he wants Octavia to produce his offspring, he might want to get around to finally meeting her. Moreover, Antony has similarly been reminded that he agreed to marry the lady and to dawdle any further would not only be interpreted as offensive, but also as a breach of contract, which in turn would result in very serious consequences and unpleasantness for him. With a sigh, Antony agrees to an engagement party organized by Enobarbus (invitations) and Agrippa (event concept and event logistics).

Torches, palm trees, Rome's top chefs, and, from the far reaches of the Empire and beyond, even enough exotic animals to start a small zoo — Agrippa has once more outdone himself. In spite of the generous layout of the venue, any narrow path to hors d'oeuvres that need to be tried or old friends who ought to be met is a narrow path indeed as the place is *packed* with Rome's upper crust and miscellaneous characters whose lack of standing is compensated by their entertainment value.

Although Enobarbus did his best, Antony is rather late to the party, but overjoyed to make the acquaintance of the charming Octaviana as soon as he has joined the social whirl. They just seem to click — at least the slightly inebriated Antony thinks so — which leads him to comment that she and he will have "the best honeymoon *ever.*" — "Wouldn't *that* be wild?!" Octaviana rejoins before she disappears in the crowd.

Exhilarated, Antony turns to Enobarbus. "What a firecracker! And that dress!"

"Isn't she a bit young?"

"Looks fertile to me. Besides, a deal is a deal."

"My lord, the person you have just spoken to is not Octavia, but Octaviana, her half-sister twelve years her junior."

"Can't we, like, do a switch?"

"No, sir, that would be most unwise. Your contract is binding. Beyond that, Octavius has given you the sister he esteems the most. Any attempt to do as you suggest would provoke outrage and scandal."

"Okay then, show me that Octavia."

"You can see her on the other side of the vestibulum, reclining on the dining couch next to Octavius."

"Her?! She looks like Octavius with tits!"

"Of the people who have had the privilege of viewing both her and Cleopatra, it is the general consensus that the beauty of the former outshines that of the latter."

"With that nose?!"

"Somewhat aquiline, granted, but may I propose we dispense with the nitpicking and make our introductions? Octavius beckons."

"Of course he does."

They approach the siblings.

"Antony, Enobarbus — may I present my sister Octavia?"

"Hi, Octavia."

"Madam."

She not too impolitely dismisses Enobarbus with a nod. "So, Antony ..." — "Yes ..." — "You are the buffoon that got my brother to kill Cicero, Rome's leading senator and the author of some of the most astute books on rhetoric and statecraft ever written. I have to say that I am quite displeased that you stopped him from completing his works."

Octavius hastens to correct his sister. "Let us not be rash in our accusations. Cicero died in a single-chariot *accident*. There was no evidence of foul play."

"Save it, brother. Antony, what do you have to say in your defense?"

"That there was no evidence of foul play?"

"A buffoon *and* a coward. A nice match you made for me, brother."

Offended, Antony is now too angry to keep up the charade any longer. "What Cicero wrote about me in the *Philippics* was way out of ... was way ... was just wrong! He *deserved* to have his cakehole shut! And don't you dare tell me that you wouldn't have done the same in my place!"

"Ye gods, I might end up having a measure of respect for you after all, husband. Now that you are in a manly mood, shall we move on to the mating part of this exercise?" She moves into close bodily contact.

"Here?!"

Octavius elaborates: "Your bridal bed is in one of the chambers above the kitchen. Octavia knows the way."

"Isn't that a bit sudden? I mean, this is just the engagement party."

"My dear husband, you have already stalled for several weeks. And since you are now getting hard, why not make the most of it?"

Once relocated and properly interlocked, Antony feels like he has just begun to enjoy himself when Octavia pushes him off. "That should do. I'll send for you if it doesn't take."

Worse than Fulvia. Just what he needed.

Checklist — How to Tell if Your Wife Is a Libyan

I. She jokes about being Libyan.

II. She has Libyan friends.

III. She spends more time with her Libyan friends than with you.

IV. She talks about going to Libya.

V. She likes to do it Libyan-style.

TOM ANDERSSON

My Other Life

O Eneas! What wil ye do?

–Geoffrey Chaucer, "The House of Fame"

Wrecked and shipwrecked, Aeneas had washed up on the African shores of Carthage. Nursed back to health by Dido, the Queen of Carthage, the military-aged male developed tender feelings for his savioress, tender feelings that were more than repaid as he became her life, her love, her lust, her lord.

Pleasure followed pleasure as day followed day as they played hide-and-seek in the palace's courtyards and passageways with the very youngest of the court, toasted each other and the sunset next to the pool at the rooftop bar, a half-finished backgammon game set to the side, were invited to and spontaneously joined an al fresco brunch they had chanced upon on one of their morning walks, explored and re-explored trendy boutiques in trendy neighbor— "Stop! You, Aeneas, are frittering away your hours! You, Aeneas, are ignoring your calling for the sake of a female! You, Aeneas, are to do your duty!"

And so, in the dead of night, he stole away from the woman he had supposedly loved, boarded his ship, and set sail for Italy. When Dido learned of this great trespass and betrayal, she cursed Aeneas and his people with the eternal enmity of her tribe and slew herself by her own hand.

Still out at sea, but making good time on his journey, Aeneas did have the thought occur to him that to ditch his soulmate for his job — which, granted, was of some importance, as it was to found and father the first dynasty of Rome — had been a dick move indeed. Although he did not turn back, this was a regret that would not be without consequence much later on.

Enobarbus Warns Antony

To Egypt or not to Egypt, that is the question.

–Per-Sekemkheperre

Enobarbus, seeking conference with Antony, finds him in his private chambers. In bed, in fact. Antony is not pleased with the intrusion. "Can't you let me sleep?"

"My lord, it is past noon."

Antony groans. "Then tell me whatever you have to tell me and be gone."

"Sir, may I ask where you were last evening? Your chambers were deserted, even at midnight."

"Looking for my little Octaviana. Everywhere. Couldn't find her."

"Lord Octavius took the precaution of putting her under house arrest in a location he will not divulge. Possibly on one of his private offshore estates."

Antony groans again. "Just let me go back to sleep."

"Sir, she knows."

"Who? Octavia?"

"Cleopatra."

"She does?"

"Yes."

"So what?"

"Lady Cleopatra has written you a letter stating that she has taken no offense, that you are most welcome to return, that her affection for you is unchanged."

"Hm, really? That doesn't sound like Cleopatra."

"Sir, she is trying to lure you back."

"Might be fun to spend some time with her, just for old times' sake."

"Not in the long run, sir. Do you remember why you left that paradise of hers in the first place?"

"My obligations as a triumvir. There were some fires I had to put out."

"Yet there had been other fires before that you had been all too happy to ignore. I dare say that you got bored in Egypt."

"It's nice to just chill for a few days."

"But for months or years, even? And have not some of your most recent actions made clear that Cleopatra didn't quite offer you enough variety?"

What might Enobarbus be referring to? Ehhh, ah, yes. It just could be, among other things, that total cock-tease of a farmer's daughter near Heraklion, Crete, whose ass Antony felt he had to grab most forcefully. Well worth the box on the ears and the ruckus caused by her fellow villagers and a fond memory for Antony overall. "Well, a man's gotta do what a man's gotta do."

"Which is exactly what I came here to discuss. But maybe over a nice breakfast?" To put his master in a more receptive mood, Enobarbus has had the foresight of asking the domestics to prepare a sumptuous little treat. One by one, servants laden with culinary goods fill Antony's room with everything that makes for a good start into a new day: bakery baskets of croissants and other flavorful breads, scrambled eggs with parsley and peppers, assorted pastries, a selection of cheeses with respectable quantities of Roquefort and Camembert, cereals, pre-sliced fresh fruits, honey, pancakes, low fat yoghurt, bacon, sausages and other meats, as well as a few hard-boiled eggs; to drink there is the usual choice of teas, coffees, juices, milks, and spirits.

"Enobarbus, not that I'm not happy, but why do I get the feeling that you're buttering me up?"

"There is no reason not to mix business and pleasure as long as one knows the place of each, sir."

Antony considers Enobarbus' point for a moment, his first half-munched croissant in hand. "Hm, can't argue with that."

"I fear that your exaggerated love for the foreign and all things new to you may prove your undoing, my lord."

"How so?"

"Rome is your city and country; this is your place, whereas you will always be a stranger in Egypt. No society truly accepts an outsider; they may be flattered that they were seen as paradise and chosen as refuge; they may even return the flattery and compose songs and erect statues in his honor; yet in the end, he will have been nothing but a diversion, a fool too stupid to know his own tribe."

"Isn't that a bit harsh?"

Enobarbus knows to apply also the carrot. "In Rome, you are loved by the people, by the soldiers, by many a senator. In Rome, you have a refined and beautiful wife, of honorable deportment —"

"Ha!" interjects Antony. "You weren't there when we were fucking."

Enobarbus waits for Antony to explain further, but as Antony seems content to honey his pancakes, he feels obliged to press on: "Did she ask you to feed on ill ground?"

"If only! Push me off is what she did."

"I heard that she had appeared rather eager to be inseminated."

"That and only that! We had barely finished the first round when she sent me packing!"

"Hm ... this is of course regrettable, but —"

"And I now totally see why Caius Marcellus didn't last two winters with that harpy. I'm telling you, I'd rather cross the river Styx than share home and hearth with such a woman."

"Let us not forget that, notwithstanding his laudable achievements, Caius Marcellus was certainly not your equal."

"You're right about that."

"And let us also not forget that your union with Octavia is mainly for politics and procreation. As long as you use discretion and do not flaunt your conquests in the amorous arena, there is no reason not to pursue your pleasure in the loose and free manner to which you are accustomed."

"But to live under the same roof as Octavia? That's going to seriously crimp my style."

"Octavia is fiercely independent and insists on having her own residence. That was already so in her marriage to Caius Marcellus."

"Hm, that could work ... You know, Enobarbus, things just make so much more sense when you're around. Why is that?"

"I couldn't possibly say, my lord."

"But to be honest, I still kind of feel that I'm missing out on something when I'm not together with my dear Cleopatra."

"Young Octaviana has already shown you that it is possible to be enchanted in Rome as well — and why not have your own Egypt in Rome? I am confident that your name and purse can procure from thence whatever your heart desires — be that the best food, the sweetest music, or the most charming companions."

"Slave girls! Why didn't I think of that! And what was that other smart thing you said, about Egypt and Rome?"

"That you can have your own Egypt in Rome. No need for a long and tiresome sea voyage."

"My 'own Egypt in Rome.' Brilliant — Enobarbus, you're a gem!"

"Thank you, sir."

Antony has decided to stay put and bloom where he's planted. Thank the gods for his reasonable Enobarbus.

Why Our Romans Are More Roman than the Roman Romans

Tests for color pigments on Roman statues and sculptures have come back positive again and again. And the aesthetics were such that the original busts of Cicero, Cato & Co. wouldn't look out of place on a merry-go-round carnival ride. So much for classical severity.

Octavia's Column

And yet ... — the most Roman Octavia, on the occasion of her thirtieth birthday, was glorified and celebrated by her loving brother Octavius Gaius Caesar Augustus in the form of a massive circular-pillar-monument ornamented with achievement-scenes widely praised for their simplicity and elegance.

Such scenes as Octavia overseeing the strategic placement of boulders in the Tiber river to reduce flow speeds and flood risks; Octavia in congress with a group of civil engineers; Octavia assessing potential sites for flood water retention ponds in Lower Umbria;

Octavia punishing wrongdoers for their incompetence; Octavia flanked and raised up by cheering city-dwellers for minimizing periodic inundation and surface runoff in Rome and its environs; Octavia presenting her book *Fluvial Geomorphology in a Roman Context* to her half-sister Octaviana; Octavia demonstrating proof of the superiority of *curved* river channeling; Octavia's *Eureka!* as she transcends boundaries by being the first to apply principles of fluid dynamics to crowd control; Octavia and Octavius entering the Senate as senators make obeisance; and, most triumphantly, Octavia being acknowledged by the river god Tiberinus who is now bound in chains.

A Roman mother, appearing miscast to us for looking barely a day over twenty, is doing a walk-by of the column with her two little boys — one hiding behind her, the other in front, but also clearly intimidated yet intrigued to the point that he has to exclaim and ask: "How *maximum* pretty she is! Is she real?"

"Yes, my dear, she's real."

Octavia is not a beautiful woman who is just a beautiful woman. There is so much more to love about Octavia — her simple but tasteful manner of dress, her attention to detail, her forthrightness, her intelligence and intellectual curiosity, her sense of justice, her loyalty to her family and friends, as well as her supreme knowledge of water resources engineering in general and of river engineering in particular.

Generations

Scientists say that little Romans see big Romans as big little Romans.

The Only Question That
Really Matters

"Hast du immer noch Herzklopfen wenn ich dich anrufe?"

Any serious Egyptologist, besides speaking fluent English and French, will have mastered German also as research papers in his field are predominantly published in one of these three languages and are very often left untranslated.

Antony Back in Alexandria

Make-up sex is the best.

Cleopatra Before Cleopatra

Cleopatra, smiling, her sunglasses moved up to near the top of her head, is sitting between Iras and Charmian on the steps in front of a massive fountain, their carrier bags at their feet. It was on that shopping trip to Athens that Cleopatra decided that these two ladies of the court, so near her in age, would become her closest attendants and constant companions.

Young-Child-Cleopatra playing the circle-running game in the sand with other children, as on so many days before; but on that day, she had the first inkling that she was to be Cleopatra.

A still very young Cleopatra sharing the pleasures of a funny-story papyrus scroll with her brother Ptolemy XIII as two female musicians look on. All of them are in a "sofa landscape" part of the royal palace, with lots and lots of cushions. That was of course a few years, but not too many years, before the relationship between the siblings turned very nasty and very, very deadly.

Cleopatra, a few weeks before her initiation as a priestess of Isis and definitely not a girl any longer, reading in solitude in the same area, in the midst of all the sofas and cushions.

Cleopatra as a personal and near-permanent guest of Julius Caesar in his villa in Rome, a worried look on her face; her suspicion that something is amiss is at first intensified by indistinct shouting, then confirmed by the blunt and stark message that Julius Caesar has just been assassinated. She went back to Egypt at once.

Liberating Syria Sucks!

The last light of day is shining over the sorry landscape of eastern Syria. A solitary fort mars the monotony of an abandoned plain — abandoned by all but a detachment of Roman troops of Legio XII Fulminata out of Raphaneae. On the uppermost level of the redoubt, leaning against the wall between two plump little towers, watching the setting sun, wishing himself in the capital, which now seems as far away as a forgotten dream, and very much part of the melancholy air is none other than Field Commander Ventidius, the very man who, only a few days ago, drove the Parthians back into Parthia.

Ventidius' melancholy, which has almost been pleasant in its unpleasantness, turns to suffering as he is approached and joined by one saluting Silius, ranked centurio. "Sir, I just had to come up here and thank and congratulate you in person!"

"Why would that be?"

Perplexed, Silius recounts the obvious: "Sir, under your leadership, we slew Pacorus, avenged Marcus Crassus, regained not one but two captured standards, and freed Syria once more. Surely that counts for something?"

"Maybe it does." Ventidius turns to leave. "Good night, Centurio."

"Sir, if I may be so bold, I would like to ask you when we shall press on and continue into Parthia?"

Field Commander Ventidius realizes he has to give the man the full treatment and stays on. "Never."

"Never? Sir, I —"

"My orders were to free and hold Syria. That I have done."

"Sir, the banks of the Euphrates are only a day's journey removed!" "And we shall be in Parthianopolis in the blink of an eye if only we could be on the wings of Pegasus. The troops we have left, the troops that have not fallen victim to sword or famine, will be out-maneuvered and eaten by a herd of cows before they ever make it over that river."

Silius doesn't give up that easily. "Surely you do not mean that, sir. The road is clear and we are ready to march!"

"Then march. Our kitchen-boys will have a few mouths fewer to feed and the Parthian ambush teams will pick you off in no time."

"Surely you do not believe those Parthian fairy tales, the propaganda of the enemy!"

Ventidius looks askance at Silius. "How did you get your field promotion again, Centurio?"

"One bad experience, sir! One bad experience that should not deter us from glory!"

"Then let us suppose that the great goddess Minerva, for reasons inexplicable even to herself, lent you her wit and favor and you succeeded in taking one of Parthia's westernmost provinces, much like Legate Sossius did not too long ago."

"Surely you would like that as well, sir!"

"Sossius was indeed flattered — elated, even — when he received a personal invitation from Antony to dine at the palace in Alexandria to celebrate his superlative exploit."

"Was the invitation not real, sir?"

"Oh, it was very real. Unfortunately, however, Sossius' happiness was short-lived, as the wine he was served on the occasion did not agree with him. It turned out that Antony had overheard a remark to the effect that with a man like Sossius, Antony would no more have need of Antony, which irked his vanity." Ventidius notices that poor, naive Silius is making a face at the revelation. "Now you know what happens when you fly too close to the sun that is Antony. Do you still want me to play Daedalus to your Icarus?"

Badly wounded, Silius decides to retreat, but finds himself checked by his master with a grip of the nastier sort. "If you are resolved to forgo answering my last question, Centurio, at least tell me what we had to eat today."

Silius has now become uncomfortable both in body and in mind. "What we had yesterday."

"And what did we have yesterday?"

"What we had the day before yesterday."

"And what did we have the day before yesterday?"

"Quite possibly what we had last week, I'm afraid."

"Would that have been slow roasted whole duck with pomegranate sauce?"

"No, sir."

"Or filet mignon with grilled asparagus, perhaps complemented by an apple-cranberry chutney?"

"No, sir."

"Or conceivably something simpler, yet still delicious? For example soft-boiled eggs in pine-nut sauce, somewhat incongruously but pleasantly accompanied by oven-fresh garlic bread and rich helpings of butter?"

"No, sir."

"What then? What did we have today, yesterday, the day before yesterday, and also not quite possibly but most definitely last week?"

"I'd rather not —"

"Say it."

"Oh, sir!"

"Say it, soldier!"

"Cold Hittite rat soup topped with irregularly shaped tree bark croutons, sir."

"Thank you!" Ventidius lets go at last. "Dismissed!"

Readers!

What are we to you?

You who are of the sick skies and glowing rectangles?
You who are of the endless calculations?
You who are of the leaders who lead from behind?
You who are of the documented life?
You who go about in big machines?
You buyers and sellers of dreams?
You who think you are free of us?
You repeaters of the past?

BOOK THREE

So Much to Learn, So Much to Understand

An Egyptian Holiday

The Nile, Kemet to the Deshret, giver of gifts, giver of *life*, is teeming with traffic: little feluccas sailing past those who come down the riverbanks to draw water and wash their garments, party boats and their noisy musicians and guests confusing the buffaloes and cows grazing on the grass, trade-galleys transporting silk and wine and grain and linen and papyrus and gold and ostrich eggs and sculptures and all sorts of things.

And in the midst of all these ships and watery waters and surrounding lands that are a mishmash and hodgepodge of farmland and natural vegetation, one stately vessel, bearing but two passengers, is slowly making its way upriver, driven on by enchanted winds. As the boat glides through an embarrassment of riches of the flowers of the motley-colored lotus and drifts by a veritable zoo of animals of legend bathing and flying and foraging and munching, a female figure emerges from the roofed section of the ship — it is of course Cleopatra, come to the prow to offer her thanks and prayers to the gods.

"Oh, Chnouphis, Chnouphis, you who are the Khnum who forged the sky and the earth, the male and the female, great is your name, and great are my thanks to your forging the bond between me and my Antony once more; respected Maat, my gratitude for your brushing my Antony's head with the tall feather of truth that let him see the truth of his heart; Hesat, Renenutet, Sheshmetet, let me be as varied and great as cow-cobra-lioness and let me walk in harvests of love for evermore! Trusty Wepwawet, dog and god and bow-wow among bow-wows, lead me with your barks and be my path-opener and wag your tail!"

Cleopatra smiles and sighs and considers and deliberates and adds an addendum: "Unut, Unut, horny rabbit-goddess of sexual intercourse and of sexual intercourse with results, bless us with the gift of many children and let them be our pride and joy and legacy!"

The queen, who has been answered with a fine spray of Nile water, withdraws to her gently snoring Antony, sits down by him, and studies his features, stroking his hair. Antony the Roman, Antony the Alexandrian, and now soon Antony the Egyptian. It was her idea to take him on this cruise — of Egypt, Antony had only really known Alexandria, and there was so much more he needed to see and understand to become one with Egypt, and it had seemed an appropriate venture to celebrate the renewal of their vows, and the time and season had just been right, and so they then set off from the seaport of Alexandria and followed the coast east to the Delta, where the great river fans out in seven different directions to finally join the Mediterranean.

Another Day at the Office

Government district. Rome. Dawn. Octavius is already seated at his desk. A cock crows, then another. Agrippa enters, strikes his chest in salute, Octavius nods, Agrippa mans a desk at right angles to that of his friend and lord. A third desk, at a respectful distance, is reserved for visitors of the first and second rank and selected personal assistants of Octavius and Agrippa.

Six go-boys, also at a respectful distance, stand at the ready. A go-boy must be quick of mind and body, with impeccable recall and legs that are firm yet lean. Beyond that, his visage must be even and regular, so as neither to disgust nor to distract by its appeal.

A kitchen-knave enters to serve a light first meal to Agrippa and Agrippa only as Octavius takes a few morsels upon rising and then goes without sustenance until midday. Throughout the morning, both men work through their respective stacks of documents, making annotations as needed, sending out the go-boys, with or without written documents, with or without verbal orders, as each situation requires. Upon a go-boy's return, he again stands at the ready until either of the two men asks to debriefed; depending on the nature of the boy's completed errand, a report may also be considered without purpose and the boy will therefore not be any further spoken to regarding that matter.

Octavius and Agrippa also know when it is opportune to consult each other: *after* Octavius has declined to participate in the upcoming Battle Regatta of the Ligurian Sea and settled on a replacement to take part in his stead, but *before* Octavius will peruse the proceedings of the XXIVth Congress on Shield Manufacture; and, in turn and in very much the same manner, only once Agrippa has written his corrigenda of the summary of the Pan-Mediterranean Workshop on the Performance of Auxiliary Troops in Intra-Town Warfare Environments, but prior to Agrippa's pondering optio turnover and how to minimize the concomitant organizational knowledge loss.

Do Octavius and Agrippa believe in lunch? Certainly, as men who know how to delegate and work efficiently also know the advantages of a relaxed environment such as a luncheon when dealing with their government and private sector contacts. A small, intimate dining room is close by; for visits by more sizeable groups, a tent is put up, weather permitting — if not, the work area can be quickly converted for the occasion.

Each and every afternoon sees Octavius and Agrippa carry their work forward on issues great and small. Once the sun has passed its apex, petitioners are received and somewhat less taxing study is done. However, as the world cannot be kept turning from one room, the men often — singly or together — take to the field: for instructions and inspections, for inflictions and interdictions, for introductions and interruptions, for insertions and incursions, for intentions and inventions.

Ahem! Although further engagements are possible in the evenings, this concludes our overview. Please note that this expert insight is given for context, in the spirit of wisdom sharing and in the hope of inspiring the next generation of Roman leaders. For additional information, please refer to the XIIth Forum Romanum keynote addresses given by General Aulus Gortyniacus, legion leader of the XXth legion at Oppidum Obiorum, and Appius Superator, Senior Vice President of Revenue and Profit Management at Satricum Metalworks.

The Delta

During their voyage through the Delta, a labyrinth of land and water that they — now on the Nile proper — cleared two days ago, Antony mostly dozed or just took in the scenery wordlessly — the last weeks in Rome must have been hectic, Cleopatra surmised. The queen herself, however, wrote a poetic diary-entry to commemorate their passage, a poetic diary-entry reminiscent of the work of another noblewoman, Sei Shonagon of the Heian court of Japan, a friend and confidante of Empress Teishi. Why this is so is a question that may be asked but that will not be answered.

Delta branches — Canopic Branch. The Bolbitinic Branch. The Sebennitic Branch. Fatmetic, Mendisy and Tanitic Branch.

The Pelusiac Branch is even more swampy than the other branches.

Barrier islands. The best barrier islands serve as habitats for migratory birds.

Settlements that are near the waterways and sometimes too near the waterways: Sais, Buto, Mendes, and also Bubastis.

Papyrus forests that try to reach to heaven but are barely tall enough for little boys to hide.

Coastal territory and coastal lagoons. Wetlands.

The Problem with Rome

We don't understand Rome because we *are* Rome.

A Stylized Hand Held
Out in Friendship

For the longest time, only the feeblest attempts were made to decipher Egyptian hieroglyphs, as they were thought to be merely wordless images, vain keys to arts and religions irretrievably lost.

Octaviana

Octaviana is dead.

Little Octaviana who was personally taken to one of Octavius' private islands by her elder half-sister Octavia, escorted by a guard of twenty lictors in front and twenty lictors in the back.

Little Octaviana who was met by philosopher-priests and their attendants.

Little Octaviana who was to study the pre-Socratics.

Little Octaviana who needed no doctrines.

Little Octaviana who was a force of nature.

Little Octaviana who beguiled-charmed-captivated everyone.

Little Octaviana who turned the island into a temple of love.

Little Octaviana who never was a one to care for minutiae.

Such as those of contraception.

Her pregnancy proved too much for this free spirit, housed in an almost ethereal body. Weakened by wine, having known no physical exertion except that of love-making, the young woman's fate was inevitable. Octaviana died in childbirth this early afternoon, having produced a stillborn son.

A Trip down Memory Lane: Cato's *Reprehensio Luxuriae Effeminatae*

It is us men who make women what they are and that is why they are nothing.
–Mirabeau

[...] men, who, considering females rather as women than human creatures, have been more anxious to make them alluring mistresses than affectionate wives and rational mothers.
–Mary Wollstonecraft

"How many of us men nowadays can call their own a wife worthy of a Cincinnatus, a wife worthy of tilling the ground with a Cincinnatus, a wife worthy of walking in the steps of a Cincinnatus, a wife worthy of enjoying the fruits of her plain and common labor with such a moral example of a man?

"This, instead, is the Roman female we have to put up with in our age and day: loud-mouthed, crass, selfish, and spoiled in every thinkable and also unthinkable sense of the word. Whereas nature teaches us that the male of species is to inspire by his brilliance and his mate is to be drab and demure — ladylike, to use a human term —, these perverted fools can think of nothing but their own splendor: to ornament themselves with false feathers of every kind, to paint their faces with colors both obscene and dissonant, to deceive and obstruct the natural attraction of pheromones by perfumes of Saba, and to dress their impoverished vocabulary with the most artificial and recherché elements of Greek oratory.

"And they have gotten fat! Oh, how they have gotten fat! And given such a luxurious and dissolute way of living, how could they not have gotten fat! They quench their thirst not with water, but with wine; they do not walk the shortest distance, but have themselves carried around in litters; and they do not procreate as wives of husbands, but yield themselves to actors and other men of lower station whose greasy cum has more calories than one can count! Certainly, there are exceptions to be found in Rome who are quite the opposite, who do not have the girth of a cow. But have those women defined their abs by principled agricultural application or by the venerated feminine art of dance? More often than not, the result was attained by exercise of the most sterile kind, in the course of which they grunted in a disconcertingly mannish manner. Daughters of Narcissus, all of them!

"O vanitas mundi! O vanitas mulierum! Where are our examples of women's marital love? Where are our examples of mothers tried and found true? Life is no longer a life of work, the feminine work that is unobtrusive and discreet and yet so essential to our society; no, life is now a life of pleasure and surfaces and impressions. All our women can dream about are clothes, ornaments, palaces, mansions ... — and the beefcakes to furnish them with all that and more! Why talk of the education of children or history or poetry or the examined life when there are toys to amass?! We have reached *peak* attention-whoring, gentlemen, and you know that by how shamelessly our womenfolk prostitute themselves for riches — who has not, for example, heard of the displays of Sapphism for the benefit of some of our more eligible bachelors? *Only* to titillate, *only* to lure, *only* to cater to the male fantasy of a threesome — for actual, honest, and unfeigned cunt-on-cunt action past a youthful stage of trepidation and insecurity is a rare bird indeed. Once a female has tasted the cock, she will not go back. And why should she, when the alternative would be so much less filling? Oh, how I long for those Romans of old who would stab their fellow-citizens for public displays of affection!

"And the costs! Oh, the costs! The jewels, the purple, the furs from Scythia, the carpets from Babylonia, and the amber from beyond Germania, from the end of the world! No cheap wine from Nomentum for *our* female nobility! By great sacrifice, Rome's soldiers and officials have brought peace and security to the world, workable international relations, communities, bridges, trade agreements, and roads! And some of us think this wonder of wonders that is our civilization serves merely to fetch them spices from far-off Malabar! And the strain is not just on SPQR coffers, but on the entire civilizational edifice: can any region of the known earth claim to have been untouched by the attendant resource wars, with deaths numbering in the thousands or more? And those rare parts that can deny such a past cannot deny fears of such a future. Think on that the next time you come across a few of our beautified sisters and their entourage of drunken flatterers!

"There must still be some difference between our women and the children nature and their spouses bequeathed to their overlooking; it only surpasses my wisdom to divine of what that difference could possibly consist. But I lay the ultimate blame not on them, but on us and our indulgence, our failure to raise them to the places for which they were meant, our sloth and false chivalry that are all too eager to accept a woman's smile as enough of an excuse for her misdeeds. To wit, our own Julius Caesar, the master of war, the tamer of the Senate, the god among men, let himself be reduced to a fool among women, most vilely by one of his mistresses, the Moorish and over-buttocked Eunoe — all that monstrous pride bartered away for an ass fetish he acquired as a pubescent stable boy!

"I leave you, my dear friends, with the solemn and beautiful words of Josephus Septentrionalis: 'We should avoid ostentation and pretentiousness in all things and always strive for more sincere ways of doing, as our lives — if they are to be taken seriously — receive their dignity from simplicity, plain dealing, and plain living.'"

Acarnanicus Severus comments: "This is a wonderful introduction to Cato! Here we have the legendary man in all his glorious contradictions: Cato the choleric, Cato the moderate, Cato the provincial, Cato the urban (and urbane!). We also get a nice sample of his long-running feud with Julius Caesar, in which neither let truth stand in the way of invention: Caesar's youth was not that of a rustic and nobody ever witnessed what Cato implies as done by the first man of Rome and the wife of King Bogudes; similarly, the Julians cast aspersions on Cato's sexual practices, libeling him as a monogamist against his will, a rather unlikely role not in keeping with

Cato's exalted position in Roman society. Another possible case of the imaginary is the concluding quote which none of my assistants could source — is this Cato the philosopher-poet speaking? "We must not forget that, in spite of all his talk of austere asceticism, Cato was also a *showman*. It is on the good authority of Rome's official chronicles that we have an account of Cato's presiding over theatrical proceedings, and how he — with his own particular flourish — presented the winning actors and dramatists not with precious tableware and other expensive gifts, but with turnips, radishes, and windfall apples. The moral lesson should be clear.

"Clarity is also the aim of this *reprehensio* and Cato again and again uses hyperbole to make his point. Thankfully, the conditions described can — sans embellishment — so far only be found in present-day Egypt and a small handful of other nations. Yet we should heed Cato and betake ourselves to the amelioration of character both male and female. If not, such corrosive and degrading influence from the Orient will prove too much even for the greatest state, Cato will have exhorted us (and exerted himself!) in vain, and Rome, too, will lapse."

The Night Sky

One of the things that you've got to get used to when in ancient Egypt — and this one is a good one because it's like *"wow!"* — is the night sky. Of course the constellations are a little bit different due to stellar trajectories and the passage of time, but because the air is still perfectly clean, there are so many more stars to see and the stars you remember truly *shine*.

By Executive Order of
Octavius Caesar

Outbreaks of fire in the city of Rome have come to be a cause for mounting concern and may do much danger as the city continues to grow and become more and more intertwined. In consequence, the likelihood of extreme events increases day by day, making this threat a matter of immediate and pressing importance.

The following security arrangements are therefore to be enacted:

I. The city is divided into 14 administrative regions, each with its own magistrate and fire brigade.

II. The duties of the fire brigade are as follows:

    i. to monitor their area for flames and smoke during all hours of the day and the night, by means of lookouts and patrols.

    ii. to educate the inhabitants of their area concerning fire safety, with particular attention paid to candles, cooking fires, and leaving emergency exits unobstructed.

    iii. to check each building under their care for a) an adequate number of emergency exits, for b) the unobstructed state of said emergency exits, for c) a number of building occupants that is within reason, for d) a permanent water reserve of at least a gallon of water per room and in each room, for e) roofs completely covered with tiles, and for f) an adequate understanding of emergency preparedness, prevention, and response by the building occupants. Moreover, the fire brigade is to g) test the structural elements under load in every new building (every five years in the case of extant buildings). The fire brigade has broad discretionary powers to tear down buildings that fail to meet even one of these criteria.

III. In case of fire, all fire brigade personnel can call upon civilians as well as combat and support formations for speedy aid.

Failure to let emergency actors employ their persons, arms, and estates as thought fit can lead to confiscation of all possessions or docked pay of no less than six months.

IV. A fire prevention think tank and research center is established.

V. The duties of the fire prevention think tank and research center are as follows:

    i. to develop a city-wide building code that can also serve as a model for other SPQR urban areas.

    ii. to develop installation-specific emergency training for critical urban infrastructures.

    iii. to develop and communicate simplified procedures for Abderites and other backward residents.

    iv. to devise, perform, and evaluate threat simulations (both single-threat and multiple-threat).

    v. to optimize real-time threat assessment methodologies.

    vi. to communicate all findings to the offices of all magistrates and to the office of Octavius Caesar.

The Pyramids at Giza

The Pyramids — what where they good for?
–Voltaire

Is this all?
–A traveler from a far-away land come to the Giza Plateau

Vanity has always built grand monuments.
–Voltaire

Antony and Cleopatra finally stand in front of those monumentally serious monuments.
"They're kind of pointy."
"Pointy?" Cleopatra is not pleased.

"Yeah, they're very big on the ground, but then they go up, they get less big, kinda small. Pointy."

"Pointy?!" Cleopatra is definitely not pleased.

"What else is there to say, baby?"

"All pyramids *are* all pyramids *are* Ra *are* Amun *are* Egypt!"

"Are you sure about that?"

It takes some effort, but Cleopatra manages to stay calm and collected, takes pity on Antony, and explains as she thinks a Roman woman would explain.

"An Egyptian legend and creation story tells of the Benu, a bird that flew over the night waters of Nun and Naunet in the beginningless beginning. The Benu at last landed on the Benben Stone, an island very much shaped like a pyramid, where the bird let out a cry that broke the silence of nothingness and spoke the world into being.

"To honor the gods that gave us life and to remind ourselves of the gods above us, we have again and again built the sacred first mountain, looking out over our earthly existence. Without ornaments — as there is no need, without function — as that would be mundane, and without time — as the Benben and Egypt are of Heh and Hehet — eternity.

"Such size, such solidity, such simplicity are the ultimate beauty of geometry. A shape so simple that even children can draw and build their own Benben — and that is what they do and that, in turn, is what makes them become as one with the Two Lands and what reaffirms and strengthens the union of the Upper and the Lower of Egypt. And so it is that not just every hill, not just every mountain, but also every sand-pyramid built by our little ones reminds us of the wonder and the glory of our world.

"And every day, the sun showers the pyramids with countless ankhs of life and moves across the sky and caresses the air and all that are beneath and lets the colors change and play in harmony and dissonance, amber and goldenrod and arylide and grain and soufrh and shaon and ochre and myelle and aureolin and berrh and kasantha and itself reddens into grapefruit soft pink as the pyramids slowly lose their yellows in the dusk.

"All of Egypt came together to build the — not out of pride, not out of ambition, not out of foolishness, but to create something wonderful and to create something wonderful as one people — to inspire men and women everywhere to go-see-know beyond what they go-see-know and what they considered possible, both in our time and in times to be."

"Okay."

Thinking Outside the Tetrahedron: The Roman Task of Opening the Egyptian Mind to the Greater Pan-Mediterranean Reality

It is a truth universally acknowledged that the sands of Egypt have not been kind to democracy. The only years when such freedom blossomed were those of *Hyksos* rule during the Second Intermediate Period — an oasis of only a few years, unfortunately, too short to establish a solid foundation, and troubled by instability and local resistance to change — change beneficial in nature, but in its contrariness to tradition a source of *friction*.

Patience, therefore, needs to be our watchword. Merely holding free elections alone will not produce instant democracy; Egyptian society, its cultural and political elite not excepted, has only known *totalitarianism and superstition* for centuries — which means that we have to prepare for a long, painful, and above all *uncertain* journey towards liberty.

It is also upon us to take into account Egyptian feelings of *envy and aggression* towards Rome. As Roman citizens, we profit from rule of law, freedom from corruption, and economic growth that benefits both the rulers and the ruled; these achievements, however, are not seen as such by *Cleopatra and her clique*, who have selfishly — and, alas, not too unsuccessfully — smeared Rome's good name among their subjects.

While Rome is not without faults and still a work in progress (albeit nearly as close to perfection as human nature permits), we are currently the only power willing and able to serve as a *counterweight* to Egyptian feminism; and any Roman not ignorant of the situation on the ground will know that we cannot have feelings substitute for the examined life, we cannot let ourselves forget the proper place of women, we cannot accept *new and absurd* notions of gender, and we cannot close our eyes to the worrying number of Egyptian females who pretend to intercourse with other females by means of carved carrots and cucumbers and other vegetables that they grow on *small plots of land* or openly procure in the common marketplace.

If we do not want our semen to become as scanty as that of the Greeks, then the moment has arrived for *extraordinary actions* to be taken — but not without a community-driven approach that is eminently understandable; and if we do not want the proverbial baboons to screech and *show us their buttocks* from a treetop, then the moment has arrived to give our counterfeminism forces all the support they require, in as expedient a manner as possible — but not without providing them with *targets and direction*; and finally, if we do not want to raise our hands in an obsequious gesture of surrender, then the moment has arrived for a war to be waged — but not without keeping in mind that *the problem of feminism* cannot be solved by military means alone, but only in tandem with a long-term humanitarian process of *development* which needs to be advanced on all levels with all the energy we have at our disposal.

I am Marcus Promptus.

What Cleopatra Didn't Tell Antony

That there are a lot of stone blocks that form the Pyramids of Giza.

That Ra is also Ra-Horakhty.

That the stone blocks that form the Pyramids of Giza are really heavy.

That the scarab-beetle god Khepri rolls the sun from horizon to horizon.

That the Pyramids of Giza themselves are also really heavy.

That the sun is not rolled from horizon to horizon and that the sun is the solar barque of Ra who sails the sky and who is accompanied by the other gods in the solar barque.

That the stone blocks that form the pyramids of Giza are really heavy and that the Pyramids of Giza themselves are also really heavy only because of gravity.

That the sun is not rolled from horizon to horizon and that the sun is not the solar barque of Ra and that the sun is given birth to by the goddess Nut every morning and that the sun is swallowed by the goddess Nut every evening.

That the Pyramids of Giza are of a precision that out-landers would find maddening.

That the sun is not rolled from horizon to horizon and that the sun is not the solar barque of Ra and that the sun is not given birth to by the goddess Nut every morning and that the sun is not swallowed by the goddess Nut every evening.

That negation need not be negation.

Octavius Withdraws to Camp Capri

It is not just Antony and Cleopatra who have left their capital — Octavius, too, has sought out the countryside. In his case, however, it is much more of a working holiday and there is only one destination on the itinerary: Camp Capri, Octavius' fortified retreat in the Gulf of Naples.

Why, then, this self-imposed exile? Why, then, this aban-
donment of the people of Rome? The official reason given is that
Octavius has gone into mourning for Octaviana and her infant
son — while this is not untrue, a weightier reason was a certain
weariness of reform on the part of the *plebs urbana*. Octavius' latest
scheme of new fire prevention measures had met with a passive-ag-
gressive response he had not seen in some time. So it was decided —
and Agrippa agreed — that the common folk should be left to stew
in their complaints and ignorance until they repented their lack of
flexibility and stopped taking Octavius' care for granted.

Cleopatra Prays to Hapy

It is trite to say and fine to know that every couple needs to spend
time together to stay together and every couple also needs to spend
time apart to stay together. So today Cleopatra has sent out Antony
to do some shopping and exploring. As it is a pharaoh's duty to move
the gods on behalf of the Two Lands, she has consecrated this day
to the worship of Hapy, the deity responsible for Egypt's freshwater
supply and freshwater habitats.

We once more find Her of the Sedge and the Bee on the Nile;
not on her boat, but astride a hippopotamus by the name of Ha-waaa-
aa-aa, a fairly large individual with funny little ears that he can twirl
in a way only the hippopotami can (the twirling increases signifi-
cantly when Cleopatra shares gentle strokes and whispers). The
queen is not wearing much; her most striking accoutrement is a
makeshift crown the materials of which she collected earlier: stalks,
flowers, and water plants.

"Hapy, Lord of the Nile, Lord of the Nile-fish, Lord of the
marshes and their birds, come and flood and nourish our lands!
Forget us not, forget not to let the Nile's blessings never drop below
historic norms! For then brother turns on brother, sister shares only
famine with sister, and we are pressed by sorrows. Instead, let the
Nile become Nachal! Overflow our banks and make us laugh and
make us smile and make us play songs for you! Forget us not, forget

not the Valley and the Delta! Let us hold grapes anew, Hapy! All that grows green we owe to you!"

Translated from middle-to-late Middle Egyptian and translated for accuracy rather than poetry, this is one of the first of many hymns, praise-songs, and incantations Cleopatra has now performed this day and the air is already thick with reed and bee symbols and the symbols of various vegetation gods.

It may be of interest to note — and this is food for thought for the serious Egyptologist as well as for the general reader — that the positioning of the hippopotamus is crucial to success: while Ha-waa-aa-aa needed to hold position in the middle of the stream and tread water and face south to the source of Nile in the case of the appeal quoted above, invocations narrowly related to agriculture and agricultural activities require a slow trot in the shallows near the shore and hymns to fertile mud and riverbed nutrients call for the company of additional hippopotami.

Ruminations on the Sexual and Romantic Vitae of Octavius Caesar

In Rome, Octavius' refusal to be near the people does not lead them to question their own behavior, but rather that of Octavius. Offended, they vent their feelings in gossip and speculation as to the goings-on at Camp Capri. Some of them, Vandals avant la lettre, express themselves by defacing property with their graffiti: "Olive oil for Capri!" (meaning obscure), "Agrippa and Octavius make the beast with two of them!" (ditto), "Oh, Octavius, how many wives and husbands you have!" and other such wisdom and observations.

The accusation of homosexual leanings and indulgence in such leanings was a tired trope in Roman politics even before Julius Caesar adopted Octavius as his son in his will. But detractors of the triumvir need not look for bumfuckery as there is scandal enough in his history with females — which may surprise some who mistook his dry and practical ways, yet it is this excess of practicality in matters of the heart that affronts: Claudia, daughter of Publius Claudius, married and given up because she was barren; Scribonia, of proven fertility and also of great physical beauty, given up because of her undue attachment to fashion and to her own will (a horse-woman, if we follow Semonides of Amorgos); and finally Livia Drusilla, daughter of Marcus Livius Drusus Claudianus, married and loved and not given up, but taken away from her then-husband Tiberius Nero when she was carrying his child. For purposes of research and intimidation, Octavius also makes it a point to commit adultery with the wives of political adversaries when there is an opportunity to do so. One may or may not approve of such a brisk handling of affairs; all the same, those who hesitate to grasp such nettles had better engage in other pursuits than that of power.

Marcus Livius Drusus Claudianus?

Yes, *the* Marcus Livius Drusus Claudianus.

Sudden Smiles All Around

For no evident reason and apropos of nothing, a smile steals across Cleopatra's face and Antony is amused also and — in their quarters and at their posts and on patrol — Enobarbus and the others are overcome by a moment of levity; and even much further afield, Octavius fails to suppress a smirk and Agrippa has to shake his head at the absurdity of it all.

Livia Drusilla Speaks for Herself

Readers of *SPQR Daily* will be pleased to learn that if any woman can lay claim to being more than "only" (!) the wife of as great and incomparable a man as Octavius, it is our beloved Livia Drusilla. And how do we know? She has written a book! Titled *True Motherhood:*

A Memoir of a Daughter of Rome, it will be out before the end of this season — soon, but not soon enough!

Livia Drusilla was not available for an interview at this time because of her now sixth pregnancy, but sent word that she was "heavy, but fine" and promised a "big boy" (whoo-hoo!) for our people! With permission of the author, we have had Marcus Promptus (fuck yeah!) pick some of the most interesting tidbits and are now making them available to the Roman people *for the very first time!*

Age 5. First visit to Alexandria. Their court, supposed to be the crown of every barbaric society, is full of Egyptians who are all too willing to speak of what they do not know; I think I am not too severe in my strictures if I also note an immoderate fondness for dress both at court and in the streets.

Marcus Promptus says: "A most perceptive young lady! The text she wrote upon her return, *Accounts of the Policy and Manners of the Pyramid People*, is a must-read!"

Age 7. [continued] When I learn that my father is the first Roman to have traversed the African coastline on foot, I resolve to do the same.

Marcus Promptus says: "And that she did, after her first pregnancy, at age 19!"

Age 7. [continued] In addition to the benefit of my father's company, I now dine nightly with men of letters and other persons of distinction. An ever-changing and most freespoken circle in which I learn to question received truths and am regularly told (with prophetic accuracy) that I am one of the most promising females to have ever graced the annals of Rome.

Marcus Promptus says: "Would we all had such company!"

Age 11. [Second visit to Alexandria, continued] Immensely struck by the matriarchal and racist relations and contradictions of the local culture. Woeful anti-Roman mindset: we are pale ghosts and do not rank among the living, we are poison to their purity, we are oppressed by male tyranny, we travel the world as Rome itself fails to satisfy, etc., etc.

Marcus Promptus says: "The writing was on the wall then already, but the plupart of us judged it as nothing more than a secondary concern. O tempora! O mores!"

Age 13. [continued] I arrive on horseback at the lawn in front of Camp Priapus. A military visit to inspire the troops with my nobility and personal assuredness. Yet it is I who am inspired even more by their selfless toil and the sacrifices and hardships our men so willingly endure for Rome and for freedom; I have been given the utmost sense of purpose by their example and am most determined to do my part as a woman of Rome. Speaking of which, I consider it worthy of mention that more than once I was there rightfully complimented on my perfect butt — those seeking to emulate my physique would be well advised to follow my equestrian regime. (I stress this as far too many of my sex let themselves go in that regard once they have secured a husband, a dereliction of duty all too prevalent in our day and age.)

Marcus Promptus says: "Res ipsa loquitur!"

Age 20. [continued, on meeting Octavius] Such clarity of mind! Such quickness of understanding! Such power and authority! I want to say yes to all he asks!

Marcus Promptus says: "Indeed!"

Age 25. [Sixth visit to Alexandria, continued] Needless to say, I anew find myself deliberating Egypt and I have to admit that I am vexed to the blood. On the one hand, everywhere you turn you see that Cleopatra continues to make her subjects' lives a complete misery: in markets Romans such as we are witness to fruit-vendors and their customers complaining about her ruthless suppression of rural small farmer movements and the resultant scarcity of food, in temples and other places of worship we overhear the faithful helplessly beseeching their gods to bring about regime change, and in private residences Egyptians of quality (such persons *do* exist!) relate how their writings are erased or wittingly misinterpreted and how they themselves are written out of the official discourse whereas those who aid and abet the narrow self-interest of Cleopatran feminism are given the most prestigious of public venues to give tongue to their folly. So much for the situation on the ground. And on the other hand, Rome is still caught up in conventional ways of thinking on Egypt, which plays right into the nefarious hands of Cleopatra and her feminist allies: instead of reaching out to the country's men's rights advocates, we sit back and do nothing; instead of putting a stop to the insidious scheming against men and boys, most detrimentally in early childhood education, we sit back and do nothing; and instead of following the wisdom our forefathers showed against Carthage, we sit back and do nothing. Make no mistake: the world is dangerous enough as it is and if we do not muster the will to challenge Cleopatra, we shall have to relearn that axiom in a most unpleasing manner.

Marcus Promptus says: "This just needed to be quoted at length!"

Age 26. [continued] I have now delivered my fifth child, and it's my fourth boy! Congratulations are coming in from every quarter! I am so lucky!

Marcus Promptus says: "We all are!"

Marcus Promptus says in conclusion: "Classic Livia Drusilla! What a way with words! What a woman! What a Roman!"

Antony Accosted by a Madman in Luxor Market

So you think you know Cleopatra? Yes? Ooooh! Ooooh!

Holy Fuck!

These camels are fucking tall!

A Bad Month for the City of Rome

Incident: charring and partial destruction of the Sublicius footbridge by fire during a nighttime river crossing march by the local militia.

Cause: still under investigation; initial reports indicate sandal friction as a possible culprit.

Incident: haystack fire in the agricultural reserve and storage area of city district VI. The fire spread and was ultimately responsible for the loss of one week's grain rations.

Cause: sunlight.

Incident: building fire in city district III that ended up wiping out more than fifty properties.

Cause: children playing with wooden sticks.

Incident: complete loss of the farmer's market adjacent to the Circus Maximus due to fire.

Cause: overripe tomatoes; weather conditions listed as dry, hot, and cloudless.

Incident: several small tourist shops near the temple of Jupiter Capitolinus damaged by fire.

Cause: divine retribution for atheism and exorbitant pricing.

Following these and further events of a similar nature, SPQRGRO, the SPQR guest relations office, issued a travel advisory advising non-residents to avoid the capital city until the streak of bad luck had passed. Non-residents currently on a visit are being evacuated by means of mail-boats and Digentia-class escort vessels awaiting them by Tiber docks I, VIII, and IX. Downed watchposts and debris in the area of Porta Capena and Egeria's Grove still need to be cleared away before the last group of visitors are free to leave.

The Wisdom of the Pharaohs

Make your bread in the morning.

An ox-cart is overturned and the donkeys play on musical instruments.

You're looking at me, crocodile, but what kind of look is this?

The Nile is a river in Egypt.

The lands of those who raise their hands against us will be flooded, but not by the Nile.

A child of water-fetching age is of water-fetching age when his or her parents judge so; they are not required to have clear knowledge or proof that a specific birthday has been reached or will be reached in the immediate future.

And in Rome, it made the ruler of the world bleed, the paper cut; helpless, tears of shame and rage in their eyes, the personal guard.

One archaeology professor, four or five graduate students — a dig waiting to happen.

When the excavation site is ready, the archaeologists appear.

All items are perishable items.

There are ten kinds of misfortune.

Egypt will be even more glorious when in ruins.

He who sits and sits on a camel can be uncameled; but he who sits and sits not on a camel cannot be uncameled.

Many men bearing arms have those who have human gods, much they march, and never do they get any nearer to the sun.

Let those tribes that are without pyramids have breakfast at expensive resorts, let those tribes that are without pyramids have expensive toys.

Egyptian cats are just "meow!"

In the African chiefdom of Punt, security boats surround the merchant vessel that arrives from abroad.

Ask what you can do for ancient Egypt.

Not having gainful employment is not having a nagging wife.

The desert knows, but you don't.

This translation was sponsored by the Nederlands Genootschap voor het Nabije Osten and the Institute for the Study of Barbaric Literature at Tokyo University and was accomplished under agreement hiero-glyphic code [low-lying sand dunes] [low-lying sand dunes] [unintelligible] [low-lying sand dunes] [third-born son]. The views and exegeses contained in this document are those of the pharaohs, translators, and Egyptologists concerned and should not be interpreted as in any way representing the official policies, either expressed or implied, of the Dutch Ministry of Defense, the Kingdom of the Netherlands, the Nippon Ministry of Education, Culture, Sports, Science and Technology, or the State of Japan.

By Popular Request, Octavius Leaves Camp Capri and Gladdens Rome with his Presence Anew

What our contempts doth often hurl from us
We wish it ours again; the present pleasure,
By revolution lowering, does become
The opposite of itself.
–Shakespeare, *Antony and Cleopatra*

Much wronged by the common body of men, but willing to forgive. Presented with laurels of honor for his personal modesty, his sense, his sincerity, and his hard work by men who were moved and encouraged by his return, by men who should not have doubted their good fortune in his love and leadership, by men who might now have learned to find their safety in following his counsel. Prompt of wit, liberal of heart, pleasant of speech, a *primus sine pari*. This is Octavius Gaius Julius Caesar.

But where is Octavia? She was last seen during the recent evacuation of tourists and must have left Rome with them. Gone are also her closest attendants; her other slaves were told she would be back from Misenum within weeks at the most, having then taken part in a seminar there on mountain snow and seasonal constraints on river levels, the learnings of which she would share with them in full. Horsemen dispatched to the town have given report that there were no sightings of the lady and any such scientific gathering could not have been but fiction. Further interrogation of Octavia's slaves and neighbors, now of the more thorough kind, proved disappointingly unproductive. All this irks Octavius considerably.

Oh, You People of Alexandria, Prepare for Pharaoh's Return!

Hornblowers, blow your horns! Make loud the day and louder still the night! Her Majesty draws near!

Poets, pipers, players! Let yourselves be called by the master of royal revelry by name and rehearse!

Craftsmen and all affiliated guilds of Alexandria! Come to the palace and present us with your schemes and gifts! In union we shall celebrate and share!

Sand-master! You who bow before Serket, preliminary the sand-judging competitions!

District administrators from Edfu and Bubastis! You who are warriors and veterans of a life of idle amusement with women and wine, take part! Intemperately, bring us Hathor accompanied by Bes! We shall roam the marshes!

The harbor of Alexandria and the adjoining sea are full of ships great and small, eager in anticipation, sporting sails in Cleopatra's colors that just happen to be *all* colors as she is not the kind of goddess who walks the earth who limits herself.

More and more camels are parked in the outskirts of the city and the city itself is becoming clogged with visitors prodding on their donkeys as artisans and traveling merchants set up their stalls.

Artistically gifted ladies of the court sketch select subjects of Cleopatra's, of both humble and honored name, their portraits to be displayed in and around the palace, such as that of two females — sisters? best friends? both? — in a loose embrace, their fashion one of simple flower motifs that add to their beauty; such as that of a young father with his even younger son, men of the desert who have journeyed far, of good cheer and wearing the colorful festival hats of the Gazelle nome; such as that of the royal soothsayer asleep in a hammock, a sheaf of scrolls on his chest; such as that of a group of giddy little children running between and underneath a group of perplexed donkeys; such as that of Princess Lintali, shy but happy, clothed in her blue djellaba that reminds us of her origin in holy Gebel Barkal.

Dates and cakes and figs and all kinds of tasty treats have arrived at the palace and those whose devoir and duty it is to unpack-taste-arrange on platters and plates the dates and cakes and figs and all kinds of tasty treats unpack-taste-arrange on platters and plates the dates and cakes and figs and all kinds of tasty treats, ready to leave the kitchens on pharaonic command.

Alexandria the Golden and the Brilliant has truly been trans-formed — and decorated and painted throughout with scenes narrating the romance of Antony and Cleopatra and decorated and complicated throughout with home-made objets d'art the Alexandrians put in their windows and on their porches and dec-orated and embellished throughout with joy flags of Alexandrian, delta-Egyptian, sub-Saharan, and other traditions — all works of ornament, none of utility.

The Bears of Cappadocia

Without much ado, the house of Octavius publishes a press release regarding Octavia. She has taken a temporary leave of absence, they say, from her works in Rome and Italy. This, we are informed, to study bears in the forests of Cappadocia. The explanation is not so absurd as to be unbelievable, but just odd enough not to be questioned. And Cappadocia is a Roman province too remote and — dare we say it? — also too unappealing for anyone but the most intrepid spirit to go and look for himself. Thank Mars and rest of his fellow gods for the far-flung corners of the Empire!

Did Anyone Even *Think* of
Not RSVP-ing "Yes"?

Clouds burst over eastern and central Africa, feeding the Nile where no Roman or Egyptian ever set foot, and Nephthys greets Isis and in Alexandria, a common donkeyteer turns out to be newly bearded Antony and a chubby market-maid turns out to be pregnant and turns out to be Cleopatra and Greek science officers talk to security detail posing as Greek science officers and there's this new thing called *theoretical* archaeology and an interdepartmental liaison says "I was born into the boatmaker caste, but I've always been an interdepartmental liaison at heart …" and the snake of time twists and turns and the all-too-attractive catering crew cruises the crowd and the guests get Baba Ganoush and flatbread and watermelon cuts and the occasional touching of hands and men and women of the papyrus industry compare figures and swap contact details for reasons professional and other and outrageous bets are placed on the tumbles of dice and gales of laughter erupt from the Sakkara Women's Pottery Collective and a visiting dignitary says "You shall all have a provisions bag with the imprint of my court!" to the women of the Sakkara Women's Pottery Collective and there are already bathers bathing in the pools and people try out the newest lutes from

Memphis and the biggest drums brought from Nubia and Cleopatra catches up with her ever-dear companions Iras and Charmian, the two squealing with joy as they see her tummy, and Antony shares his adventures with his troops, his gestures as grandiose as his stories, and his troops are happy to have him back and the Alexandrians are happy to have him back and the Alexandrians are euphoric that two are to become three and a German mercenary says "Noch ein Stückchen Pflaumenkuchen, bitte!" and the Nabatean warrior rain god Hubal is eating all the pretzels and a port infrastructure architect tells the staff how a freshly squeezed orange juice *really* ought to be done and Antony is presented with a golden breastplate and Cleopatra rubs her belly in front of yet another group and grins and talks about the best and most fun baby-making techniques and the soothsayer is reminded of the end of the world and more food is brought in and the air is heavy with perfumes of lotus blue and lotus white and there is music played by fourscore men and possibly also a few monkeys and a cat and there is dancing and table-top dancing and merry-making and nobody knows how many cocktails they've had and everybody behaves as if they had just turned seventeen again — what a night!

And, As Always, There Are Those Who Can Do Nothing but Criticize

In the Bastet Lounge, otherwise such a lovely space with an abundance of pillows and carpets and naturally motifs of lionesses throughout — solitary, with their lions, with their cubs, at play, at rest, hunting —, envious whispers abound.

"She has really packed on the pounds."

"Even before the pregnancy."

"Even then, yes."

"Too much food and drink."

"Just as debauched as the last pharaoh."

"With him, at least the flute-playing wasn't second-rate."

"And those pretensions to girlishness."

"At that age."

"Embarrassing."

"And that Antony."

"Arsinoe would never have befriended such a fool."

"If only *she* were pharaoh."

"At least Arsinoe does not have to witness such lowly things as we."

"So much decadence, so many people who are empty inside and who try to fill that emptiness with false riches."

"Quite worse than our court's bondage to the Romans is our court's bondage to deluded pleasures."

"The Egyptian people have become a dog with a leash in its snout, seeking out masters in all places."

"Is it just us who have not lost themselves?"

"If only we were with our Arsinoe."

"Agreed."

"Languishing in exile on Ephesus would be better than this."

Straight Talk from Agrippa

The Greeks are not as insane as the Egyptians, but that is why the Greeks are perhaps even more dangerous. Yes, Greek sculptures are beautiful and fittingly complement our richest villas; yes, Greek cuisine has its moments; yes, Greek music is pleasing to the ear; yes, Greek scientists and philosophers have taught us much. Admittedly, we have stood on the shoulders of giants, but now that we have become giants ourselves, they cannot and should not any longer enjoy the same stature. For what would happen if they did? We would *stagnate* as the intellectual groundskeepers of a spent force; we would *stagnate* as the tribute-bearers and trumpeters of men too awkward to take their women from the front; and, worst of all, we would *stagnate* as *Romans*.

And what are we Romans, really? *We are the student that outshines his master.* Our shields were first Argosian, second Sabinian, and then our own; strength in numbers was the advantage of the

Spaniards, and then our own; cunning was the forte of Carthage, and then our own; bravery in battle was the boast of the Gauls, and then our own. Would that the Greeks had such lack of conceit to learn from Rome!

Those in search of valor, discipline, grit of which there is no equal *look to us* and those in need of carpentry, engineering, accounting that is second to none *call our name and our name alone*, to give but the most obvious examples. Such marks of honor, such breed and disposition!

Yet still do the Greeks consider Romans inferior company and come to us as saints to whores! As if we had bestowed lesser favors on them than they on us! That a group of has-beens indulges in such pretensions may move some to laughter, but what of our legacy, what of our renown, what of the future? New generations will hear from the one who talks, not the one who does, and it is no secret that the Greeks are an overmatch in the fraternity of historians, nor that we can expect anything resembling justice from the likes of Antipater of Tarsus and Musonius Rufus. Why expect understanding from those for whom cultural imperialism has been a way of life? Magnanimous and great as we are, Greek historians will *naturally* be uncharitable, Greek historians will *naturally* invoke Demetrius of Phaleron, Greek historians will *naturally* forever portray us as the stupid geese that vainly tried to equal their swans!

And so I ask you, my fellow doers: what will you do to right this wrong?

Memories and Awakenings

Antony, having failed to find his bed, is dozing on a sofa in the Nekhbet Lounge and dreaming a dream that is as much reminiscence as a dream. Cleopatra. The first time with Cleopatra.

Cleopatra was wearing nothing but a "City of Rome" T-shirt and placed one hand on Antony's shoulder and ran her other hand over his ass and Antony was naked and Cleopatra was naked and Antony was not ashamed and Cleopatra was not ashamed and Cleopatra told Antony her Isis name and Antony told Cleopatra his Dionysus name and a couple of klicks from that other place, some, like, fuzzy minutes somewhat after an unknowable hour somehow rooted in Egyptian time drenched in an eternal past of the present gone today, a bull met his cow and the union was most sublime and kisses were given and given and given and given and a prospectus from the Aswan tourist office ("Become 'as-wan' with Egypt in Aswan") is used to thwack Antony on the back of his head.

"Huh?!"

Enobarbus and Octavia, her arms folded and the rolled-up prospectus still in her right hand, come into view.

"What are you guys doing here?"

Enobarbus looks at Octavia. "I'm really doing this against my better judgment."

"We've been over this. Give the man the sobering-up potion and let us wait until he has become fully conscious. I will most likely have to repeat myself enough as it is."

Enobarbus does as he is told and Antony drinks while he considers Octavia. She really is a Quintia — no feminine charms and no grace at all in spite of her shapely legs, her perfectly symmetrical face, her impressive breasts and some of the trimmest abs he has ever seen on a woman not an athlete or a dancer — huh? What has happened to her abs? Something's not right.

"Octavia, have you started skipping abs day?"

"I'm pregnant, husband."

"Pregnant, huh."

Antony, his eyes barely open, scratches his head and addresses Enobarbus.

"What is it with all these pregnant women these days?"

Octavia answers in his stead.

"I'm not certain, husband, but it might have something to do with your dick."

Antony needs a moment. "Right, right ..." He rubs his forehead and stretches his arms. "So where were we?"

"I need you to attack Parthia."

"You're funny. I didn't know. Or is that the blue lotus in you, Octavia? Did you have a bit too much of the blue lotus, Octavia?"

"I didn't participate in your depravity. I am as sober and serious as always and I need you to attack Parthia."

"Yes, why not? Attack Parthia. And maybe also outdo Alexander? And pluck a few stars from the heavens, just for you?" Octavia turns to Enobarbus. "He seems to have regained whatever mental capacity he usually has to do with. Fill him in."

Before Enobarbus has a chance to begin, Antony interrupts, somewhat churlishly. "Yeah, fill me in. Why are you taking orders from her and not from me?"

"Sir, as much as it pains me to say this, I have to tell you that it is not I who abandoned you, but you who abandoned me, and not only me but also your rightfully wedded wife and common sense itself when you left Rome so abruptly to rejoin your mistress here in Egypt."

"Yeah, but still ..."

"Luckily, Lady Octavia recognized my talents and I am now in her employ. I will gladly talk to you about personal matters, sir, when we have the time. But now, frankly, we don't."

"Oh-kaaaay ... — woman, do you have *any* idea how *big* Parthia is?"

Octavia just gives Antony a dirty look for supposing her ignorance in such a matter.

It is clear to Enobarbus that it is still his turn to explain. "Her Ladyship is not asking you to *conquer* Parthia — that, under present circumstances, would be a feat beyond any Roman's genius."

"Then what? *Kiss and caress* Parthia?"

Enobarbus is too professional to be aggrieved by such sarcasm. "Our idea is that you take your troops and ransack some outlying parts of Parthia." He produces an annotated map and shows it to Antony. "Here, here, and here. We believe the spoils worth the effort."

Antony reacts with what seems to be a non sequitur. "Were you guys here for the party?"

"We were witness to some of the festivi-"

"So you know that things are pretty peachy here. I even got a golden breastplate, just like that. So why go to Parthia? Mostly it's just dirt and sheep-fuckers, anyway."

"Sir, Octavius has already sidelined Lepidus and we have very good reason to believe that it is only a matter of time until he has fully effectuated your fall from power. Public opinion in Rome now leans much in his favor, especially since you abandoned your wife and his sister in so outrageous a manner. Militarily, Octavius will have you at a disadvantage in less than a year if you do nothing. And then, to put it as bluntly as possible, it will not be sheep, but you, sir, who will get fucked, and not in a good way."

"Really? Octavia, you came all the way to Egypt for that? And brought Enobarbus, too? Do you care for me so much?"

"No, I don't. I do, however, care for Rome and its people. If there is another civil war, a significant number of Roman troops will die and towns throughout Italy and the rest of the civilized world will suffer hunger and starvation. As a consequence, the entire Empire will be weakened, up to six legions will be lost, and we will not be able to hold our current borders, with our Gallic provinces most likely the first to suffer destabilization."

"Gallic provinces, then, huh? Would be a shame about the wine, but I think I'll be able to live with that."

"No, you won't, because before that happens, you will be dead. All your friends will be dead. Cleopatra will be —"

"Dead. I get it, I get it. And a little trip to Parthia is going to prevent all that?"

"Power in Parthia is much less centralized in Parthianopolis than you might think. The Parthian government is more fractured — federal, if you want to use another word — than ours. Most provinces have sizeable treasuries, and we think we do not assume too much if we say that we also know two sites within reach where bows and arrows and other weapons are produced that are superior to regular SPQR military equipment. Husband, it is our calculation that even if you only manage to loot sixty-five percent of the targets we suggest, it would amount to enough deterrence to negotiate a lasting truce with my brother."

"This *is* starting to sound interesting. Maybe I'll send a lieutenant to hit one or two provinces, just to get a taste."

"You really *are* a coward. Enobarbus, tell my husband why he has to lead the campaign in person, why the targets need to be taken out in rapid succession, and why there is no other course of action open to him."

Antony rolls his eyes. "This conversation is going to be the end of me. But go on, Enobarbus, by all means say what you have to say."

"Thank you, sir. Firstly, Lord Antony, if you lead this effort, it will not only counter your reputation of debauchery and dissolution, but it will also force our easternmost provinces and client kingdoms into renewed enmity with Parthia and consequently bind their allegiance to you even more strongly. Secondly, if you do not overwhelm your Parthian targets quickly, too many reinforcements from other Parthian commanderies will have time to pour into your mission zone, thereby severely limiting any chance of success. At present, Parthia's forces are rather evenly distributed within their empire; our intelligence assumes that this is so because you are not seen as a serious threat."

"'Not a serious threat.' Hm. And thirdly?"

"And thirdly, Lady Octavia and I have worked through dozens of possible geopolitical scenarios: a new front in Dacia, a provocation by Libya, an Athenian offensive, retaliation by Sparta, multiple concurrent insurrections in Italy, theaterwide natural disasters, subversion in Macedonia, the untimely death of King Herod of Judea, the loss of legions stationed along the Rhine — to name but a few. You are free to peruse our findings, but the long and short of it is that you need to attack Parthia to be safe."

"And you're certain?"

"No, sir."

"No?"

"There is no such thing as absolute certainty when planning for the future. Notwithstanding this caveat, sir, your doom is all but assured in over ninety percent of our scenarios should you fail to act as we suggest."

"Okay. I guess I'll think about it, then."

Octavia is ready to leave. "Fine. Enobarbus, you are detached to Antony to assist him here in Alexandria with administrative and logistical concerns. I myself will return to Rome to do what I can on that end. I honestly hope, husband, that you will do the right thing, just for once."

After all this hectoring, Antony is not willing to let Octavia have the last word. "You know, Octavia, you're smart and hot and all that, but you really have to work on being more womanly — maybe Cleopatra or some blue lotus could help?"

This only sets off another lecture. "Taking drugs in my pregnant state would be the height of irresponsibility. Moreover, my femininity is not contingent upon my engaging in frivolous behavior. To use intoxicants, to give myself inordinately to the all-too-common pleasures of food, sloth, and intercourse while there are weightier matters to be attended to — those would be the marks not of a lady, but of a pig wallowing in mud. Goodbye, Antony."

Octavia has now indeed had the last word, but not the last grunt, so to speak, as she considers the pig noises Antony makes in reply unworthy of a response.

BOOK FOUR

Sabotage

Preparing the Battleground

A for *Ape*. The ape is not indigenous to the Italian Peninsula and is therefore a *Foreigner*.
–Roman schoolbook

I do not know a more contemptible people than the Egyptians; there must have always been a radical vice in their character and government to make them such vile slaves. Throughout history they were subjugated by whoever bothered to try: by the Assyrians, by the Greeks, by the Romans, by the Arabs, by the Mamelukes, by the Turks — by the entire world, basically.
–Voltaire

There is perhaps only one thing that is not reprehensible when it comes to the nation of Egypt: that those who are ridiculous enough to worship a cow will not dare to ask those who worship a monkey to change their faith.
–Voltaire

Not just the local intelligentsia, but also many fans of master actor Porcus Quintus have gathered together tonight, at SPQRITPA Capua (SPQRITPAC), where the famous Acarnanicus Severus once more interviews a leading figure of Roman culture as well as further guests. The evening begins with two actors practicing dance steps or rather pretending to be practicing dance steps, ever converting apprehensions of failure into astonishment at their choreography. As Porcus Quintus grape-walks onto the stage and joins the formation's movements, he is greeted with much applause, some of the more enthusiastic audience members even standing up or at least calling out his name. Before long, the dancers abandon Porcus and the stage, and are replaced by Acarnanicus Severus who enters clapping hands, shouting, grinning, waving, throwing kisses to the crowd.

The two great men finally settle into their chairs.

"Good to have you, Porcus!"

"Good to have you have me, Acarnanicus!"

"How about that dance?!"

"Yeah!"

"So, what's the name of that new Porcus Quintus project of yours?"

Porcus smiles. "Just that."

A moment passes and then the penny drops. "*New Porcus Quintus Project* — I love it! Brilliant! Form follows function!" Acarnanicus remembers not just to flatter but to also satisfy the audience's curiosity. "Now tell us, how was prep?"

"Awful, oh just awful. We had some Egyptian dialogue in the play, for 'realism' because I'm boinking the pharaoh, you know — such a pain in the ass, all that weird gobbledygook. And I said, 'Why don't we just take it out? We're Romans, real Romans, and I don't need this shit.'" The crowd cannot but applaud such rectitude.

"You got it taken out?"

"I'm Porcus Quintus. Of course I got it taken out." A decisive measure, rewarded with even more applause.

"Did you make any new friends during rehearsals?"

"Among the actors? Not really. But there was this art department researcher who had an ass I couldn't just pass up on."

"It's good to hear you're staying true to yourself."

"Yeah, it keeps me grounded and satisfied and all that."

"Now I hate to bring this up, but there have also been protests by some rather shrill characters …"

"I don't know what their problem is." Porcus takes some time to reflect before he elaborates. "I know what they *say* their problem is. But I think they're just messed up. Unhappy childhood, something like that. Or just confused. But I've heard that you have a political guest on, too, so maybe he can make more sense of it than me."

"That's exactly why we have one on board tonight. But before we ask him to the stage, let us not forget to tell our friends where they can see you in action. I understand this spectacle is intended for first performance in Rome?"

"That's right. We're starting big, then go on tour a bit — I think we're also doing one or two performances here in Capua, no, I'm sure of that, really — and then we come full circle, finish big in Rome again."

"And now let us put our hands together for a fearless intellectual, Ra-Ptahhotep II, the spokesman for the Romans for a Free Egypt!" Acarnanicus leads a round of applause and offers Ra-Ptahhotep II the chair to his left.

"Thank you, thank you!"

As Ra-Ptahhotep II is not quite as famous as Porcus Quintus, Acarnanicus Severus feels the need to fill in the blanks for the audience, consulting his notes while doing so. "You have quite a curriculum vitae, R-P — is it okay if we call you R-P?"

"Certainly, yes, of course."

"You grew up in bitter, unimaginable poverty in rural Egypt, became a scribe in the department of agriculture, first in your nome, then at Alexandria — and then, just when your career was really taking off, you decided to give it all up by coming forward with an insider's account that shocked the civilized world."

"You mean my book *Egypt Abandoned by Itself*."

"Yes, and I have to admit, it was so depressing and at the same time also so infuriating that I didn't know if I should cry or pull out my hair. How could any society let itself go that badly?"

"In one word? Cleopatra. The ruler of Egypt — not democratically elected, not risen through the ranks by merit, but simply born into power — is a woman, a decadent woman who has stooped to publicly expressing desire for sexual intercourse."

Porcus' interest is piqued. "Now that doesn't sound so bad to me."

Acarnanicus laughs. "We know, we know!"

"It is no laughing matter when the woman in question is a head of state. Cleopatra and the rest of her court live in a world of their own making, a debauched, decadent, most unreasonable world, while the people of Egypt suffer the consequences."

"But you're not too gentle with the common folks, either. In your next book, *Quo Vadis Egypt?*, you called Egypt an 'idiot-majority country.'"

"It *is* an idiot-majority country. Officially, sixty-two percent of the population can't read or write; but the real situation is much worse. People who can scribble their own name are not included, so what you will find is that they have a terrifying *ninety-eight percent* suffering from functional illiteracy. Only an excruciatingly small minority of traders, scribes, and courtiers are not outdone by SPQR schoolchildren."

"So what's the solution, teach?"

"The boys of Egypt. In my work with the SPQR Freedom Forum, we have shown that if you educate a seemingly negligible percentage of boys, the others will want to have the same skills and will also be able to acquire the same skills. Competition, knowledge, and male common sense go hand in hand."

"But instead they have feminism."

"And *escalating* feminism at that, which threatens to engulf the entire region. Every time I travel to Africa and the Near East, people tell me that this perversion needs to be stopped."

"Is there any hope that the people of Egypt will be able to resolve this crisis on their own?"

"Before I answer specifically, let me just point out that this is no longer an Egyptian problem, but a question of international security — ERPSA, the East Roman Politics and Society Assembly, a deliberative body I very much respect and with whom I have a very good working relationship, has stated that the south-eastern Mediterranean situation is of 'serious and rising concern.' Egyptians, sad to say, tend to put together their incongruous worldview from sources as disparate as village gossip, pharaonic propaganda, and even their own half-baked thoughts. They believe in the vows of Cleopatra and blame the followers of Arsinoe and — more often than not — the Roman Empire for what they think is amiss. So I'm very pessimistic about independent progress, but I also want to emphasize that I'm very optimistic about education and its potential."

"What about national pride? Don't they want their own country to do better? Don't they want to help themselves do better?"

"Egyptians are stirred and intoxicated by national pride, but it is a national pride which is mere emotional wallowing. The excruciatingly vast majority are not able to engage intellectually, they do not understand what is necessary to put the nation back on track."

"Thank you, R-P. Porcus Quintus, any last words before we call it a night?"

"You know, this intellectual discussion thing is not really my thing, but it's been good to hear somebody argue so convincingly about Mediterranean politics and the need to take action."

Acarnanicus Severus nods and is about to make his farewell comment; Porcus Quintus, however, is not quite done yet. "Maybe this wasn't talked about because it's so obvious it's absurd, but what is also messed up in Egypt is all that stuff with the animal-headed gods. I mean, all that superstition is a snake that needs to be put to rest."

"I completely agree with that. But as for *your* snake, does it ever get *any* rest?" This particular zinger generates much laughter and much mirth throughout the room; Porcus Quintus, used to such gentle ribbing among friends, also rather enjoys the joke and hams it up, pretending to be offended and stung and just plain shocked.

On Acarnanicus' cue, musicians begin to play. The audience gives a final round of applause as the triumvirs of reason rise from their chairs and bow and then, too, their hands over their heads, applaud the crowd.

What is SPQRITPA?

The SPQR Institute for Theater, Performance, and Art (SPQRITPA) is a Roman institute focusing on theater, performance, and art. It was created in the first year of the reign of Julius Caesar. Originally limited to two small venues in the capital, one of which was and still is devoted to theory only, it has now been expanded to also include subsidiary posts in six towns in the Italian provinces (peripheral territory excepted). SPRQITPA is under the triple supervision of the Senate, the Commission for Drama and Rhetoric, and the City of Rome.

A Fond Farewell for Antony

At the Thoth Gate of the Palace, Antony, sober, shaved, and in military uniform, is making sure of the readiness of his men and their kits — actually, to be *perfectly* frank, Enobarbus is doing it for him while Antony stands by. But not for long, as Iras and Charmian just must, must, *must* do some of their own inspecting — so many dashing troops!

"Oh, Antony! Why haven't you told us about your new friends? They're almost as strapping as you are!" Iras.

Now Charmian: "But you really must do away with those cheek guards! How can a girl adore cheekbones when she can't see them!"

Before Antony can reply, more from Iras: "Do we get to see them run about?! We'd just *love* to see them huff and puff!" Charmian nods eagerly in agreement and both of them look at Antony expectantly.

Antony, flattered, has forgotten about his bad mood, and jokingly suggests the impossible: "If you come to Syria with us, you can."

Enobarbus jerks his head as violently as if he had been punched in the face. "Sir! Until now, not even your personal guard knew this detail! No more sharing of information! Our mission is a top secret SPQR matter and I have to ask you to treat it as such!" He turns to the soldiers and officers and warns them: "If you are to speak about this to *anyone*, you *will be* executed. Do not be unwise."

Antony sees no harm done. "Oh, *everything* is top secret nowadays."

Enobarbus considers making a reply, but thinks better of it. For the time being, at least.

Iras and Charmian, on the other hand, are not quite that taciturn and have also started tugging Antony by his uniform. "Please! We want to go to Damascus!" "The shopping arcades there are just so pretty!" "And retro-chic!" "And we can buy Syrian baby clothes for the baby!" "And Syrian shawls for us!" "And watch people from the Palm Tree Café!" "And brag about it when we get back!" That last idea has both ladies-in-waiting clap their hands like fluttering birds.

Antony is bemused by all this enthusiasm. "Now, now, girls — you know you have to look after your mistress here, now more than ever. But I'll have the quartermaster load one of our ships with such purchases on the way back."

Iras kisses Antony on the left, Charmian kisses him on the right, and off they race to bring Cleopatra the good news.

It will be many months, however, before Antony's return, and then there will be no such treasures to bring home.

Parthian Intelligence and Counter-Intelligence Is the Most Capable Intelligence and Counter-Intelligence Outfit in All of Western Asia, Part 1

DROMEDARY CHATTER STANDING EAGLE ROCKER ROCKER ROCKER

Threat Level Dark Olive Green

Are isolated crocodile sightings off the Italian coast signs of an impending Egyptian invasion?

The Great God Thoth Speaks and Shares His Wisdom Either as Ibis-Bird or as Baboon Depending on Circumstance

Delta poems. Desert nights. Cleopatra elaborating on the pyramids. Pharaonic proverbs. Scenes at court. All this is not enough. You want more. You need more. Your hunger-love-desire for Egypt has been awakened and is getting worse and worse and will never be satisfied. And you never want it to be satisfied, you never want it to stop. The Great God Thoth provides holy medicine; take an overdose from Thoth!

His Sacredness recommends that you continue your journey with *Strong Bulls that Rise in Truth*, scriptures that instruct you on how to mount the cows of challenge in your path with profit; read and pay homage to all Strong Bulls and read with particular application the second, sixth, and eighth Strong Bull.

In addition and for contrast, engage with *The Pharaonic Day-Book of Neferhotep XXV*, a beautiful text written in non-rhyming prose by the dullest and in all likelihood also the dumbest of all pharaohs, mixing everyday observations with not much else.

Next, do treat yourself to any number of early pyramid-building treatises by Imhotep, all rather serious and droll.

So as not to neglect the feminine, turn to *I Shall Recount and I Shall Relate: Selected Mother-Daughter Correspondences of the New Kingdom*. At a minimum, browse one of the *Cloudless Sky* editions; peruse the *Stars That Come Out at Night* commentary edition if you want to be given all that can be given.

Then examine the *Nile Protocols*, in spite of its title a compendium of maps and the most imaginative-misleading-willful compendium of maps of its kind, covering not only Egypt's fertile river lands but also the country's arid mountain and desert regions.

Furthermore, do not tarry in reaching for and unbundling the *Onomasticon of Amenemope*, containing all the words Ptah used to say Egypt into being — there is no rival to the Kahun-Hetepsenusret Archives version, of course.

A barbarian's account that simply cannot be excluded and that needs no further introduction is the popular yet truthful *Sandal-Bearing: Tasks, Trials, Triumphs* by the Cypriote Under-Secretary of State for Foreign Affairs. *I Know That Pyramid!* is by the same author and is not to be read by children over the age of five.

And now firmly arriving in the present, make certain use of the papyrus *Cleopatra When She Tilts Her Head and Smiles*, which principally consists of queries of an aesthetic, cultural, or sublime nature and the advisory opinions received from Cleopatra or her staff.

All these writings are readily available for consultation-study-rapturous delight at the Library of Alexandria.

Octavia on Her Way Back to Rome from Egypt

Acting as a lookout on her ship, the ever more heavily pregnant Octavia cannot currently see anything but blue water and a sky almost as empty as the surface of the sea, bar a few small white clouds. But she notices something else, something that even an experienced mariner might not have realized at first, had he been inattentive: the rowing done by the port oarsmen seems to have become just a hint more sluggish than that done by the starboard oarsmen.

Not one to take such a development in stride, Octavia immediately descends below deck, surveys the scenery of men grinding away, spots the one man too tired to do more than to go through the motions, goes up to him, kicks him off his bench, and starts rowing herself.

In Octavia's mind, there is no excuse for sloth or neglect: not inexperience, not ignorance, not sickness, not exhaustion, not anything else.

And if Octavia had not reacted in the way she had, she would have considered herself at least as guilty. Anyone on board a ship is responsible not only for his own narrow task, but also for ship-handling in general and may not shy away from doing the work of others if the current situation requires it. To take the initiative is to take responsibility.

Very Rich, Very Fat, Very Successful: Croesus

Most noted for his counsels *contra* Gallic separatism and resource nationalism. Few, if any, quotes publicly available and verified. Said to inhabit an advisory rather than an operational role in the running of the Empire. Nonresident Senior Fellow of the Consultative Office for Common Enterprise; otherwise an éminence grise. Numerous geostrategic friends.

"Obviously, the Gauls and all the other shaggy-bearded guys are our *de jure* vassals and tributaries, so to speak, but that's not the whole picture. Sure, we've had our wars and ups and downs and so forth, I won't deny it, but I think we all know we're all in this *together. De facto* we're like a big family, if I may say so. Sometimes we even play golf together."

All You Legions

You just cannot believe all the legions that Antony has pulled together at the military settlement of Zeugma in north-eastern Syria: both Gallica and Antiqua out of Raphanea, Ferrata out of Judea and also Raphanea, Fretensis out of Judea and Syria, and coming with him out of Alexandria and Upper Egypt, so many cohorts of Deiotariana and Cyrenaica that Cleopatra's safety is barely guaranteed. In addition, the main force will be joined en route by the client kings Polemon of Pontos and Artavasdes of Armenia with their men, bringing the total not to ten, not to twelve, not to fourteen, but to *sixteen* legions. Enough to conquer the world, one would think.

We Have Some Serious Activity in the Forested Areas of Italy

Octavius has named engineers of forests and trees and auxiliary engineers to spread over the home regions and — as most available information is out of date on many points — to take new knowledge of present conditions and to *act* on that knowledge. They are currently directing farmers and other local residents by power of imperial edict to clear the woods of any materials they have deemed suitable for the building of adversarial sea-going craft. The trees are then readied for transport and make their way to the natural harbor north of Palinurus, which the first loads have already reached. More and more of them arrive there every passing day.

The Exarcheia Fragment

It must be borne in mind that my design is not to write histories, but lives. And the most glorious exploits do not always furnish us with the clearest discoveries of virtue or vice in men; sometimes a matter of less moment, an expression or a jest, informs us better of their characters and inclinations, than the most famous sieges, the greatest armaments, or the bloodiest battles whatsoever.

–Plutarch

If we take Plutarch (he of the *Parallel Lives* and the *Moralia*) as our starting point and inspiration, we might draw the same comparison between history's loudest and most principal actors and those who seem to have a bit part at the most or none at all — yet they are that vast majority without which nothing can be done (as Bertolt Brecht so wryly reminds us in his poem "Fragen eines lesenden Arbeiters," Julius Caesar surely couldn't have conquered Gaul all by himself and must at a minimum have had a cook in tow). So let us not spurn a cheap ostracon with much surface damage and several bits broken off, found over twenty centuries later, not in a palace or a temple, but in the Exarcheia district of Athens due to construction work.

While we do not wish to circumscribe the reader's interpretation (or, rather, interpretations, plural), it might be worth pointing out that said district in which said ostracon was dug up (or, rather, will be dug up, if we apply the perspective of our characters) has quite a reputation for being an "alternative" hotspot, full of anarchists and iconoclasts and poseurs who fancy themselves as such — it is even worse than Berlin Kreuzberg, some would say. Has Exarcheia inherited its genius loci from ancient times? If so, is our ostracon a case in point? Moreover, to what extent is the take given representative of wider demographics and how did this outlook affect the course of history as such?

But enough of all that! The original text (or, rather, its remnants and lacunae) reads as follows:

[...] afford? [...] inasmuch as this is not the sort of feminism [...] in appearance [...] or those gynocrats who take some perverse pleasure [...] sisters into copycat men until there are no women left? Strong and independent my cunt.

Other artefacts found close by as well as textual and handwriting analyses suggest female authorship.

Cleopatra Is Just Bored-Bored-Bored

It has not been *that* much time since the grand-excessive-exquisite festivities at Alexandria, and yet Cleopatra is just terribly bored and feels the anticlimactic post-party ennui most acutely. Reclining on a chaise longue in the Tefnut Lounge and absent-mindedly exploring the texture of said piece of furniture with her beautifully manicured hands, the petite queen looks out over the infinity pool. Her tea, her biscuits, her chaise longue, the deck chairs, the attendants, the quintet of softly playing musicians — all seems lazy and worn thin, in spite of not being so.

What to do, what to do? Can dullness increase even more? How could she be feeling so jaded, so blasé, so just plain bored when she is pharaoh and pharaoh with child? Maybe a fashion show, right here, in the Tefnut Lounge? No. She has done that enough times already. Or a baby fashion show? Or a kids' fashion show with her Caesarion? Maybe that could be fun. Or maybe not. Where *is* that little tyke, anyway?

Or pose for a portrait? By moonlight, when the moon is the most generous? Or try her own hand at portraiture? But it takes so long to make art that is magical-intriguing-inspiring and more than workmanlike. Funny word that, workmanlike. Work-man-like. And just to become sufficiently proficient to make art that can be called workmanlike is a process that can take several changes of seasons. To become a mere common artist, what an immortal shame! Cleopatra will always be Cleopatra and never be common!

So it is decided. A portrait will be taken that will grace the moon with her companionship, reflecting Cleopatra's royal light! Who should paint it, of all the painters at court? But hasn't the Crown Princess of Libya done that before, isn't that exactly the reason for her now having this idea? Yes, she's sure of it. Nix the lunar portrait, in that case. To imitate a woman of lower rank!

Nevertheless, it would perhaps not be below her station to visit the Libyan aristocrat. Or maybe have the Crown Princess visit her? It's been so many years, so why shouldn't a meeting be interesting-enriching-stimulating? Charmian could write out an invitation and have it sent by secure camel. Then again, there are reasons why it's been so many years …

If only Cleopatra weren't pregnant, just for a few weeks, then she might go and climb new mountains and stand on their summits! Being pregnant, however, Cleopatra might still be able to travel to some of the wilderness marshes of the Delta she has not yet had a chance to explore. Wouldn't that be a nice escape, just roughing it with an elementary entourage of about thirty, thirty-five? But all the places she would have to pass through that she has already seen often enough!

Something in Alexandria, then. Stage a competition — any kind of competition, as long as it's not a fashion show again —, a test of strength or skill or cunning? What sort of competition would be appropriate? Hmmm. On further reflection, none. There is something not very feminine about competing rather than cooperating, something insecure, something mean-spirited, something masculine and sweaty in the worst of ways. Audience, encouragement, let alone participation are out of the question.

All the same, Cleopatra wonders what it would be like to watch her Antony perform his feats of arms in Parthia! To sit on a horse, to shout at troops, to lead the charge! Oh, when her man of men stormed her own fortress of love! Such a story and epic needs to be written a thousand times, in a thousand forms, in a thousand tongues!

Reading, why hasn't Cleopatra thought of reading?! How many new worlds has she discovered through the written word, how many heroes, how many geographies and philosophies and psychologies and chemistries and technologies! And yet. And yet. Lately, it seems, the words have become just scribbles, the witty asides turned pre-dictable, the stories only permutations of the ever-same. Isn't it so that all stories in the end are reduced to the same twelve stories? And isn't all knowledge vanity?

Oh, to know nothing and be a stupid little fool! Or a big fool, like those self-important asses from Rome and Carthage and Atlantis and whatever other distant empires there were, fixing their thoughts on ambition and nothing but ambition instead of simply enjoying life and then calling themselves world-conquerors, in total denial of the immensity of the 7,128,943 realms! Each and every one of those dreamers eventually fell by the wayside, grown old and fat, the ants together with their ant-heaps. To march in triumph! Over what? How silly!

King Artavasdes of Armenia
Takes His Leave

Much to Our dismay and consternation, Our Majesty has been forced to come to the conclusion that Our military alliance with Antony has proven unsatisfactory and cannot be continued in good conscience. While We remain a friend and partner of Rome, the triumvir and his command have 1) not shown proper deference to Our royal rank, 2) shown themselves utterly lacking in cross-cultural awareness, 3) failed to view geopolitics as anything other than armed confrontation with enemies of their own making, 4) ridiculed Our attempts to initiate a peace process, 5) remained stubbornly stuck in anti-Parthian ideology despite Our best efforts to help them to transcend their infantile convictions, and 6) generally adhered to a modus operandi of doing much while knowing little. We and Our men-at-arms thus take our leave and return to Our homeland.

How Is Good Old Lepidus
These Days?

How indeed! While we do not comment on individual cases, what we can confirm is that either Lepidus is still actively enlisting his personal physician Gaetanos to aid him in improving his health or maybe not. In the former as well as the latter case, Lepidus would still liaise with other officials responsible for safeguarding Rome's sovereignty and imperial rights and interests. Africa Nova. Africa Proconsularis. Numidia. *Absence makes the heart grow fonder.* Good old Lepidus!

Who, why, and how many? We shall not ascribe motives to our friend, but let it be said that a man who knows how to deftly avoid his crone of a wife in the narrow confines of their unified bed need not be a man who fails to see that young women are too impulsive in their love-making to properly please a man and are of a general restlessness that aggravates and does not soothe a man with enough on his mind as it is. Nor need such a man be a man who has come to the conclusion that a *femme de trente ans* — or two or more — is what it takes to at least momentarily relieve the crushing banality of existence. *Accurate assessments.* And we may also state in the most unreserved manner that slave sex is not sex as a slave is not a person even if not underage and thus any such slave sex is mere masturbation, an activity which no philosopher of good standing has ever equated with stepping outside one's marriage — this particular debate we need not repeat here. *There are no records of extramarital activities and the issue of adultery simply does not arise.*

Finally, the above meditation on African activities exclusively concerns the perils of inter-gender relationships and romance and fucky-fucky and is not to be interpreted as anything other than that. *Frame of reference.* To presume that the information given implies respective troop strengths at Clupea, Hadrumetum, Ruspina, Thapsus, and so forth would be a forced sense-making from a foreign policy perspective and one of the worst examples of reader response theory in classical history. Nor should these words be misconstrued or overgeneralized as pronouncements of the triumvir's political plans or as analyses of his expeditionary infrastructure. *Immaterial and unsupported.*

Statianus and Antony React to Artavasdes' Departure

Enobarbus stayed behind in Alexandria to serve as a local liaison, but a staff officer named Statianus very much serves Antony on this campaign as Enobarbus would. Statianus makes answer to the accusations and to the desertion of the Armenian king: "Antony and his command regard the recent criticisms by Artavasdes as unjustified. Furthermore, we do not regret the loss of such a conflict-averse ally. A leader of his people who keeps getting lost in discussions of terminology, who chronically underestimates the Parthian threat, who desperately wants to believe that every conflict can be solved by words and the gifting of fruit baskets, who uses Armenian thinking to avoid shouldering his share, and who is unwilling to make and implement the hard decisions that reality forces upon us is a man who will prove the undoing of himself and all who are foolhardy enough to yoke their fate to his."

Antony expresses the same sentiment in a rather less verbose manner: "Good riddance to that dweeb!"

Parthian Intelligence and Counter-Intelligence Is the Most Capable Intelligence and Counter-Intelligence Outfit in All of Western Asia, Part 2

SEATED MERCHANT BONGO BONGO BONGO

Cybele Will Not Stand for This

The taking of her children in unprecedented numbers has angered Cybele greatly. The men who have so plundered her dominion she has already had visited by night by her divine companion and sharer Attis to give them nightmares of themselves as trees uprooted and pained and cut up. As this seems to have been of no avail, Cybele now feels she has been provoked to resort to more drastic action. So she will shortly ask her friend Pomona who is the goddess of fruit produced by trees and who is also of her mind in this matter as in all matters to call in a favor from a goddess of fate to whom they once offered shelter and sanctuary.

Earlier sins and infractions — chief of which was and continues to be excessive cattle farming leading to a barrening of the soil and general disharmony — were for the most part soothed by prayers and gifts in Cybele's places of worship. But now that the two-legged beasts of the Italian Peninsula have abused their progress in forestry studies in so gross a manner, Cybele has firmly turned against them.

Octavia Arrives at Ostia Antica and Makes the Acquaintance of Gnaeus Elaboratus

This very early morning, at daybreak, Octavia finally makes landfall on Italian soil, at Ostia Antica, the main naval and maritime hub of the Roman Empire, only a few hours' journey from the capital.

At the pier, she and her retinue are recognized by an assistant fleet paymaster and invited to breakfast with Gnaeus Elaboratus, the one and only senior fleet paymaster. Octavia accepts and before long finds herself placed opposite Gnaeus and in conversation with the man.

"Thank you, Senior Fleet Paymaster, for receiving us at your table in such a spontaneous manner."

"Oh, it's nothing. And just call me Gnaeus."

"Gnaeus, then. You have had quite a sumptuous breakfast prepared, as if you had been expecting guests, yet you could not have known that we would be coming hither."

"We have breakfasts like this every day. It's normal."

"Normal?!"

"We have very complex accounting and logistics work to do. You cannot think on a hungry stomach, Lady Octavia."

"While this cannot be disputed, are you sure you are not erring in the other direction? I could not help but notice that you and your staff are —"

"Fat? Oh yes, we are! And I insist on hiring only portly personnel. My philosophy is that every man is greedy one way or another, for fame, food, riches, sex ..." Gnaeus winks at Octavia, which she — though annoyed — chooses to ignore. "Food is the most innocent weakness. We have to handle large sums of money in our line of work and I cannot have any coin-hoarders around."

"Interesting." The newly philosophical turn of this tête-à-tête almost makes up for the man's lewdness and Octavia, curious, decides to continue in this vein. "Is it not so, Gnaeus, that everybody, when given a chance, hires underlings based not on their qualifications, but based on their likeness to themselves?"

"Hmm. Let me tell you something. How I became senior fleet paymaster. And that is that something." Gnaeus Elaboratus' manner of speaking is at times constrained by his concurrent feeding and picking of the next culinary delicacy. "My house is honored by connections with the descendants of Romulus and the house of Scipio. We Elaborati are met at the Senate, in Gaul with high commanders ..." — time to chew on another morsel — "... with high commanders, as I said, in Roman trade missions to the Greek city-states and Africa. I am not baseborn."

One lady of Octavia's complement can barely stifle a laugh at this assertion. It is now Gnaeus' turn to be offended, but like Octavia before, he decides to refrain from reacting to the affront.

"But if I had not become industrious in finance before the age of six, but if I had not endeavored to become a fellow at the Naval College, but if I had not distinguished myself enough to be named Honorable Member of the SPQR Society of Monetary ... — I forget the full name, I have so many honors, but it's something really important and respected; but the long and short of it is that if I had not applied myself, I would not have had the career I now rightfully enjoy. Unlike other positions in society, that of senior fleet paymaster can only be achieved by merit."

Octavia is about to say something, but Gnaeus, having gathered speed and oblivious to their respective positions in life, plows on. "And one of my achievements here at Ostia Antica is a highly sophisticated recruiting process that was lauded by none other than Marcus Promptus. So to answer your question, a man's girth is only one of many prerequisites to his being promoted to the privilege of working at my side."

Octavia, not quite sure what to make of what she considers to be a provocation — out of ill will or out of sheer boorishness? — for now reacts in a noncommittal fashion: "That was quite a reply, Gnaeus Elaboratus."

"I know."

"I think I remember your name from another context. Are you not cousin by marriage to Heliogabalus Oratorus, the philosopher?"

"I am. I am not surprised that you have heard of him. Heliogabalus is a philosopher of major repute, Lady Octavia."

"That is one way of putting it. His book *Defense of Whoredom* was the talk of the town a few years ago, was it not?"

"It sure was and it sure got him into trouble. But in the last quinquennium I have been too busy with the Roman navy to read it. Besides, the prostitutes of harbor towns like ours need no defending."

"Really, Gnaeus Elaboratus?"

"They make enough money as it is."

"What do you think they make of their lot in life?"

"Once a slut, always a slut."

Before Octavia can think of an answer to this succinct bon mot, their meal is interrupted by one Centurio Volusus Cyrenaeus, who — without any sort of reluctance or reserve — storms into the dining hall and salutes her Ladyship. "Salutations, most noble Octavia, and welcome home! I, Centurio Volusus Cyrenaeus, am to convey to you your brother's heartfelt greetings and to ensure your safe and quick return to Rome. My centuria of heavy infantry as well as some prize cavalry, a contingent of personal maids, and your litter are at the ready to transport you, your party, and your belongings to your destination."

Centurio Volusus, posted at Ostia Antiqua for the sole purpose of meeting Octavia in case her return would lead her through this area, has been here for several weeks and, in consequence, has had quite some time to practice this little speech, which, as a result, he delivered flawlessly.

Octavia, not a woman of many feelings, has experienced enough bad ones this morning to be touched more than she would have thought by this eager expression of benevolence. "Thank you, Centurio! And thank you, Gnaeus Elaboratus, for sharing your food, time, and above all your *opinions* so freely. It is time for us to take our leave." And leave she does, as fast as possible.

The Wisdom of Rome

Octavius has named engineers of boats and engineers of applied mathematics and auxiliary engineers to explore various ship shapes and find the figure that is most commodious for naval warfare needs; particular attention is to be paid to maneuverability ergo to bringing down the waterline-to-beam ratio without fear of capsizing. Progress varying between very moderate and rather significant has already been made on several fronts: hull development, damage limitation analysis, equations on unsteady flow blue water environments, and a partial deconstruction of the "ungainliness" paradigm.

And all this seventeen centuries before Huygens!

Philosophy, Geology, Psychology

Cleopatra! Queen of queens! Woman of legend! Pride of Egypt! Cleopatra, who like no other has had a way of "to elder statesmen's cobwebbed schlongs restless make"!

For the yearly no swimsuit issue of the *Heidelberger Journal der vorderasiatischen Weiberkunde,* Cleopatra has granted us a rare interview. We beg our readers' forgiveness for not being able to grant them a look at Cleopatra unveiled due to royal decorum; however, we very much hope that the accompanying artistic sketches that were provided to us are adequate compensation. Magnificently done by her gentlewoman Iras, Cleopatra still shows herself as we have never seen her before: feminine beauty on the ramparts of Alexandria, tenderness set against stone, in the loosest and most exquisite of garments, the wind playing with her hair — oh, to be one of the elements to be nearest Cleopatra!

"If we may begin with Semonides of Amorgos ..."

Cleopatra smiles. "We may."

"You evidently know the philosopher and his philosophy."

"Of course. At court, we have amused ourselves greatly by assigning the right animals to women of our acquaintance and to women of general renown. I have to admit that this helped us pass the time more than once, when we did not know what else to do. We also considered if the same or other animals would be most appropriate for men and what animal Semonides would be if he were female."

"And?"

"Dog or bee."

"And you yourself are ... ?"

"As Cleopatra and as Pharaoh, I transcend such limitations. I am a goddess. But if I *had* to choose, then the very highest expression of fox, with some horse of the most fabulous kind thrown in for good measure."

"You have a very healthy ego."

"I am the ultimate flowering of Egypt. Why shouldn't I?"

"You certainly are to be complimented on your collaboration with Iras on your portraits — could you tell us more about your process there?"

"Oh, we were just doing our thing, Iras drawing and me posing next to the sandstone or limestone — I keep forgetting: is that particular stretch of rock sandstone from Gebel Silsila or limestone from Tura? Or do I have it all backwards and it is *limestone* from Gebel Silsila? Or perhaps even sandstone from Tura?"

"Hard to say."

"But I do want you to know that, in spite of my ignorance, I would just *love* to go on a quarry expedition and get the hands of my personal entourage dirty: to personally oversee the earth giving up alabaster at Hatnub, granite at Aswan, and gold near Fort Ikkur!"

"That would be quite the trip."

"Wouldn't it?! Oh, and I totally forgot the turquoise mines at Serabit! I am such a goof today! My condition of pregnancy must be at fault!"

"Would turquoise be your favorite, now that you mention it with such emotion?"

"Absolutely, yes, and basalt and granite and diorite and granodiorite and alabaster and carnelian and even those terribly common tectosilicates such as feldspar and quartz as long as they are from my soil — maybe not gold, as it has become *so* predictable in royal environs lately."

"And you wouldn't want to be predictable."

"I don't want to be predictable, I just don't. It wouldn't behoove a queen of the name Cleopatra VII Thea Philopator Thea Neotera and it just wouldn't be me. With the only exception that I prefer to be predictable when it is predictable to be unpredictable."

"You surely stunned the world with your choice of man to father your first child. And after that, nobody would have thought that you would choose the same kind of mate again."

"Same kind of mate? Really? A Roman Atlas once more, yes, but things are so much more relaxed with Antony. I would like to think that life is a beach, but Julius literally needed to be dragged to the beach, supremely worded to shed all his armor and then dragged further into the waters. Never had I suspected that having fun could be such a chore."

"You went skinny-dipping with Julius Caesar?!"

"What else is there to do at 3 a.m.?" Cleopatra turns serious again. "You have no idea how much cajoling that took — there was so much tension and restlessness in that man. He was always on the move, always scheming, always trying to do everything at once. Even the sex was just go-go-go! I was able to teach him to let go and let himself go momentarily, but not more than momentarily."

"And now you're together with Antony."

"And now I'm together with Antony and finally feel I have *arrived*, not as pharaoh and ruler of Egypt which I did so long ago I don't want to be reminded, but as a *woman*. I at last feel *truly womanly* in all respects. Antony and I are just *so compatible* — sexually, emotionally, intelle— okay, maybe not intellectually, but he knows how to have fun — I'm sure he's having fun now out east with all the boys, running around and fighting and feasting and doing the gods know what else — he knows how to have fun and that was what I missed *so badly* when I was together with Julius, despite all his other merits, some of which were just exceptional, as we are all aware. Last question, now."

"Last question. The end of the world is never far from our minds these days, so let me ask you: is the apocalypse going to be an apocalypse of fire or an apocalypse of water?"

"Love. It will be an apocalypse of love."

The interview was conducted at the The Name of Hathor Flourishes Through Jubilation Collection of the Library of Alexandria.

Asia Minor Is Fucking Boring!

It is day twenty-one of Antony's Parthian campaign. Or is it day twenty-three? It's all the same. Once you have left behind the coastal area of the Mediterranean Sea, the scenery gets very old very fast. Shrubs and bushes and more shrubs and bushes and plains and mountains that just go on and on and on. And the villages, if there are any, are squalid and the females they encounter are just too fucking sad to fuck, even for the lowest and most proletarian of the men. The proper Parthian females are said to be so beautiful that their skin glows like honey, but they are far away, in Parthianopolis or thereabouts. Here you have nothing but inbred wretches — every few five-miles or so, as in between there is just nothing. Antony, especially, experiences the monotony most acutely and has to admit to himself that he misses not only Alexandria and Cleopatra, but Octavia — Octavia! —, too. The days of battle cannot come soon enough.

Lions, Lawlessness, and Rome's Sins of Omission — A Book Review by Acarnanicus Severus

Full disclosure, right at the start: Ra-Ptahhotep II, the author of this book, is someone I have now known for quite a while and someone I very much respect both on a personal and professional level. Ra-Ptahhotep II has never been a partisan in politics but has always followed his own conscience and reasoning, wherever it might lead him: so we find him a progressive when it comes to mixed-race intimacy, of which he is a staunch advocate and practitioner, but we also find him an imperial security conservative ("that is the foundation we cannot do without," he has told me, more than once).

So I'm honored and pleased that the *Roman Gazette* has asked me to review his latest offering. But I'm also surprised. *Lions, Lawlessness, and Rome's Sins of Omission* (not his punchiest title, so I'll call it *LLRSO* from here on) takes us to Nubia, of all places, and documents the wildlife crisis there, also a first for R-P. We learn that Egypt's pharaohs have had a thing for lions and cats for longer than anyone can remember (or wants to remember), and their obsession with those kitties has resulted in a dearth of these creatures roaming free — the ones that are left are mostly reduced to living as pets, only shadows of what their ancestors were in the wild. And now, because they can't find them in their own country anymore, those monarchists have taken their hunting chariots south of the border. Now I hear you ask: "Why should we Romans care?" I'll tell you why: the Nubian Alliance, though not an SPQR province, is an important ally and trading partner. We have signed several treaties with them and have committed ourselves to local infrastructure support (mostly trade-related stuff: designs for customs, markets, etc.) and also to making sure their strike force is up to scratch. For reasons that are too complicated to get into here, the removal of the big cats from the fragile Nubian ecosystem that is underway these days is a disaster, first upsetting their wildlife, then their agriculture, and finally the Nubians' own survival (famines, malnourishment, low birth weight infants — you get the picture).

If we Romans simply accept those repeated incursions into the sovereign lands of our friends, if Nubia is undermined, if Nubia falls, then we will not only have lost a trade route and a partner, but also — deservedly — the respect of the civilized world. To quote from the book:

> From the perspective of the Nubian Alliance, Egyptian hunting in Nubian territory is illegal. Our position, too, can only be that this is egregiously unlawful. This is a position that we may not concede if we do not want to concurrently abandon Nubia and our standing at home and abroad. It would be remiss of us not to make clear to the House of the Ptolemies the costs of their unilateral actions. What would happen without Roman leadership? (*LLRSO*, p. 638)

I think we all know the answer to that one. But do we also act on it? At the moment, we are in danger of lapsing into isolationism: too many of our politicians in Rome are too busy with their petty squabbles to really *think* about the Egyptian question, too many of our citizens still react phlegmatically to outbreaks of feminism, too many of our allies look to us to "provide policy alternatives in the Two Lands region," as *LLRSO* puts it, and instead only see nonintervention and withdrawal.

R-P's new book is another reminder that Cleopatra's cult of personality (which has already infected an alarming number of the world's deviants and sentimentalists, even here in the center) and Egyptian ultra-nationalism have no place in our midst. There is recklessness and there is caution, but too much caution is not only weakness, but also recklessness in and of itself. Thank you, R-P, for telling us. Thank you, R-P, for fighting the good fight.

P.S. I have to react to another review of *LLRSO* that has unfortunately managed to cause a stir. Written by one "Hathormose of Egypt" (surely a pseudonym, always a sign of cowardice), it's a hatchet job that tries to discredit the book and its author on the basis of something called SVA (Statistical Vocabulary Analysis). Just to give you a taste of how wacko this is, here's a direct quote:

> The words "penetrate," "penetrated," and "unpenetrated" occur in total eighty-six times in the opening fifty-one pages, while there is a short and concentrated burst of "embrace," "embraced," "hug," "hugged," and "hugging" in chapter thirty-two, again in a purely technical/political science context, numbering in combination twenty-five entries.

This claptrap has the crude title "Ra-Ptahhotep II's Hate-Boner for Cleopatra" and wants to sell us the idea that there is a "hidden psycho-sexual aspect." If that were not enough, R-P is also accused of narcolepsy, autism, and obesity — all diagnosed based on his style of writing (the real content of the book is barely referred to). R-P is not a native speaker of Latin and he can be a bit ponderous at times, but if his carefully reasoned and very thorough argument can only be attacked on those superficial grounds, then that anal-retentive word-counter Hathormose and other jackasses of his ilk should just admit defeat and leave important debates concerning the future of our society to levelheaded individuals who know how to have a mature dialogue and how to behave themselves in public.

Acarnanicus Severus, recipient of the Ra-Ptahhotep II Award, is one of Rome's leading intellectuals and sits on the boards of ERPSA and the SPQR Freedom Forum. He is also the editor and co-author of the recently published anthology In Loco Parentis: How We Can Impart Realism and Moderation to the Egyptian Character.

Is a Senior Fleet Paymaster Still a Senior Fleet Paymaster When He Has Lost His Job?

Within a week of meeting Octavia, Senior Fleet Paymaster Gnaeus Elaboratus is forced to retire without pension.

What led Octavia to have the overweight executive removed from his post? The mere sight of him? Or his want of moderation? Or his unchaste choice of words? Or that he kept licking his lips? Or that he had suffered his first cousin Tertia to marry the unsavory Heliogabalus Oratorus, whose contributions to gender studies (key quote: "a woman investigates a book and fails and a thousand women investigate a book and fail also") had always irritated Octavia greatly? Or that Gnaeus himself, by deriding women impelled to sell their love, gave offense to the sisterhood and thus to the woman who considered herself its champion and queen? Or the sum of all that and more?

While we may never divine the answers to those questions, one thing is certain: no matter how important and indispensable we may think we are, to sour the mood of persons more powerful than ourselves is ill afforded and not to be done lightly.

Whatever Happened to Cybele's Revenge?

Give it time. A quick revenge is rarely ever the best revenge. The theft-rape-pillage that took place in the Roman woods will eventually bring dark fortune to those responsible.

An Egyptian Perspective on Deserts

Nubia is a desert. And Arabia is a desert. And Libya is a desert. And Judea is a desert. And Carthage is a desert. And all of Parthia is a desert. And the entire Roman Empire and all its provinces are deserts. And how can they not be deserts? Any place whose pyramids are lacking in number and craftsmanship is a desert. Any place that is without tombs that are hidden-decorated-eternal is a desert. Any place that does not keep the worship of Maat is a desert. Any place that is without hieroglyphs is a desert. Any place that is not home to the world's only donkey night race in which the donkeys swerve to avoid the temples is a desert. Any place that does not feel right to you because it somehow seems off-wrong-faulty to you is a desert. Any place that is not guarded-protected-cursed by the venom of snakes and scorpions is a desert. Any place that is without the Egyptian tongue and instead with tongues that are imperfect-inept-senseless is a desert. Any place that is without crocodiles or does not respect-recognize-cherish crocodiles as sons and daughters of Sobek who is the son of Neith and the lord of the Faiyum and the holder and steward of one of the four elements is a desert. Any place that is not to an archaeologist what a flower in bloom is to a honeybee is a desert. Any place that cannot boast of being the heart and wonder and treasure of the world is a desert. Come home from desolation! Come home to Egypt!

King Polemon Is a Fount of Information Indeed

As a reward for King Polemon's constant and loyal service during this campaign so far, Antony lets the man ride side by side with him today, a decision he comes to regret in short order, as Polemon proves to be all too chatty.

"Say, Lord Antony, I have to wonder that your campaign relies so much on foot soldiers rather than horsed men. This, if I remember my Roman military history correctly and I think I do, is nearly the same ratio of infantry to cavalry Marcus Crassus chose when he invaded Parthia with such dismal results. Much like yourself, he relied on allies of varying reliability, the worst being Prince Alchaudonius of Arabia — how Crassus could have ever considered such a man so inadequate and full of himself an ally is anyone's guess —, Prince Alchaudonius of Arabia, as I said, who very much reminds me of King Artavasdes of Armenia in more ways than one, and of course also Regent Abgarus of Osrhoene. Abgarus of Osrhoene, a tricky and devious character, to say the least. To pretend to engage in reconnaissance against the enemy and in reality to proceed to inform the enemy of the exact state and aims of the Roman expedition. How treacherous! And to have the gall to lead Crassus through terrain so advantageous to the Parthians, I say! How very treacherous indeed! But to return to the topic of infantry and cavalry. The Roman over-reliance on slow-moving infantry proved fatal in combat with the Parthians, as I'm sure you're aware. Yet many historians say that it was not the Roman over-reliance on slow-moving infantry *per se* that proved fatal to the Parthian campaign of Marcus Crassus, but the very person of Marcus Crassus himself! How could such an experienced Roman military leader blunder so badly? Rejecting the advice of both local guides and trustworthy members of his own staff such as Cassius, a most eminent military commander in his own right? Being such a bad judge of character, not only in the case of Abgarus of Osrhoene, but also in several others, most probably and most perniciously concerning himself? Not knowing he was too old and grown too mentally inflexible for such a venture? A bad judge of character, indeed, I say! And then, already rather deep in Parthia, the olive branch extended by the Parthian envoy Vagises, to avoid unnecessary bloodshed on either side and to save face on both, dismissed out of hand! What an affront, I say! And then, the utterly tragic and shameful battle at Carrhae! Inexorable and inevitable, I must say! To have outnumbered the Parthians three to one and to have lost! What a tragedy! What a shame! Bows and arrows, that is what it was all about, bows and arrows, I say. Shield-piercing arrows, grievous, most grievous. The Romans might as well have thrown away their shields for all the good they did them. And

the loss of three quarters of over forty thousand men, including the elite cohorts under Legate Vargunteius! What a disgrace! What a —"
In the last minute, Antony has hatched a battle plan of his own.
"King Polemon!"
"Yes, Lord Antony?"
"I have to make you a compliment. You are a very knowledgeable man."
"Thank you, sir! But I have to say that —"
"Just shut up and listen. I have decided that your obvious talents would stand my man Statianus in good stead. He is a good officer and that is why I gave him and his two legions the job of escorting the siege engines convoy. But he still has a lot to learn. I'm therefore detaching you to Statianus *immediately*. Don't be sparing in your advice and don't take no for an answer."
"Thank you very much, sir! I cannot say how flattered —"
"Now get your ass to Statianus!"
"Of course, sir! Thank you, sir!"

Everything Is Going According to Plan

Is it the fresh sea air? Or the more southerly climate? Or the restful nights, far from the din of Rome? Or that his desk job has become less of a desk job and more of a job of being out and about and checking things and giving orders and saluting and being saluted? Or the splendor of so many able-bodied men working together and busied in their diverse functions to end in one common purpose? Or chiefly the sight of those of the men that are the rowers sinking their oars into the water in perfect harmony again and again? Or that the first intimations that Antony's Parthian campaign has gone balls-up have by this time reached even Palinurus? Or the prospect of the victory to come? Or the cumulation or indeed multiplication of all these factors? Agrippa's testosterone levels have of course always been as high as behooves a Roman leader and man of action, but they may now have surpassed those of his youth and he feels himself pitching a tent on the slightest provocation.

Nagging Out Loud

Khamerernebty is the eldest daughter in a big family and also a mother herself.

Khamerernebty is barely twenty-two years old, but due to her plural output and intemperate diet no longer to be considered shapely by any stretch of the imagination. Khamerernebty is not happy with the way things are. Khamerernebty is a self-styled exponent of wisdom and men's studies authority who passes judgment on the world from a menstrual hut in Upper Egypt's Field Mouse nome, far-far-far from the fashionable world of Alexandria, a nome that has never been fashionable itself, a nome that is home to a verily disappointing number of Egypt's 11,839 archaeological sites and points of interest, a nome whose only claim to fame is to have postulated and dubiously so that it was part of the legendary pharaoh Hatshepsut's coronation route and that said menstrual hut was built on the spot where the queen-to-be-crowned had her period and stayed the night.

Khamerernebty proclaims: "Roman men who hold themselves so much more the men as they are Roman men are the worst of men! They say they give birth to life-stability-culture, they say they care and share, they say they welcome debate, they talk of friends and partners. Oh, they are whole and skillful and subtle, indeed! They are as those that hunt gazelles from a chariot! They eat rapidly, they all dress the same, they only hear what they want to hear! Lords of capriciousness, they call us infantile-petulant-aberrant, they probe and test, they offer false counsel, they are adept at interest and subjection, they do not know they are the most enslaved! In sum, they are as those that conceit themselves seated on a mat that is the mat of verdant-lush-fruitful Osiris yet they are too sick with their sickness of death. And we are *above* their bare esteem. Romans! Men! All that coarseness! All that bluster! And war! What a sausagefest!"

All this she says from an edifice in dire need of repairs, in a state of advanced collapse, nearly in ruins.

Roman experts agree that Egypt's infrastructure needs very much work.

A Note on Egyptian Menstrual Huts

There are those huts that are designated menstrual huts and only serve as such, just as there are other specific huts and also ordinary huts. However, if when in the course of hut-to-hut-to-hut-to-hut-to-hut-to-hut travel which in Egypt is one of the most common kinds of travel, it is that time of the month for a female guest of a specific or ordinary hut, that hut relinquishes its other functions and becomes a menstrual hut for the duration of her stay.

It Is the Self-Inflicted Wounds That Hurt the Most

Antony successfully got rid of over-communicative King Polemon by sending him to Statianus, but might have done otherwise had he really considered the likely consequences of putting those two men in close contact in such a manner. In Statianus' place, Enobarbus would have handled the situation with aplomb. Statianus, however, although almost as glib of tongue as Enobarbus, had been a field officer and as such was much less willing to suffer fools gladly, royalty notwithstanding.

What must have happened is that Statianus hit the king on his head for his forwardness; with the king not relenting, Statianus must have then pulled Polemon off his horse, whereupon the Pontic troops, offended in their honor, doubtlessly offered violence to the Roman; as a result, the men of Legio Fretensis and Legio Ferrata most certainly entered the fray — this, if we are to believe the few survivors of this melee.

So: Legio Fretensis wiped out, Legio Ferrata wiped out, and the allied Pontic troops wiped out; with the Armenian troops already gone, the former sixteen legions are now only little more than half that many. And not to forget the irreparable damage to the siege engines that now need to be abandoned, most notably the fifty-foot-long battering rams, wood for which cannot be gotten in these parts. All this without the meanest assistance of the Parthian military, which has so far refused to show itself.

Parthian Intelligence and Counter-Intelligence Is the Most Capable Intelligence and Counter-Intelligence Outfit in All of Western Asia, Part 3

HENHOUSE OTHER IRREFUTABLE

Marcus Promptus Gets to Interview Agrippa

Marcus Promptus — son, boatman, administrator, SPQR naval safety center deputy commander, politico-military prodigy, senator in the making, utterly suave, devastatingly knowledgeable, and simply *hot* in every sense of the word — has traveled to Palinurus to interview Agrippa for the *Roman Gazette*.

The two men talk to each other while seated on the al fresco deck of the officers' mess overlooking the waterfront and bay. A pair of staff clerks — two, since one is none — take notes and subsequently put together the transcript of the conversation, which will be further edited for cogency and coherence — not that there would be much need for that, of course — by Marcus Promptus' own hand. Readers will be interested to learn that Marcus Promptus has not written down any questions in preparation for this encounter as only people of lesser intelligence are forced to resort to such a crutch; moreover, to cling on to checklists of any kind in non-technical pursuits is a mark of the petit bourgeois and therefore to be avoided by an up-and-coming hero of Rome.

"Most esteemed Agrippa, let me begin by confessing freely that you and your work have been a constant inspiration in my life and career. I do not want to bore you by going through the many occasions on which your example stimulated me to rethink and expand my approach; instead, let me only thank you once more for your inviting me to lecture at Sora last winter — I could not imagine a more productive way of spending the solstice than having you and your graduate class hearing me out on the subject of post-discipline practice and pushing me to further refine my arguments regarding the nexus of practice-based research and research-based practice."

"Duly noted; and let *me*, most respectful and therefore most respected Marcus Promptus, again thank you for sharing your views with us at Sora Military Academy. Particularly absorbing, in my estimation, were your groundbreaking concepts of theory as practice."

"My gratitude to you, Agrippa — and of course very much to the point, as my passion is to provide an integrated framework that serves as a useful basis for concrete and comprehensive action. But on to the unavoidable topic, on to what we are all too aware of, on to what needs to be dealt with: the threat of a belligerent Egypt. Quo vadis Euro-African security?"

"Sad but true. Lupus Septimus, head of the Africa Program at the Rome Group, perhaps the most accomplished expert at the most accomplished policy forum we can ask for, put it this way: the bad news is that for far too long Egypt has proven a disruptive element; the good news, however, is that finally every right-thinking Roman knows and agrees that bold and stringent security measures are needed to curtail the threat."

"Lupus Septimus — isn't he the one with the small teeth and a slight lisp?"

"No, Marcus Promptus. That is another Lupus Septimus, the spokesman for the Ministry of Military Transportation and Mobility."

"I stand corrected. While we certainly all concur with the assessment of Lupus Septimus, could you maybe elaborate and share your perspective — which, from your lofty vantage point, I am sure, will not fail to teach me and the readers of the *Roman Gazette* something new."

"Although I am not at liberty to divulge everything ..." — here Marcus Promptus nods sympathetically, as he understands the need for discretion in such challenging times — "... let me tell you the following: One. There are indeed patterns of suspicious behavior by the Egyptians and they have increased in number and frequency in recent times. Two. Roman naval archery and anti-piracy units have now taken care of some of the most egregious excesses. It is to be remarked that our men achieved this without stepping onto Egyptian soil. It is also to be remarked that those actions were taken with the full support of the Mediterranean community. And I repeat — and this bears repeating — that at no time did any of our SPQR troops violate Egyptian territorial sovereignty. Article 651 was therefore not contravened. Three. Data supplied by the SPQR Water and Land Data Center (SPQRWLDC) in Ancona has proven to be reliable and actionable intelligence and will continue to be applied to in-theater scenarios in the foreseeable future. Four. We are very close to 'Drusus' level combat ready status, meaning that we will be a) ready to fully monitor shipping activities in all crucial sea areas, b) ready to fully answer any further provocative behavior by Egypt, c) ready to fully provide timely disaster relief to our allies in the region, d) ready to fully perform naval maintenance and repairs as needed, and e) ready to then undertake the steps to reach 'Romulus' level combat ready status."

"In spite of the —"

"I am very sorry, Marcus Promptus. I have to cut our conversation short. While my schedule is always full, these days this is more the case than ever. Thank you, Marcus Promptus, for coming to Palinurus. You will see yourself out?"

Rather taken aback, Marcus Promptus gets up and says the only thing that can be said in such a situation. "Thank you for your time, Agrippa."

The Fennec Fox

Known to bark-purr-snarl. Foreshadows impossibility. Precautious. Good listener and friend in solitude. Loved especially by young children. Native to northern Africa and to no other place. Slandered as docile.

All You Need to Know Is Everything

By now, you should have learned that there is no salvation outside Egypt. There just isn't.

You can't waste your time on other cultures and general introductions to ancient civilizations.

You can't rely on "best of Egypt" compilations on your quest, as everything is the best in Egypt.

You can't make use of executive summaries, as your path is not that of the executive but that of the rudderless-lost-incomplete who wants to acquire the attributes of the initiate worthy of the revered Fennec Fox.

Instead, it is upon you to learn all there is to learn about your real home. And "all" means *all*. You are to consult *all* the material you can.

Only from Pliny the Elder do we get a description of the pyramids that is both haughty-quaint-contemptuous and unsatisfactory-dull-brisk.

Only in the writings of Julius Africanus is there a proper explanation of why the women of Egypt bear twins and triplets much more frequently than women of lesser tribes.

Only the *Proceedings of the Eighth Astronomical and Gods of Egypt Technical Seminar* yield to us information about the Neteru's construction of the sun and moon within the nothingness of the first waters.

Only in the *Memphis High Court Reports* — and not in the otherwise more inclusive *All Egypt Legal Decisions* — do we find a nomarch's futile attempt to be given the right to import monkeys for non-pharaonic entertainment purposes (to perform music and to dance, for the nomarch of the Helpful Soil nome, in the reign of Psamtek II; see also the Two Lands Simian Assessment Act written into law in the reign of Psamtek III).

Only the *Ode to a Pomegranate Tree As the Very Joy of Egypt*, authored by an anonymous farmer near Asyut (find-spot), offers us a botanical praise-song that is not too heavily biased towards fig trees, palm trees, or other traditional plants of the genre.

Make yourself scarce and befriend the staff of rare book and manuscript collections and the staff of departments of Egyptian antiquities at major museums and the staff of departments of Egyptology at overfunded research universities. Consider no countries other than Egypt. Listen to no music other than that of lutes and sistrums and tambourines. Look at nothing but beautiful coffee-table books on Egypt. Talk about nothing but king lists and commemorative scarabs and six-stepped pyramids and rescue archaeology and the falcon-god Khonsu. Think about nothing but your reclamation of the blessed land ...

A Bold Visionary Helps
Antony to Regain Hope

Antony is sitting outside his general's tent, sulking. This Parthian campaign was cursed, he thinks to himself. All those plans and theories of Octavia and Enobarbus that sounded so convincing in

Alexandria have proven to be useless. Things just have a way of going wrong. Which shouldn't have been a surprise considering some of the idiots involved. Artavasdes. Polemon. Statianus. Hard to tell which of those idiots was the biggest idiot. All this effort, all these troops, all that adversity endured — it was all for nothing. And now the siege engines are gone, too. How can you crack walnuts when you have nothing to crack walnuts with? The gold reserves of the Parthian city of Tabriz would be seriously worth it, but now he can't take Tabriz, not in this reduced state.

Antony is not aware that he has started speaking out loud, and neither is he aware that Centurio Silius of Legio Antiqua has been waiting to speak to him.

"Forget the gold, sir!"

"Sossius?!"

"Silius, sir! Centurio of Legio Antiqua, at your command!"

"What are you talking about, Centurio?"

"Sir, forget the gold, sir! We cannot take Tabriz now, sir, and we have to accept that. But I have come to see you, sir, because I have a very useful new plan, sir!"

"Centurio, I'm really not in a good mood. So if this plan is a stinker, I just might have you flogged for wasting my time."

"I understand, sir! I propose a nighttime attack of the fortifications of Phraaspa, Phraapa, and Phraata, sir!"

"Fortifications means for-ti-fied; we have no siege material, remember, Centurio?"

"That is why we should not attempt to take them!"

"Come again? What's the point of attacking, then?"

"Surely they will shoot at us with their superior arrows, sir!"

"You got that right. If you have a death wish, I can have that taken care of right now. Guards!"

Two burly men appear.

"Get rid of that centurio for me, will you?"

As they are about to do just that, Silius makes haste to persuade Antony. "Baggage-wagons! We put our baggage-wagons in front! The arrows will then be ours!"

"Guards, unhand him and leave us!"

They again do as they are told.

"That is not a bad idea, Centurio. Not a bad idea at all! I have to say that I'm impressed."

"Thank you, sir!"

"What's your name again, soldier?"

"Silius, sir! Centurio of Legio Antiqua!"

"Antiqua. Hmmm. Weren't they destroyed in that tussle with Polemon's men?"

"That was Legio Ferrata, sir! Not Antiqua!"

"Right, right. And the nighttime thing is that they don't see that they are shooting at our baggage-wagons and not at us?"

"That's correct, sir!"

Antony makes his decision quickly as he has not been able to come up with any other workable ideas in the days since the most recent severe loss of troops and materials. "Okay. Let's give it a go, then."

Parthian Intelligence and Counter-Intelligence Is the Most Capable Intelligence and Counter-Intelligence Outfit in All of Western Asia, Part 4

HIGHBALL BORROWED IF OBVIOUS PRANCING THEN MINTAGE FRONT COUNTERMARK

An Ignorant and Reductionistic Misinterpretation, but Not Surprising at All, Sadly

In Athens, the Egyptian consulate general to the Greek city-states heaps scorn on the exchange between Marcus Promptus and Agrippa, saying that it was "just so much military porn."

Some people *never* learn. *That*, if anything, is to be decried here.

Might Not a Woman Try to Save the World?

If, when leaving the capital city, you take a long and winding road, you are either drunk or actually not in Italy, but in remote-bewildering-inefficient Mesopotamia, outside the gates of Babylon; all the roads leaving Rome are as straight as the current state of Roman civil engineering and its mastery over the terrain permit.

To begin again: if, when leaving the bounds of Rome, you take a certain *straight* road that is called the *Appian Way* and that (you should know this) pursues a south-easterly direction, you might notice a sizeable group of temporary tents not too far off the route's twenty-five mile marker, literally but perhaps not figuratively under some quite dark clouds; not surprising, really, as the weather has been uniformly bad all the way from the capital. This ad hoc military settlement has sprung into existence to give a group of hand-picked cadres the chance to personally learn from Octavius — officially. Unofficially, it is a test of their ability to mobilize and march their troops to a new location at the briefest notice and in inclement conditions; and it is also an opportunity for the triumvir to informally assess their personalities and interpersonal dynamics; beyond that, Octavius considers it necessary to convey an image of himself as a successful military strategist — while it has proven wise to delegate such matters to the more suited Agrippa, Octavius cannot afford to seem to be eclipsed by his friend's generalship.

So: as all the soldiers on guard duty — and they are numerous indeed, given the status of the men they have to protect — start making faces because the drizzle is threatening to become rain proper again and war on their relative comfort, the "elite" are indoors and dry and ... therefore to be envied? Not in their estimate. Octavius is personally conducting a high-level seminar on his use of, improvements on, and thoughts about Etruscan hand-signaling techniques during decisive battle moments. The fourth unbroken hour of this has begun and there is still no end in sight. The officers, men of action unused to excessive theory, are *not* happy and a number of them have started to question whether their allegiance should not really lie with Antony, who, though also an ass in a different way, at least knows how to party.

Imagine their relief, then, when following a confusion of voices without doors, Octavia — tired-looking, but determined as always — enters the tent with a crying baby in her arms. "Ave, my dear brother!"

Octavius cannot hide his indignation and surprise. "Octavia! What are you doing here? Can't you see I'm in a meeting?"

"And can't *you* see that your men need a break?"

"Fine. Officers, do a perimeter check and then break for refreshments."

The cadres do not need to be told twice.

"Why this groundless intrusion?"

"Is this the way to talk to your sister and the wife of your brother in arms? Who has selflessly come to see you on a matter of great importance? Who has had to give birth on the roadside less than an hour ago, in view of the troops accompanying her?"

"Is it a boy?"

"No, it's not a boy, it's a girl. Your niece, if you follow. I was going to let you name her, but I'm not so sure anymore. Not after this frosty reception."

Octavius decides that it is in his own interest to become more welcoming towards Octavia and forces himself to be the diplomat rather than the military man. "Please have a seat, sister. Congratulations on your newborn child."

"Thank you, brother."

"I apologize for my manners — I have been so busy with my legions and officers lately that I must have forgotten that there is also a civilian sphere of life."

"Apology accepted, then. You say that you have been busy with your legions and officers — doing what exactly?"

"Routine capacity building."

"Routine capacity building? Is that genuinely so, brother? With what aims in mind?"

"Your curiosity, sister, has led you to make worthy breakthroughs in river management and I and the Roman people are grateful for that. But when it comes to military matters, you really do not need to concern yourself on my behalf."

"I don't?"

"That's right, sister. You don't."

"Then explain to me why your men were just about to gang up on you and murder you in self-defense before you bored them to death with your silly pantomime? Why I just happened to save your life?"

"My men were not bored, but merely trying to hide their double fascination for me and the very latest in battlecraft. That you as a woman and even as a very intelligent woman cannot understand the intricate facets of male psychology is forgivable and therefore forgiven."

"You sound as if you were an Antony that suddenly got the smarts of an Enobarbus, but none of his insight. So let me avoid any further misunderstandings by being as blunt and clear as possible: you and Agrippa are preparing for war on Antony, but I will not let you tear the Republic apart in a civil war. Not now, not at the moment when the world needs the Roman Empire more than ever."

"Speak further."

"When it comes to weapons and legions, you think you will soon more than match Antony. This is true. However, you should know that I have had my husband raid selected Parthian armories. This means that any troops you send his way will be badly wounded or killed even if they achieve some of their objectives. Brother, please think on this! Do you really want to throw away so many good men only for your glory? Orphan so many children?"

"I have done quite a lot of thinking concerning the strategic challenges of Rome, thank you very much. You stress the importance of Roman leadership. How, I ask you, can we lead and assist the world when one of our foremost men is an inveterate and incompetent troublemaker and blunderer? Antony, not I, has an unquenchable thirst for glory that makes him blind to his own faults. If he does not presently step down, the only way to stability and peace will be war indeed."

The exhaustion from the stress of giving birth and her diplomatic efforts has finally caught up with Octavia and so she lets Octavius speak on, herself now unable to respond in a timely manner.

"And I suspect you know that any Parthian campaign is fraught with difficulties and therefore doubtful of success, particularly with a foolhardy general such as Antony at the helm. It has been most unwise of you to involve yourself in this dispute. In the end, your meddling may hasten Antony's fall from power, in which case you will have done the world a great service. Even so, the facts are that you absented yourself from Italy without leave and then fully took the side of a man who has not only cheated on you personally, but who more importantly also has a history of flouting negotiated solutions of a political nature. I cannot allow any more interference of this kind. I am of half a mind to exile you to Cappadocia, de facto and irrevocably this time; yet as I suspect that you might be able to stir up trouble even there, I am sending you back to Rome where you will be under house arrest and close guard. Consider this a kindness; anyone else I would have put to death for such disobedience. Make no mistake, however: if you again attempt to instigate irregularities, you and your daughter will suffer an accident fatal to you both."

Octavia cannot believe what she is hearing — is she hallucinating? That a brother, a brother with whom she has been raised and instructed and bonded as only family could have been, would treat her so wickedly? "Is this what you honestly want to do to your sister? Does our common past mean nothing to you?"

"You chose to force my hand. The day is too advanced for you to begin your return journey. I will instruct my quartermaster to prepare lodging for you and your child. You will set out for Rome by daybreak. Goodbye, Octavia."

A Night of Trouble, a Night of Battle and War

Make bright the shields! Gather the arrows! In the Middle East, darkness has fallen what feels like only a little time ago, and strong-beyond-strong jackals have already begun pulling the solar barque of the Egyptian sun god Ra over the sands of the underworld, now in the first duat, and then in the eleven duats to come, as they are wont to do.

Devise and prepare the ambushes! Antony has put Silius in charge of tonight's trickery of the Parthians. The baggage wagons have been filled with straw to rightly catch the fiendish weapons of war, and the essentials unloaded and distributed among the infantry and the cavalry.

Off to Phraaspa! The baggage wagons placed in front, the Parthians in the fortification provoked, the arrows received, the siege withdrawn, Silius commended by Antony.

Off to Phraapa! Once more, the baggage wagons placed in front, the Parthians in the fortification provoked, the arrows received, the siege withdrawn, Silius commended by Antony.

Dreadful combat! On the way to Phraata, the Romans are inconvenienced and denied passage and attacked by a major land force led by King Phraates of Parthia. The baggage wagons are heavy and the Romans are premature in victory and the wind has changed not a point but in entirety. The throne of King Phraates is most powerful! Antony realizes that they have to flee west and tells Silius and Silius tells Antony "Save yourself, my Emperor, and leave me to my fate!" and Silius and Legio Antiqua stem the Parthian tide as Antony and the rest abandon all and Silius and Legio Antiqua are torn apart and rent asunder and stomped upon by the rage that is Parthia.

History Does Repeat Itself

And what should they know of England who only England know?
–Kipling

Egypt. There were problems quite a few years before Antony's escapades, you know. Roman troops posted to Alexandria by General Gabinius during the reign of Ptolemy Auletes, the pharaoh before

Cleopatra, ceased to worship at the altar of Disciplina, the goddess of Roman military discipline, and went native and married the local women and produced bastard offspring, shocking all upstanding citizens in the process. And when there were problems in Syria — what is it with that country? — and the Roman governor Calpurnius Bibulus sent his two sons to get reinforcements from the land of the pyramids, the Gabinians did not want to be uprooted and to prevent that thought to outright kill both of them, which they did. To keep the peace with Rome and to smooth some very ruffled feathers, Cleopatra — by then the new pharaoh — had the ringleaders arrested and taken away to be dealt with by Roman justice.

There has to be something in the siren call of Egyptian pussy and the lunatic ways of those womenfolk to lead some hitherto stoic and reliable men on to the path of destruction. What exactly it is we may never know, but one idea for future reference must certainly be strictly limited tours of duty.

Straight Out of Sicily

Nobody in their right mind would launch an attack on Palinurus. Octavius and Agrippa have been massing troops there for months now, making it one of the biggest concentrations of Roman military in the entire Empire.

But not everybody is in their right mind. Sextus Pompey, for example. Renegade Roman, party king, self-proclaimed ruler of Sicily. Octavius and Agrippa are aware of the man and the small-scale pirating he engages in to keep himself and his followers in bountiful provisions — and have dismissed him as lazy, nothing more than a nuisance and of no importance in their grand strategy calculations, and rightfully so. Yet they neglected to consider his equally mad and much more ambitious second Menas, who has now most violently entered the picture and upset their plans in a very unpleasant fashion.

Menas, an eager beaver keen to impress his master, and also egged on by others, chose to do some rowing — not the kind of rowing that is leisurely and lackadaisical and brief, but the kind of rowing that takes you over 150 nautical miles in a matter of days, the kind of rowing that scorns coast-hugging routes for the open sea, the kind of rowing that is simply not believed until it has been done. It does not matter how many guards you have on duty at your base or camp or fortification: when it is the middle of the night, when the attackers are stealthy and not at all expected, when then there is doubt if the attackers really are hostiles and not a patrol of your own, when the rest of your men first need to be roused from their sleep — then the defense is not what it could have been.

All you need are a few good axes, a few good torches, and a few good men and it is amazing how many wooden ships you can sink and burn in quite a short period of time. Quite a sight, too!

There is, of course, the double snag that once you have begun injuring a giant, the giant will start striking back and that casualties will be inevitable — Menas, his madness notwithstanding, was enough of an officer to know this, but did not feel it necessary to overcommunicate that particular fact to his posse. Besides, it was worth the price.

Menas thought to return triumphant — which he did, for about a quarter of a nautical mile. He had been almost unable to tear himself away from the obliteration ("just one more ship, just one more ship!" he kept thinking) and when he did finally make his escape he had pushed his luck too far. The Octavians that gave chase were in no mood to deviate from their purpose and put an end to his madcap existence soon enough. Only a minority of the attackers managed to return to Sextus' private kingdom.

It was not much of a revenge, though, as the damage had been done: destruction and smoke as far as the eye could see, the Octavian naval forces in near complete disarray. What must be nothing more than a curious coincidence is that the amount of wood lost during the onslaught is the exact amount of wood taken from the realm of the Roman nature goddess Cybele.

Not All Is Lost and Torn Down

Even on this black day, there has been *some* good news. We have just received word that Croesus has officially announced and endorsed Marcus Promptus as the latest Croesus Fellow — a much-coveted title that should smooth the young man's career immeasurably. The official acknowledgment lauds him for his mission-driven acts of bravery and purpose-focused civic-mindedness. There is hope in this world!

Antony Retreats Through Hostile Lands

One would think that when every day is almost the same as the day gone before, life would simply be boring, as when Antony rode into Parthia. Or life could be nasty instead of boring, as when Antony lost yet another legion and barely escaped the clusterfuck so skillfully arranged and executed by King Phraates. But now that Antony and his troops are retreating westwards to the far-off coast, life is both boring and nasty. Food and water are scarce, there are barely enough baggage horses to carry the sick and wounded, the terrain is also a pain in the ass, morale, needless to say, is at an all-time low, and to top it all off, those Parthian degenerates keep showing up to re-engage the withdrawing Romans in hit-and-run attacks, wearing them down by attrition. Not every day, to be sure, but often and unpredictably enough, at intervals that seem arbitrary, but are not (you may call this variety, but to call this variety is to make a mockery of variety). When, once a pattern has been set, the Romans might think that they have to endure just one skirmish a day, there are more than that; when they assume that a massed Parthian presence is a sign of all-out attack, the enemy is content to just observe and follow them from a safe distance, only to vanish after a few hours; and when, after one or more days without sighting the foe, Antony's troops feel that they have outpaced the threat and no longer need to be on their guard and can finally relax, King Phraates suddenly comes upon them with a strong party of horse.

Once that particular episode is over and another loss has been sustained, Antony cries out: "Those damn Parthians with their damn superior horsemanship!" The only consolation Antony has at this point — and it is a very minor consolation — is that his Parthian campaign has been nearly as catastrophic as that of Crassus, but not quite.

BOOK FIVE

New Possibilities, New Plans

What Do Little Egyptian Children Do When They Make a Mistake?

They cry "stinky camel poopy!" and — not always, but more often than not — they then laugh it off.

Octavia Most Diligently Attended to in Rome

It has now been over a day since Palinurus was overwhelmed by chaos and disrepute, since Palinurus was almost lost to infamy, since Palinurus brought most dreadful shame to Octavius and his men. Agrippa, a high achiever all too used to success, is still in denial, having never known the bitterness of a major defeat before. "How is this possible?! How could they have done this?!" is what he keeps asking himself and everyone else on site.

Octavius, on the other hand, is still enjoying the bliss of ignorance — and also, in the master bedroom of a secluded villa, the bliss of a proconsul's wife, even if the pleasure is very much his and not hers. But what had she expected when she prostituted herself for power by way of marriage? And is she not for the moment the consort of heady might itself, as she had once desired so fervently? Stupid young thing, to make a complete abnegation of herself for the supposed privilege of plopping her butt onto a front-row seat! Would she had heeded Velleius Paterculus on the demands of great posts!

Another female who once fancied herself as some manly Venus and who in consequence likewise has to suffer Octavius' authority is his sister Octavia: now in Rome, now under house arrest in a luxurious villa on the Palatine, and now very much on her own — that is, if we do not count the baby she is currently nursing, if we do not count the villa's household staff, if we do not count the Octavian guards, and if we do not count General Caudinus who has just invited himself in — but who amongst them is not a stranger to Octavia?

"My apologies, General, if I stay seated and keep my child to my breast during your visit."

"Lady Octavia, there is no need to apologize. I was just in the neighborhood and all of a sudden I realized that you would by this time be in residence in these parts. I just had to see if you had settled in all right."

Octavia looks at the guard by her side and sighs. "As much as my present station in life allows."

"Guard, why don't you leave us alone for a while?"

"Sir, General, sir, I must not, sir!"

"Why, so few words, and so much flattery and disobedience at the same time." General Caudinus' tone now becomes much less jocular. "Guard, you are dismissed."

"Sir, General, sir, I cannot comply with that order, sir!"

"And why is that?"

"Sir, General, sir, Lord Octavius gave express command to the contrary and said that his command superseded that of any officer or magistrate who tried to pull rank on us, sir!"

"'Superseded'? 'Pull rank'? My, Lady Octavia, what fortune you have to have such a brother.'

"Indeed. He cares for me greatly."

"How great, exactly, is that care? Guard, how many of you nitwits are there in this house?"

"Sir, General, sir, I am not at liberty to disclose that information, sir!"

"'Not at liberty to disclose that information' — madder and madder still. You have parrots for guards, Lady Octavia, and what wonderful words they have been taught!"

If her change had not been not so dire, Octavia would have smiled at such a remark. "I don't know how many there are. And I'm not sure they themselves know when the others come and go and exactly how many there will be in a few hours, let alone the next day."

"Interesting. I, at least, know that I am here with one of my centurios and a complement of ninety-four foot. Ninety-eight, in principle. Four of them are on errands that are all classified. As for the select company you have to endure, I have seen no more than five so far. Maybe twelve in total, two posted at the rear, one in the kitchen getting in the way of the chef and the maids, and the rest off-duty and playing dice in some dreary servant's chamber, ready to spring into action should you decide to make a run for it, hmm?"

What a man this Caudinus is turning out to be — *her* kind of intelligent, *her* kind of sarcastic, and very much in control. But why this visit? Octavia has an idea, but is not sure she likes it. "Purely arithmetically speaking, you seem to care even more for me than my brother does. Much more."

"Purely arithmetically speaking, ninety-six is of course a much bigger number than twelve." The general addresses the other person in the room without taking his eyes off Octavia. "Wouldn't you concur, guard?"

"Sir, General, sir, I couldn't possibly say, sir!"

For a bit, nobody speaks. Not the guard, because it is not up to him to make conversation; not Octavia, because caution seems to be most warranted; not Caudinus, because he wants the awkwardness of the guard's reply to sink in even further.

It is the general who resumes. "Speaking of troops and numbers, I assume you have heard?"

"Heard what?"

"In that case, you haven't. Palinurus. Almost done away with by the forces of Sextus Pompey."

Octavia does not know what to make of this. "You are not without humor, but if this is a joke, I don't follow."

"Not a joke. Sextus took everyone by surprise. Most out of character. Primarily a loss of sea-going craft rather than men, but of what use are they if they have to swim to meet their foe?"

"If this is true, then the balance of power is quite likely going to be upset."

"And Antony might still come out on top. That Parthian gamble you had him take — even if it concludes in only a partial success …"

Octavia refrains from speculations of her own. "The last time I spoke with my brother, he was rather certain that my husband would make a mess of it."

"Octavius ascribes much of his success to his orderliness and looks down on more adventurous spirits who have other qualities that *he* lacks. Antony may yet outdo him."

"General Caudinus, I thought you were an Octavian, not an Antonian. Or do your emblems belie your allegiance?"

"Lady Octavia, it is good to learn that your fiery spirit has not been broken by your house arrest … yet." As Octavia makes no reply, he speaks on. "To answer your question, it is my duty to my master to worry about things that he might not take seriously."

"Such as a potential attack on his most important naval base? Why have you really come to see me, General?"

"To thank you."

"To thank me?"

"If it were not for you, I and a few of my friends would have learned far too much about Etruscan hand-signaling techniques."

"You were there in the tent with my brother."

"Yes. Who, by the way, has spontaneously and therefore most unusually decided to take a few days' leave. People aren't even apprised of where he is at present."

What is this? To thank her? Much too flimsy. And the show of strength, an entire centuria at her doorsteps, if Caudinus is to be believed? Within the capital, even if they were not in uniform? Highly irregular. Was this about a coup?! She could be at liberty within minutes. But what chaos might ensue if Antony, though bound to her by marriage, had free reign? There is no doubt, however, that this is not a social call, despite all the general's jokes and chattiness; and his gaze never once strayed south of her face, although she is only sloppily covered (Octavia has never been a coy one about anything). Almost too intelligent. Not the kind of man to take such a parlous risk. Then again, it is an attribute of their sex to act rashly. And what of Palinurus? All she can rely on is hearsay, from someone she barely knows. Agrippa, not Caudinus, would be blamed for that. She is now leaning towards the suspicion she had earlier: that this is a test, orchestrated by her brother in absentia. If it were just her own fate and not also that of her baby daughter whom she has now decided to name Octaviana …

"May I have an answer, Lady Octavia?"

No, no more trying to beat men at their own game. And is it not the hand that rocks the cradle the hand that rules the world? From this moment onwards she shall be loving-veiled-incidental and loving-veiled-incidental alone. How strange! Why would she put it like that?

"Yes and no."

"Yes and no?"

She extends her hand. "Yes, you may kiss me goodbye, and no, you may not see me or come to my house ever again."

The general betrays no reaction and does as he is told. "Good day, Lady Octavia."

Cleopatra Is Growing More Impatient by the Day

Robbed tombs and besmirched monuments! By the four sons of Horus! *Where* is my *man*?!

What Else Is Happening in the World?

Mediterranean: Rome calls for "immediate" surrender of Sextus Pompey; Egypt: eating disorders among camels on the rise; feminist outbreaks in Gaul — Roman tourists sealifted to Ostia Antica; Cleopatra's Egypt, having alienated everyone, now paying price; patterns of suspicious behavior in Iberian Peninsula; Alexandria fails to meet local needs in 35 of 42 nomes (by Marcus Promptus and Ra-Ptahhotep II); moist Pannonian gals want to meet and bang; SPQR officials warn that Roman Empire "only remaining pillar" of international community; experts discuss if Antony has joined Parthian cause; Livia Drusilla visits orphanage with her new baby boy, helps children with their Latin grammar; interim Roman governor of Syria to deliver Croesus Lectures in the Humanities at Sora; analysts say that Antony "could be very useful" to King Phraates;

nine in ten Egyptians worse off under Cleopatra (by Ra-Ptahhotep I, Ra-Ptahhotep II, and Ra-Ptahhotep III); runaway Vestal Virgins demand you take off their sandals and togas — slowly! — and teach them the ways of love; Antony found to have plagiarized Veranius Flaccus, an action roundly condemned by the first scholars of Rome; King Herod of Judea "personally witnessed" Egyptian efforts to bribe his subjects, "only a matter of time" before entire region "riven by sectarian conflicts" unless world turns "suitably punitive"; Kerasos by the Pontos finally recognized as the Empire's sweet-cherry town; Nubia co-sponsors SPQR initiative on counterfeminism strategy; highly coveted Deutsche Orient Gesellschaft field journals and scribal palettes presently on sale and ten to twenty percent off while supplies last; "no factual basis" in Porcus Quintus domestic staff assault case; massive Egyptian troop build-up near Libyan border — Libyan crown princess assured of "unqualified" Roman support; "subversive" female prostitutes arrested by Athenian security forces; Acarnanicus Severus compares self to Porcus Quintus; anonymous officials and oracles alarmed that Senate majority "sympathetic or very sympathetic" to King Phraates; Agrippa marks Palinurus as "momentary setback," promises "sustained effort" until time of victory; Greek sluts now waiting for you on the beaches of Aegean.

Regarding General Caudinus

Further reflection convinces Octavia of the rightness of her response.

Antony Is Back in Alexandria

Another day has broken and another day finds Antony in a funk, refusing to get out of bed. Although Antony's bed is *soooo* soft and comfortable, as soft and comfortable as can be, although this is paradise beyond compare to anyone who has just returned — safe and sound, no less — from an ordeal as grueling as that of a really, really fucked-up trip to Parthia's least touristy parts, although Antony should rejoice at being again united with the love of his life, although everything thinkable is done to cheer him up, Antony is glum-cranky-depressed. To have put in such an effort and to be rewarded with less than nothing, to have to await now certain destruction at the hands of Octavius' minions is more than Antony can take. Only five legions left. Or five and a half legions, as Cleopatra keeps reminding him. And everything so much worse for wear. Octavius can now finish them off even sooner. All Antony does these days — besides sleeping and napping and dozing and offering a blank stare to the world, that is — is to pig out on pots of ice-cream brought to his side and to insist that the storytellers recite to him the ever-same poems — in the main from the *Hesperian Verses*, the *Trove of Libya* and the *Altägyptische Sauf- und Abendlieder* —, often one particular stanza more than a dozen times in a row.

Cleopatra seems rather unimpressed by the whole fiasco. The only change one can discern is that her use of pastels has abated a bit, making way for more muted colors. But it is almost impossible to really fathom a woman's true heart and mind, anyway.

And Enobarbus? Enobarbus is making the most of it, reviewing personnel files and reorganizing the remaining soldiery. Having known Antony for quite a while, he gave Octavia's Parthian plan — a plan Enobarbus considered noble in its intentions, but flawed in its design — a mere twenty-five to thirty percent chance of success due to her husband's ill qualification for such a venture and his general proneness to messing up. Enobarbus knew that he was in no position to persuade or even cross either spouse when it came to the Parthian project, so he did the next best thing: he used the coming disaster to purge the ranks of slackers, men otherwise lacking in discipline, troops of questionable loyalty, and hotheads whose ambition outstripped their ability — simply by picking them to march on Parthia under Antony; all the capable and reliable units stayed on in Egypt and at their garrisons in the eastern Mediterranean. As not all of the undesirables failed to return, Enobarbus is now busy redistributing them among the legions in such a manner as to minimize any detrimental impact they might effect.

Yet if Antony's Parthian effort had been well-soldiered and well-officered, might it not have worked?

The End of Rome?

Antony's Parthian fiasco cannot but have emboldened King Phraates of Parthia — another Hannibal by all accounts and reports — into thinking that Rome is weak. And we are weak — as long as our eastern dominions are in the unsure hand of Antony. Syria remains unstable and if Syria falls, Judea falls. And if Judea falls, Arabia falls. And if Arabia falls, we might as well surrender Egypt with the whore and the amateur and all else it contains and guarantees: no more grain ships, no more free passage through Mare Rubrum, no more trade with eastern Africa and India. At this time, it seems not too cautious a move to start a revival of the Roman agriculture of old, costs be damned.

Another Question
Concerning Enobarbus

If Enobarbus is so good at shitcanning losers, what is he still doing in Alexandria?

Sextus!

On the mild Tyrrhenian Sea a big rudderless raft sluggishly bobs up and down, moves to and fro in the most dullish manner, and generally stays where it is. This big rudderless raft, utterly in the open in the waters between Sicily and mainland Italy, virginal and naked and exposed to archery and attack, is where Octavius and Sextus Pompey have agreed to meet and negotiate. Valuable hostages have been exchanged and three warships on each side have now approached close enough to complete a loose and less-than-intimate circle, as prescribed and consented. While the Octavian and ... Sextan? Sextonian? Sextusial? — Sexto-Pompeyan! forces keep a good distance, four men each are lowered to the wet surface in little rowboats.

Once the trip has been done and the raft has been boarded, we see that there are two personal guards in each group of four; on the Octavian side, Octavian and Agrippa, of course; on the Sexto-Pompeyan side, Sextus Pompey, the man himself, and his new numbers man, Gnaeus Elaboratus, a bit shaky on his chubby legs. While the guards take up their positions in the corners of the raft, the others meet in the middle.

"Hey guys!" So Sextus Pompey.

Octavius and Agrippa are not in the mood for salutations; however, Agrippa has a question: "Who is this sidekick of yours?"

"Oh, that's Gnaeus Elaboratus! Your hot sister got him kicked out of Ostia Antica, remember?!"

"I do not have a sister."

"Too bad! Ah, you're the Agrippa guy! I have been away from Rome too long! What's it been? Four years?"

"More like three years and eight months."

"You *did* miss me! Oh, I *really* should have visited you all in Rome, but we've been *so* busy having fun! We now have opulent vineyards that are just fan-fucking-tastic! And we also just imported new dancers from Africa — black and sultry and terribly young and unspoiled. Did you know that they believe they could get pregnant from a kiss?"

"No."

Octavius has decided that enough time has been spent on frivolities. "We are here to talk about Palinurus."

"Oh, what about that! What about that! What about that! That Menas really had it in him. Who would have thought!"

"That was not done as a Roman. That was terrorism." Agrippa seems to be a chatty one today. In comparison to Octavius, at least. And definitely in comparison to Gnaeus Elaboratus who so far has said nothing, being too busy balancing on the raft's logs and generally feeling unwell.

"Oh, just a little sneak attack. Boom! A ship one down! Boom! A ship two down! Boom-boom! A ship a three and a ship a four down, down, down! Ka-boom-boom-boom! A five, a six, a seven, an eight, a nine, all down, down, down!" Sextus Pompey does a little victory dance, shaking his hips, caressing his breasts and thighs. "Boom-ba-ba-boom! Ka-boom-boom-boom! Boom-ba-ba-boom! Ka-boom-boom-boom!" Agrippa and Octavius are becoming rather unnerved, even more so as his voice now drops to a whisper before rising up to a crescendo as he acts the boxer who acts the dancer. "Ka-boom-boom! Ka-boom-boom! Ka-boom-boom-boom! And boom! And boom! And boom! Boo-boom-boom!"

Agrippa goes for the obvious putdown: "Have you considered seeking professional help from a trained psychotherapist?"

"I have *ten* psychotherapists, each better than the other. 'And we're all talking *with each other*, and we're all loving *with each other* ...'"

Octavius once again attempts to cut to the chase: "What do you have to say to our demand of Sexto-Pompeyan reparations, both in sesterces and goods, our demand of freedom of navigation in the Tyrrhenian under Octavian arbitration, our demand of unfettered Octavian access to all Sicilian vessels and ports, our demand of permanent Octavian bases in Agrigentum, Panormus, Messana, Calana, and Syracuse?"

"Well, I don't know about 'demands' and 'Octavian this' and 'Octavian that' ..." Sextus Pompey takes a moment to reflect, then — in conspiratorial fashion — moves in closer, puts his right hand on Agrippa's shoulder, puts his left hand on Octavius' shoulder, and looks them straight in the eyes. "But to be honest with you fellows, you seem like you are way too anal and really need to loosen up those scrunched-up sphincters of yours. So how about some serious oral and vaginal penetration — you come over, and we gangbang those African chicks the way they need it?"

Octavius has had enough. "Will you let go of me?"

Sextus Pompey lets go, of Octavius ... and of Agrippa, too, after an uncomfortable second. "Let go, let go, let go! Let go, let go, let go! Let go, let go, let go! Oh, oh, oh, oh!" Having sung his little song, all the while clapping his hands, Sextus turns, signals to his guards, and together with Gnaeus Elaboratus — steady now! — they leave the raft and board their little rowboat. "Feel free to visit anytime! Mi isla es su isla! And bring some Falernian — we're fresh out!" The four men left behind on the raft and the all-too-visible fury emanating from them are a sight to behold.

Fuck Like an Emperor

Julia, the only daughter of Octavius, would — in time — have very much agreed with the assessment given by Sextus Pompey. Now only a child, she will in her teenage years be harshly criticized by many of the most prominent men of Rome for her ruinous shopping sprees, her penchant for orgies, and her lack of any forethought or reputation management. Then personally urged by Consul Arruntius to follow the moral example and discretion of her father, Julia defends her expenses and wantonness thus: "Not only are my father's prim attitudes towards debauchery outdated and hidebound and misguided, my father also forgets that the manners of a lowly file clerk ill suit the towering station he inhabits. I, however, know that it is my threefold responsibility as the emperor's daughter to be an irritable socialite, an icon of luxury and waste, and a powerful sexual predator. And you should also know that if you ever again dare to impose on my time like this, I shall without preamble kick you in the nuts and have you defrocked."

We have this on the authority of Macrobius of Thubursicum Numidarum who relates that Vettius Praetextatus said as much.

Antony's Speech to the Roman Chamber of Commerce in Alexandria (Full Text)

Cancelled due to hangover.

Certainly Good Enough to Be Read Out Loud to Iras and Charmian to Effect and Share Hilarity-Mirth-Amusement, and Just As Certainly Insufficient Cause for Anything Else

I greet Superlative Cleopatra who is second to none but me and me alone!

You who are my Fellow Marvel of the Desert have beyond all doubt proven your fecundity and Egyptocity by producing twins. Here in my royal seat at Petra I have heard their names: Cleopatra Selene and Alexander Helios! It is most fitting of you to have named your issue the moon and the sun, as you yourself have already filled the heavens with stars!

And I also praise your most noble Antony for his sacrifice and martyrdom in Parthia and his valorous defeat of Palinurus — I rejoice in his having crushed that sedentary Octavius and that Agrippa whose words and garments are those of an incurable sodomite and I say bravo to that! Bra-vo!

In order to strengthen the bond between our two houses, in order to celebrate your powers that are now very much crescent, and in order to gratify posterity with our copious offspring regal and majestic I proudly submit to you that I am ready to strike, to slide my erect phallus into your gate of joy, and to plow you in an exquisite contradiction that is both most unrelenting and most gentle — to make love in the Nabatean fashion as only a true Nabatean of the highest birth can make love and as I dictate these words I assure you I am most aroused and mighty. And when you and I are in congress you will find that I am the food and drink that finally answer your hunger and thirst.

In turn, Antony very generously may of course canoodle and entwine with as many of my wives as he is able to properly service in the course of a splendid night and day spent here in supreme Petra.

In our procreations we will not complete verses begun by others or prevaricate or calculate, but sing new songs! Of daughters and sons to outshine even the likes of us! Of their deeds and new worlds and cities yet to be built! Geographical and metaphorical and literal and biological and agricultural!

I who am the one who has enchanted the Four Parts and their Quintessence, I who am the one who has scoffed at those who have grappled with their lives, and I who am my father's son now send you many kisses and kiss your hands, arms, neck, cheeks, forehead, and above all your lips most lovingly and longingly.

With the perfume of numberless roses, I approach you in delight!

Malchus, King and Lord and Chief and Prime and First and Master of Rabbits

The Negotiations Between
Sextus Pompey and Octavius
and Agrippa, Reconsidered

Were you really persuaded that it was not out of character for Octavius to negotiate with a known pirate and terrorist supporter? With an amoral pervert? With a man who had utterly broken with Rome and proven himself a major security risk? To chance a meeting *in person* with such an individual? Not to set a trap to deal with this stain on his honor once and for all?

Not after Palinurus.

The meeting *did* take place, but it was not the fantasy conjured up by Sextus Pompey's ego: the two times three warships indeed formed that circle, the little rowboats indeed met in the center, four men each indeed set foot on the raft. Much to Sextus' frustration and disadvantage, however, he was met by four gladiators in the guise of eminent Romans. They, having been promised their freedom from the arena on condition of their success, wasted no time in thoroughly knifing their ill-prepared victims and unceremoniously kicking them into the water.

That day consequently also marked the end of the Octavian hostages delivered unto the Sexto-Pompeyans. While some of those hostages had been quite valuable — for the ruse to work, they had to be —, Octavius and Agrippa considered their loss regrettable yet acceptable, as this gambit not only yielded to them the neutralization of the crackpot, but also the free use of Demochares and Appolophanes, two Sexto-Pompeyan admirals with a sound grasp of changing requirements, quick, and now in their power. They already proved their worth in the ensuing sea battle: although one of the Octavian warships was lost, so were two of the three enemy ships, the third taking flight badly reduced.

Time-Keeping

Philip K. Dick — Philip K. Dick, ladies and gentlemen! — Philip K. Dick said something like "I, Philip K. Dick, say that the Empire never ended." And this is most true in the count of our days. The Gregorian calendar which has finally gone global is nothing but a very minor correction of the calendar that Julius Caesar installed once upon a time and decided to call — can you guess? — the *Julian* calendar.

The result? No more "once upon a time," but a direct assault on all that is fair and fairy! The months are named no longer after radiant stars and goddesses of plenty, but many a time only numbered or commemorating war males such as Julius and Augustus and their war god Mars. The unholy shedding of blood is *locked in*, and desecrated is the holy shedding of blood during the female menstrual flux as the moon cycle of twenty-eight days was replaced by an off-kilter "moon" jerked from thirty to thirty-one days and back again. That only one pitiful month retains the natural rhythm, barely more often than not, completes the mockery.

If you don't "buy" this explanation, it is only further proof.

Of what?

Exactly.

What Egyptian Noblewomen See
in a Man Such as King Malchus

King Malchus is not exactly the kind of king who tickles Cleopatra's fancy, that's for sure. Is he Charmian's type, then? Hardly. Iras, on the other hand, would not *overly* mind being fawned upon by His Royal Wonder provided he were not such a forgettably dressed individual, his table manners were equal or superior to those of a lady of the Alexandrian court, he had spent his youth properly developing his skills as a raconteur, he could tell apart the poems of the Early Middle Kingdom, the Middle Middle Kingdom, and the Late Middle Kingdom at least by their differences in *either* phrasing *or* symbology, and he did not while away so much time puttering around in his private zoo and more often left the feeding and care of the animals to the keepers.

Further Remarks on Time-
Keeping and Related Matters

This was one of the things that Napoleon tried to fix. The new French months of Aubade, Lavande, Rêve des Fleurs, Gamine, Nonpareil, Douceur, Bonhomme, J'adore, Voulez-Vous, Fraternité, Rivière, and Bel Esprit — just like the original Egyptian months with which we are all so familiar-endeared-enchanted — were *a healing potion.*

Nobody is saying that Napoleon was an Egyptian pharaoh or temple priest in another life.

Napoleon's short-lived conquest of Egypt was a trick to lure *les bif-steaks anglais* to that country and make them dream Egyptian!

The Rosetta Stone, written in the trinity of Egyptian demotic and hieroglyphic and Greek — for a very short while in possession of the French, now in the British Museum — was *tactically* lost!

Vive la France! Vive l'Empereur!

Skeptical? Then the French Ministry of Culture has this to say to you, in modern hieroglyphic: puny monkey, British flag; big frog, roar of the triumphant one, French flag!

Geminius in Egypt

You can't always eat at the palace. Well, you could, but *someone* needs to take it upon themselves to try out the new restaurants in town to keep the local economy going. Besides, news of the Octavian setback at Palinurus has finally been relayed by several traders making port in Alexandria and the general mood has swung from despondent to kind of hopeful — at least a minor celebration seems to be in order. So we find Antony and his Roman staff at this new Nubian place that above all prides itself on its oak-grilled crocodile flesh, hand-torn by alpha males of Nubian warrior caste extraction — word is that they even spit on it to add their signature testosterone to the dish.
  "To Geminius!"
  "Geminius!"
  "To Geminius!"
  "To Geminius!"
  "Geminius!"
  "Welcome, Geminius." Enobarbus. Not exactly one of the boys. Can't keep his phrasing simple. Avoids exclamation marks. Has to be different. His own man. Geminius is a bit like that. But awkward and of more average intelligence.

Antony takes the lead: "Our Geminius! Fresh off the boat! So how are things in Rome?"

"Bad."

"Bad bad?"

"'Bad bad?' Yes, my lord."

"Bad bad bad?"

"No, my lord."

"So: bad bad, but not bad bad bad." Antony turns to the others. "Our boy here came all the way to tell us that: bad bad, but not bad bad bad. Bad bad, but not *bad* bad bad."

A bad (!) start for Geminius, but at least he remembers not to speak unless spoken to, a most worthy maxim when in the company of one's superiors.

Once the laughter has died down, Antony resumes: "What, then, is so bad bad?"

"As my lord knows, I'm here representing a group of Roman senators that all consider themselves Antonians —"

"But that's good! Not bad! Not bad at all! No?"

"Certainly, of course, sir."

"Bad?"

"Good, sir."

"'Good sir!'" Antony provokes more chuckles among his men. "And would good Geminius pray tell us what is bad, good sir?"

"In short, sir, we fear a coming Octavian tyranny."

Antony, slightly more pensive, gnaws at his crocodile bit, gives up on gnawing at his crocodile bit, and gesticulates with it instead. "Good Octavius a tyrant? With good Agrippa by his side? Wouldn't he be a good tyrant, then?"

"My lord, we have credible intelligence that —"

Enobarbus suspects where this might be going and feels compelled to intervene. "Perhaps this venue is not sufficiently private for this type of discussion."

Antony, as usual, chooses to override such petty concerns. "Never mind. Out with it, Geminius!"

"As you wish, sir. The Octavians have somehow gotten ahold of a booty of Parthian arrows. They're reverse-engineering them and planning mass production."

"Oh-kay ... that *could* be a problem. What else?"

"Octavius has shown his heavy hand against your wife, my lord. He put her under the most shameful house arrest. Almost no communication with the outside world, and threats against her life and that of your daughter."

"My daughter ... so it's a girl, then. That whole Octavia pregnancy thing slipped my mind *completely*. Must have been the rushed conception, I guess."

"If this behavior towards your wife is indicative —"

"Hold on! My wife?! My wife is Cleopatra, not that other chick!"

"As you say, sir, of course, sir. But speaking of which, we Antonians in the capital are worried not only about what your current dalliance has done to your reputation in the Senate, but also about the possibility that her feminine wiles may have begun to cloud your judgment. A senatorial committee —"

"Get up!"

"My lord?"

"Get up from your fucking chair, get the fuck back to Rome, and don't let the fucking door hit your fucking ass on the fucking way out!"

"Sir, of course, sir."

That Napoleon Fellow

You shall find attached, General, an order to take command of the army. [...] I abandon Egypt with the greatest regret. The interests of France and the extraordinary events of these days oblige me to pass through enemy lines to return my presence to Europe.

–Napoleon, in a letter left behind at army headquarters in Alexandria, addressed to the unsuspecting General Kléber.

What a mess a "great man" can make! Italy lost almost as soon as she had been gained, Egypt a French graveyard, and the most staggering madness, Russia, yet to come.

"How many miles to Moscow, officers?" — "Too many."

They knew, but they followed him anyway. Such is the wondrous nature of man.

The Russians disappointed Napoleon by running away, leaving him to practice all his super-duper battle tactics on no one. They even turned their capital and crown jewel into a ghost town. Napoleon, sitting in the Kremlin all alone, is said to have been seriously unnerved by the crowing of the crows. The snow took care of the rest.

Lepidus Makes His Move

It is a mistake to think that because Lepidus is driven by gluttony, he is only driven by that particular vice. He cannot but be also a slave to power, greed, and his own ego or he would never have become a triumvir in the first place, even if the role assigned to him was merely that of a figurehead.

And, as Sicily and the North African coast are not much more than a few miles apart (okay, fine, we hear you, a few *generous* miles apart), it should not come as a surprise that Lepidus was nudged — nay, *shoved* — by his varied hungers to open secret negotiations with the Sexto-Pompeyans almost as soon as he had so prudently and preemptively exiled himself from the homeland.

Those negotiations brought to fruition a trade treaty. Lepidus began to supply Sicily with every kind of want and desire: African dancers and domestics, blue lotus in immense quantities and also the "chefs" to properly store and prepare the hallucinogenic, other plants for more prosaic purposes, and a whole menagerie of North African fauna (cats of prey such as leopards, lions, and cheetahs, but also giraffes, scimitar oryxes, striped hyenas, Barbary macaques, and several breeds of gazelles — anything, basically, that would impress even the more well-traveled among Sextus Pompey's under-lings and blow the minds of the many Sexto-Pompeyans who had been nothing but hicks until they joined their master on his isle). All these imports helped to give the maverick Roman's kingdom an otherworldly, even dream-like veneer.

In return, Sextus Pompey provided Lepidus with one thing only, the thing whose dearth Lepidus had whined and whinged about to no end during their first meetings: troops, drawn from both Sextus' own contingents and also from other sources (hapless merchants and their crews, for the most part, press-ganged during their business trips).

Commerce between the two realms was not a one-time exchange, but a steady flow, as the poor beasts expired quickly in Sexto-Pompeyan care and needed to be replaced — some would say that was due to Sicily belonging to a different biogeographical region, but why, then, did the Sexto-Pompeyans also keep asking for additional entertainers and servants? The lotus, too, was a taste acquired and kept.

Funny, isn't it, that Sextus in turn provided Lepidus with his own invasion force? Grown men, some of them less than talented in the arts of war, sure, but in comparison to which the African "manpower" sent the other way was hilariously inept on the battlefield: depending on the purpose, either pretty and talented, precocious, even, or masculine yet as a rule too dumb to know their ass from their elbow — Lepidus' people made certain of that.

Once Lepidus learned of the deadly trap that had been sprung on Sextus by Octavius and Agrippa and the major dent it put into the Sexto-Pompeyan navy, he had his forces simply overrun the island, meeting with next to no resistance from the leaderless and dazed troops — some of the more alert ones even tried to escape on giraffes, can you imagine that?

Why We Egyptians Need a New Vision

> We are always in peril, always in a bad plight, just on the
> edge of destruction, and only to be saved by invention and
> courage.
> –Emerson

Feminist alterations of laws and customs. Advancement of unworthy persons. Pussywhipped officials. Factions as diverse as desert nomads, basket weavers, and translators of trade-related texts grown desperate. Widespread impotence. An economy in the doldrums. Girl bands. Plant food shortages. The overflowing of marshes and streams. Gender-based harassment. Rock collapses. Astrology. And no justice but the whims of pharaoh.

Our country is on the ropes, dear friends. Cleopatra, a brutal feminist, has stirred up and brainwashed our women, has put it in their heads that women are not to serve men, but men are to serve women, and that all are to put their trust in her and her coterie of sensualists and delinquents. Feminism itself may be a fantasy, but these Cleopatran notions of gender difference have had very real consequences across the board — as absurd as it seems, our once-proud civilization has become the victim of one woman's unresolved daddy issues.

Cleopatra's physical father Ptolemy Auletes (a.k.a. "the flute-player") was a weak ruler, easily manipulated by Egyptian courtiers and Roman powerbrokers alike. Even at a young age, Cleopatra must have sensed that the man was not her equal, neither in intellect nor in grace (these qualities, although used to nefarious ends, we are in all honesty forced to grant the current pharaoh), and in all likelihood generalized that disparity to encompass the entirety of both sexes.

The late, great Julius Caesar inadvertently compounded the problem when, having met the then newly womanly Cleopatra in intimacy, he promoted her to bear rule above Alexandria and the rest of the Two Lands region. Caesar's genius brought peace and unity to an almost irreparably divided and blood-soaked Gaul, but in Egypt it failed him utterly. By adding a second father-figure to the still-evolving psyche of the inexperienced *kindfrau* Cleopatra, Caesar introduced an overpowering tension into her personality that she has very obviously been unable to overcome to this very day: is a man to be outdone as a matter of course or is a man an earthly god she can never hope to rival? In only a few years, this confusion has turned a once vibrant society into an object lesson of how mismanagement ensues from female hysteria.

In contrast to Nubia, a country that not too long ago was even more primitive than ours, but that has had the recent good fortune of a string of pragmatists and realists as its rulers, all men (surely no coincidence) who conscientiously strove to effect positive change and to adjust to the new reality, Egypt has gone backwards. We shall name but a few symptoms of this neurosis:

[little bird hieroglyph] Cleopatra's reign has seen Alexandria supplying hyper-nationalistic textbooks to our classrooms that completely lack self-criticism, that exonerate Cleopatra's administration of any wrongdoing, and that are full of negative stereotypes of "detractor" cultures, of which Rome is of course the most maligned.

[little bird hieroglyph] [little bird hieroglyph] The proliferation of signifiers of female promiscuity: ducks, acrobats, convolvulus leaves, gazelles, musical instruments, hip girdles, lotus flowers, swimmers, and various other Hathorian symbols.

[little bird hieroglyph] [little bird hieroglyph] [little bird hieroglyph] At the same time, Alexandria's crackdown on independent organizations and charities is another consequence of Cleopatra's deep wariness of anyone with a penis. Greatly respected institutions such as the Adonis Center for Virility and Democracy (ACVD) and the Roman-Egyptian Men's Council (REMC) were accused of "operating as masculinist agents" and so had to vacate their offices and abandon their projects in Egypt. The large-scale archaeological surveys conducted under the auspices of the ACVD had offered thousands of restless young Egyptian men more than just something to do, they had offered them a *future*. And who is at present in a position to fill the sandals of the experts of the REMC to teach Latin to Egyptian schoolboys, as Egypt increasingly looks inward? All that, and much, much more, is now irrevocably gone.

What are men to do if they want to do more than commiserate like a bunch of washerwomen? As dire as the situation seems at the moment, it is crucial that we do not give in to despair, but focus on how we can return to the Egyptian values of old and restore Egypt to its unsullied prime. Remember that many others also think like you and consider making *daily* efforts such as these:

[bird of prey hieroglyph] In conversation with male children and youth, set an example both morally and intellectually. Question Cleopatran narratives, question the arguments and paradigms of lettered mercenaries, and question the false generalizations and partial use of sources found in the demagoguery that masquerades as history.

[bird of prey hieroglyph] [bird of prey hieroglyph] Engage and encourage moderate feminists. Like very beautiful sheep that have been led astray and are now lost, they eagerly seek and accept the guidance of a certain hand that they can follow back onto the path of righteousness. To quote a dear, dear soul who fears feminist reprisals and therefore wishes to stay anonymous: "As an insecure teenager, I used to look up to Cleopatra and dreamed of being as elegant and confident as her. It was a dream my younger self decided to call feminism. Little did I know that the real Cleopatra is overbearing, scornful, and much too fond of herself — to the exclusion of everyone else. If that is feminism, I want no part of it. Luckily for me, my cousin is an Egyptian domestic policy expert with a research group in Memphis. It is he who took me under his wings and set the record straight."

[bird of prey hieroglyph] [bird of prey hieroglyph] [bird of prey hieroglyph] Some of you may have wives that have become stubborn feminists under Cleopatra's reign and in consequence have also become closed off to reason — by no longer doing your bidding, they are doing that of their queen. You are literally sleeping with the enemy. You may of course continue to entreat-petition-negotiate from a position of weakness. Or you could try to bring her to her senses by forswearing-skipping-withholding relations of the flesh. Take your business elsewhere. If you are the loyal type and your wife still passes the boner test, resort to an anti-aphrodisiac (personally, we have had very good results with a cocktail of mandragora and the urine of the *male* jackal, collected and bottled *at dusk* — imbibe regularly and liberally, and your libido will rest and not awaken from its slumber).

While we should not limit ourselves to these action points, they are a good start. And start we should. It is not a disgrace to lapse into passivity-lethargy-apathy for once, but to stay there. Either we keep tolerating an unnatural social pyramid of injustice and thereby remain part of the problem ourselves, or we take feminism to task by powerful speech-action-more action. It is time we look to ourselves and our brothers. It is time we answer the call for renewal. It is time we become heroes.

Seb XII is the director of a number of research groups in Lower Egypt and the Romulus Professor of Near Eastern and Feminist Politics at Rome University's Octavius Caesar School of International Studies. He is the author of Besotted by Their Superiority: Cleopatran Feminism as the Seed of Its Own Destruction, The Mental World of Egyptian Jealousy, *and* In Search of Old Alexandria. *In addition, Seb XII co-authored (with Ra-Ptahhotep II and Ra-Ptahhotep III) the seminal pamphlet "Unlearning from Cleopatra VII: Toward a Democratic Theory for Feminist Societies." He has been praised as "provocative-deep-wise" and "our own Marcus Promptus" by Ra-Ptahhotep I and listed by* Imperial Policy *as one of the top five Egyptian thinkers and one of the top 350 Mediterranean ("Mare Nostrum") minds for several consecutive years.*

Madu I is an Egyptian economist and exile in Rome. For over twenty years, he has served as the macro-economic advisor to groups as diverse as Romans Concerned for North African Peace and the Near Eastern SPQR Planning Board. His numerous publications include Taxation in New Kingdom Egypt, Egyptian Tax Laws, Proposed Changes to Egyptian Tax Laws, Egyptian Tax Laws Reconsidered, A New Perspective on Egyptian Tax Laws, Some Serious Questions About Egyptian Tax Laws, Why Egyptian Tax Laws Need to Be Reformed, Egyptian Tax Laws Cannot Continue Such as They Are *and the landmark* The Whore's Rhetoric: How Cleopatra VII Cheated-Duped-Misinformed Egypt for Shameful Profit and Gain. *Madu I has been hailed by Croesus as "the doyen of Egyptian economics" and the elderly émigré's recent forays into social criticism and the linguistic analysis of his homeland's power structure brought him kudos from none other than Marcus Agrippa: "A new and thoughtful critic of Pharaonic Egypt has emerged and his name is Madu I. The* Whore's Rhetoric *is a game-changer of a book that instantly established its author as one of Egypt's most original polymaths. Read his effort to truly understand the signal threat selfish persuasion poses to international co-operation."*

Octavius' and Agrippa's Public Reactions to Lepidus' Exploit, in Summary

Timely intervention. Just demise of Sexto-Pompeyans. Puerile, disruptive, misguided. Sexto-Pompeyans showed themselves to be man-children that refused to grow up. Cult of personality centered on Sextus Pompey. Arbitrary actions. Animal rights. Antonians and Egyptian feminists stayed silent. Lepidus vindicated. Bold, decisive, and strictly limited. Importance of North African presence. Analysts agree. A triumvir's duty performed. True tradition of consuls. Good old Lepidus. Stalwart, forthright, expansive. Shared values. Friend and partner. Much-needed sobriety in Roman affairs. Freedom, liberty, and safety in conjunction with commerce, trade, and navigation. Original shipment routes being restored. Repatriation programs. Lepidus managing transition in Sicily.

The Senate Learns Antony's Secrets

Cato once said: "A man without honor is without friends; and a man without friends is a man without honor." And he is right. If there is no respect, if there is no modesty, if there is no reticence — then how can a man call himself a friend and ask others to be his friends? Geminius is not a big man, is still finding his way in this world, is only "a beardless baby senator of 24," as Antony puts it, but can a mouse not help a lion? What greater good is there than serving your brother, and what greater affront than to strike at a helping hand?

Geminius may have considered himself insulted beyond reason, may have been perplexed by his master's actions, may have questioned his own wisdom in following such a rager and howler, but wavered only in thought, not deed. Fellow Antonians Titius and Plancus, however, men of consular dignity, big men, experienced men, were also sported with by both Antony and Cleopatra during a much longer stay in Alexandria and took it ill — so ill, in fact, that they came over to Octavius' side and — out of sheer spite — proffered him their help and intelligence, which he of course accepted.

And so Octavius, with more than a few lictors, paid Rome's Vestal Virgins a visit one beautiful morning. The triumvir was courteous enough, but brisk and serious, as were his men — the Octavians would brook neither delay, nor questions, nor any resorting to legal niceties, that was clear, and they got what they came for.

Now that the Senate is in extraordinary session, Octavius reveals the personal papers of his brother in empire: "I have here in my hand, senators, the last will and testament of Mark Antony …"

Is he dead? There is much concern and unrest and whispering in the ranks.

"No, Antony is not dead. Antony is alive, yet not well."

Again the audience is unsettled. To proclaim a man's final directives before his time is unheard of and without precedent in the history of Rome.

"Respected senators, I ask your forbearance! Although Antony still is among the living, you will learn today that he unfortunately died to us and our observances a long time ago. We have lost a friend, a capable commander, and a true Roman ... to a venomous woman who ensnared him, took him from us, and subverted him in her manifold and treacherous ways. My father barely escaped her clutches and now she has all the more dug her nails into Antony's back."

The Senate is still disoriented, but now seems more ready and inclined to follow the narrative Octavius has begun to lay out for them.

"Weep with me as I tell you that Antony wishes to sell off all his assets and holdings in Italy, Gaul, and Greece.

"Weep with me as I tell you that Antony wishes to name the Royal Treasury of Egypt as recipient of the monies obtained from said liquidations.

"Weep with me as I tell you that Antony wishes to name said treasury also as claimant of any debts incurred against his name.

"Weep with me as I tell you that Antony wishes to sponsor a chair for Egypto-African cultural studies at the Egypto-African Institute of Alexandria.

"Weep with me as I tell you that Antony wishes to be acknowledged as a son of Egypt and wishes to have said country authorize stelae and murals to that end.

"Weep with me as I tell you that Antony wishes to name his children Alexander Helios and Cleopatra Selene as his divine successors in rule and religion.

"Weep with me as I tell you that Antony wishes to be buried in Egypt, in a ceremony attended by Cleopatra and her priests."

That last one did it in particular. This is all so outrageous, so unthinkable, so absurd that at this point Octavius can do with the Senate whatever he may please.

Do Octavius and Agrippa Really Approve of Lepidus' Invading Sicily?

Why shouldn't they? Sextus was not only responsible for acts of terrorism great (Palinurus) and small (continued piracy off the Italian coast), but also a bad influence on the populace, making them believe that "fun" is more fun than work and that the only sin is not to have "fun" — no matter how depraved. He and the rest of the lowlifes needed to go, and if Lepidus wanted to do the mop-up operation, why should another triumvir and his aide object? No Octavian forces needed to be diverted, neither for Sicily's taking nor for its administration. In fact, Lepidus was treated to a pleasant surprise when Agrippa took it upon himself to visit the man and offer congratulations and gifts: a selection of some of Rome's choicest cakes as well as new female companions, obtained from certain houses in between the Viminal and Esquiline hills (wink, wink).

However, Octavius' and Agrippa's private views on Lepidus as a personal friend fail to track their public stance. The man can be useful, yes, but they regard him as too fat and silly to be respected as a true peer. In truth, Lepidus is like a lot of other officers of high rank and honor: a bit over the hill, a bit on the portly side, a bit more smug than he deserves to be, but still quite capable and ambitious in spite of being a somewhat ordinary chap. Not a Caesar, not a Cassius, not a Sextus Pompey. Then again, rather a Lepidus than any one of those three.

And, to remind Lepidus that it is best to be a Lepidus, Agrippa warned him of the grave consequences of imperial overstretch: that wherever our men are spread too thin, attacks on soldiers going about their duty naturally increase; that this is especially true in North Africa, where troublesome semi-nomadic tribes — jealous, insolent, and ideologically beyond the pale — would not hesitate to interrupt routine military operations and stir up general unrest; and that Agrippa's Egyptian contacts advised that Cleopatra looked westward and — in all her lawlessness — might use Antony to do to Lepidus what Lepidus did to Sextus Pompey.

Some Things Never Seem to Change

"Soothsayer!"

"Oh, Soothsayer!"

The man addressed is in transit from the library to his private study, laden with *Eclipses in the Sun and Moon and their Sequent Effects, Saturnine Axioms and Theorems, Hildesheimer Astrologische Beiträge* (first and second volume only), *Recueil du XXIII Rencontre Astrologique à Fribourg, Comets in Chaldean Astrology,* and some other scrolls.

He is far too deep in thought to notice Iras and Charmian at first, but has no other choice once they flank him and touch his arms.

"Oh, Soothsayer, we've been talking about love!"

"And the love of love!"

"We'd love to set you up!"

"So you need to tell us!"

"Tell us who's your type!"

The soothsayer reflects for a moment and then recalls the exact answer to the question. "There are only two-hundred-and-one types of people: firstly, those that have never been to Egypt and never will; secondly, those that, though strangers to us, have kindled the love of Egypt in their hearts; thirdly, those that —"

Finally impossible to suppress, a fit of giggles from the girls and they run off to their next adventure — be it another palatial encounter, a journey of discovery from market stall to market stall, or a new spa treatment they haven't had a chance to indulge in before.

The War to Liberate Egypt? It's On!

"We the senators of Rome speak with one voice and speak thus: by unanimous decree Rome is to end the tyranny of Queen Cleopatra VII of Egypt. Her provocative unilateral actions have proven to be too many and too egregious to further ignore: non-Egyptian merchants and traders submitted to insults, annoyances, and unjust exactions; the poisoning of the mind of a Roman triumvir, to a point where he has become unproductive and delusional — frolicking on the seashore at Canopus and publicly 'giving' her ownership of kingdoms and provinces in the Donations of Alexandria; and, to crown her hybrid war against civilization and humanity, the unremitting spreading of the doctrine of what she calls feminism, a new philosophy whose sole aim and purpose is to remake and subvert the world in Egypt's image.

"And the image of Egypt is one of sorrow and despair. When Cleopatra came to power, the country was already in a hallucinatory fever: a topsy-turvy world in which their pets had been elevated to gods, with the population languishing in an effeminate state of half-dreaming and half-sleeping in a perfumed air. She took advantage of this sad state to further her own agenda to the full, with the result that, within the few short years of her misrule, the subjection of men to women has become a universal custom, any departure from it appearing quite unnatural. Such policy must not be mistaken as a mere harboring of animosity toward the stronger sex; rather, it is a combination of that and political opportunism in order to impose a completely Cleopatra-centric regime on her society.

"Cleopatra is a victim of her own propagandistic narrative in which she has become completely caught up: having played Omphale to Antony's Hercules, Cleopatra has set her sights on the international community in general and Rome in particular to do the same; Rome being the main target as we have confronted and questioned radical feminism harder than all other Mediterranean nations combined. Styling herself a diva sui generis and citing a nebulous devotion to 'femininity-culture-love' (a term that she has refused to define anywhere in her copious proclamations), she now megalomaniacally wishes to make the entire known world her jurisdiction.

"Absent Egyptian feminism, absent Egyptian impudence, absent Egyptian intransigence, the Levant would not be unstable, Africa would not be in crisis, Rome would not be forced to take substantial countermeasures — such is the trouble an absolute monarch can create in the face of initial indifference. But no more! We who are Rome have in reasoned and protracted dialogue come to the irrefutable conclusion that serious intervention is required in the form of committed military engagement so that the free world may again live in peace and a normalised Egypt will once more be able to take its rightful place in this brotherhood of nations, under stable and harmonious governance.

"Further, we wish to impress upon those who doubt this long overdue course of action firstly the fundamental dangers both of a) politically expedient point-scoring and of b) being tempted into exaggerated caution; secondly our duty to our friends and partners; and thirdly and most importantly that while those under Cleopatra's influence may not be interested in human rights and democracy (such as our Antony who is, alas, not our Antony anymore), a moral Roman Empire cannot stay idle when its central values are under such insidious attack. Virtue will not be marginalized!

"Once Egypt has been reintegrated into the real world, the Cleopatran elite will be no longer in a position to foment Mediterranean disunity, divisive Egyptian exceptionalism will give way to cooperation and multilateralism (as will petulance to maturity), false creeds of feminism and Egyptophobia will be supplanted by the rule of law and the philosophy of peace, and the people of Egypt will be living real lives instead of serving as mere playthings in a mentally unstable individual's fantasy world.

"We ask the people of our great nation to abandon any accommodationist pretensions and support our soldiery in their great task. We thank you."

And in front of the temple of Bellona, the foremost men of Rome watch Octavius throw the ceremonial spear of war over the marked boundary line.

And as of 0500 this morning, the first Octavian warships from points of origin throughout the Tyrrhenian, Adriatic, and Ionian have set sail for Panormus on the Greek coast, their intermediate port of call where they shall congregate before crossing to oppressed Egypt.

Antony Disses Octavius

It has come to my lofty attention that the dorky upstart by the name of Octavius has provoked the Senate into promising my wife a licking. What a bunch of idiots and girly-men! Is this Rome still? Can I not leave the capital for a few years without everything going to the dogs?

This is what happens when a person of unworthy blood is adopted into power! Was that really in Caesar's testament or just some low fakery? Whoever pulled this (and I *include* Julius Caesar in this estimate!) was in thrall to Discordia! Is it not enough that the Greeks have Eris? Apparently not!

How unworthy is the blood of that boy, really? He keeps referring to Caesar as "father," but his real father was one unremarkable praetor and later governor of Macedonia (seriously!) whose most telling achievement must have been naming both of his daughters Octavia! Of similarly stolid and embarrassing stock is the rest of the ancestry: a first cousin once removed married a merchant who got rich off Faliscan sausages; another first cousin once removed is a career coach in the country town of Clampetia; two other relatives "saw action" in Gaul — one of them a centurio who dishonorably let himself be wounded by a *swineherd* of the tribe of the Belgae and the other a hornblower third class (and we all know how homo those guys are!) who *of course* returned home unscathed; one of Octavius' maternal great-grandmothers once had an affair with a subordinate official employed at Ostia Antica and later married a coast guard officer who was then posted to *Lake Benacus* and there commanded much respect from fellow fresh-water sailors; and is *anyone* really surprised that his great-great-great-grandfather of unbroken male lineage stayed an amanuensis his entire life?

And this is the sum of the man who is now pitting himself against rare Cleopatra!

Cleopatra Disses Octavius

Octavius? Hmmm. Oh, *that* Octavius. What a talented boy! So studious! He does know a great deal about a great many things, that Octavius. Is there anything he does not know — about government, trade, politics — or any other topic that keeps him up-up-up-and-coming? So much stuff he has stuffed into that fresh-faced little head of his! So knowledgeable on every concern! So very much in command of the facts! Well, I guess that's what happens when your tent-royal is an office and all your visitors are such sufficient scholars.

And the way he dots his i's and crosses his t's — most remarkable! So punctilious! He must have gotten very good marks at school when he was even younger — and no beatings at all, at least not from his teacher. So clever!

And is it not wonderful that he has announced his wish to come and see me in person here in Alexandria! All this time I have considered myself the blessed paragon of Egypt and Octavius is to embark on a long journey to cure me of my folly — and is it not most gracious of him to endeavor to teach a half-witted woman such as I, uninstructed in the use of reason, unaware of the false-sloppy-confused nature of her judgment, and unable to understand the superiority of Roman practices and ethics? I most eagerly await this education in critical thought — especially on why the sine qua non of statecraft happen to be pricks.

BOOK SIX

Actium

Tourism

Is Antony still in Egypt? Is Cleopatra still in Egypt? Is Enobarbus still in Egypt? No, no, and no. Thrice no, that is.

They are summering in Greece, together with five hundred warships, a hundred thousand foot, and twelve thousand horse. Some noteworthy fellow vacationers of the party include King Bocchus of Libya, King Tarcondemus of the Upper Cilicia, King Archelaus of Cappadocia, King Philadelphus of Paphlagonia, King Mithridates of Commagene, and King Sadalas of Thrace — a group of men Antony keeps referring to as the "vassal king dudes." (King Herod of Judea and King Amyntas of Lycaonia and Galatia were empeched due to prior obligations and thus not able to make the Greek journey in person, but sent some of their guys as representatives.)

This military-style getaway involves many new experiences such as learning traditional breadmaking in sedate mountain villages, enjoying the hospitality and local authentic cuisine provided by the native populace, tasting street food with an Asia Minor twist, and of course also getting a bit tipsy and — boys will be boys — acting all scrappy and starting fights in quaint little bars.

Yet the Epirus region offers other delights to the discriminating visitor besides those of the culinary variety: fun holiday activities include playing hide-and-seek with Octavian advance scouts, fortifying history-rich beach resorts, turning tranquil fishing villages into design-forward army and navy barracks, getting an intimate behind-the-scenes peek with resident families going from house to house during counterinsurgency inspections, levying a liberty tax on curmudgeonly old farmers, acquiring statement-making armor and weapons of Hellenic design, keeping seafront watch standing next to a flickering campfire, and roughing it in swampland tents.

Unfortunately, a great many of the soldiers are not used to Greek living and are forced to keep withdrawing their presence due to health reasons. To make up for those losses, Cleopatra's husband simply continues to invite more and more locals to join their revelries.

The Octavians on the Offensive

That Agrippa simply has no manners! It was only logical for the Octavians to cross most directly from Italy to the northerly Strait of Otranto — which the majority of them eventually did —, but Agrippa of course first had to take a naval task force to attack and destroy Methone, Greece's south-westernmost port until then held by the Antonians. How, Agrippa, are Antony's forces now to be supplied from Egypt without running into *you*? How?! Hmmm! Hmmm!

And Octavius … Octavius … Octavius, birds of a feather they say, don't they? Snatching up Antonian strongholds coming south just like that, most uncivil, most uncivil. And, as Cleopatra reminds us, most unoriginal — pincer movements in military campaigns are so passé and have been done to death and went out of style altogether generations ago.

Antony rallies and scrambles and repels the Octavians from the center and masses in and around the almost completely landlocked Gulf of Ambracia, to which Actium is the entry point. "This is where we stand, this is where we fight, this is where we prevail. And that snot-nosed kid will finally rue the day he turned against me."

The snot-nosed kid in question, however, is not yet done with his little victories and also secures Leucas and Patrae.

But What Does the Man in the Street Have to Say About the Latest Action?

While one half of the Senate is sport-fucking Pannonian hetaerae and the other half of the Senate is getting Rhaetian cock-rubs,

Octavius and Agrippa are finally doing something about the Egyptian question. One can only approve.

General Canidius and Antony Discuss Military Matters

One good thing about war is that the tents of masters and emperors are always spic-and-span and roomy and just plain marvelous. This may be the reason why Antony can — with the help of a native philosopher and a few trinkets the two of them keep moving around — currently afford to be utterly engrossed in a series of Greek paradoxes and forget all about the mundane necessities of camp and soldiers and campaign. "Now this Zeno — did he *know* Achilles?"

"I think not, my lord."

"Because why pick Achilles to run a footrace against a *tortoise*, of all beasts great and small? I'm telling you, Zeno must have had an aggro thing against Achilles."

"I would not know, my lord, but it is certainly a way of —"

Enter General Canidius, commander of Antony's land legions, and with him all the mundane necessities of camp and soldiers and campaign. "Hail, Antony!"

"Canidius, how are you doing?! I'm kind of in the middle of something ..."

Canidius sees the attendant book-clutcher and a toy tortoise and puts two and two together. "Zeno's paradoxes. All total bull."

"You sure?"

"Oh, I'm sure. What I'm not sure about is how you intend to proceed regarding the real world. Oh, and nerd boy? Get your ass out of here."

The philosopher looks at Antony, who smiles and shrugs. Correctly taking this as his cue to leave, the man makes for the exit, but not before attempting to retrieve his materials. "The tortoise stays here!" Antony has spoken and so he leaves empty-handed — not an ideal outcome, to be sure, but not too bad a fate for having had an encounter with the mighty and powerful.

"Canidius, you were saying?"

"The Octavians have battered our forces more than enough and we need to strike hard and we need to strike fast!"

"We are well-fortified here — why not wait and have them come to us?"

"Why not? I'll tell you why not. Octavius may only have twelve legions to throw at our sixteen, but those are well-trained and Italian. Whereas our men are anything but — Greeks, Egyptians, Syrians, bastards of every description; and they would be the dregs of any army: slaves, rejects, turncoats, press-ganged thugs, mercenaries only in it for the money. You just can't hold such a military together for long. Time *really* is of the essence, my lord."

"Aren't you exaggerating this a bit?"

"Not by much."

"Hmmm."

"Exactly, sir."

"What does Enobarbus have to say about all this?"

"Enobarbus, my lord, was caught snooping around the northern perimeter, on a patrol I accompanied myself, no less. I had him executed on the spot."

"Are you convinced he wasn't just doing, like, necessary research?"

"Had his briefcase with him, too. Just in time for those perimeter shift changes. Highly suspicious, if you ask me."

"Well, I guess that's it then for Enobarbus."

"Yes, sir."

"But are you sure he was guilty of desertion?"

"Philadelphus of Paphlagonia has already taken all his men over to the Octavians. Would you have wanted me to risk letting one of your highest-ranking staff betray you to the enemy, sir?"

"Well, if you put it like that ..."

"We have to stop the bleeding before this gets any worse."

Over Lunch, One of the Octavians Confides in a Friend

Numerius can talk about nothing but trireme manning requirements. Now, as this is also my job, I'm okay with discussing water displacement issues, seating arrangements, multi-role training programs, shouters/oarsmen ratios, and whatnot. But he really needs to watch it with other people.

Antony's Narrow Escapes

I verily envy your costly teachers who — for a lot of money and I presently shall expatiate on the pertinent bills item by item — have taught you to know nothing, you dolt!
–Cicero, addressing Antony in absentia during the second of his *Philippics*

Antony has been in tight spots before. There was that little trip to Parthia that is most recent in memory, but also worthy of record are his altercation with Marcus Brutus and Cassius Longinus at Philippi (which *easily* could have gone the other way if not for some self-inflicted snafus on the part of the regicides), the time when he was sent to re-install Cleopatra's father on his throne and — Antony's entire company nearly delirious from lack of sleep — during which mission he missed a literal viper's nest by just a few steps on his way through the Delta while another officer wasn't so lucky, or last year's "domestic" episode when Antony and Cleopatra roamed nighttime Alexandria disguised as commoners as they were wont to do and got utterly lost in a very bad and very oddly laid out neighborhood only to be rescued by a Libyan weather forecaster, of all people. There were further incidents, most of them admittedly less dire and more trivial, but — save the worst for last — it was during his exile in Gaul that Antony reached his all-time low; objectively, Parthia might have been just as bad, but life's reversals make more of an impression when you are still young and hopeful and not jaded and middle-aged.

Not that this happened to Antony in his first blush of youth; he had already proven himself as Julius Caesar's right-hand man and just as importantly restored order in Rome after his superior's assassination, no mean feat for a soldier who had never had any love for administrative work.

Yet no good deed goes unpunished, especially if you underestimate some determined little fucker styling himself Caesar — Octavius had been properly schooled in politics by his mentor alright and before Antony knew it, the impertinent schemer had amassed quite the following: senators, veterans, and that pompous ass by the name of Marcus Tullius Cicero (when the primus of Rome's public intellectuals was eventually wrong-footed by the boy, too, Antony at least got a day's worth of perverse satisfaction). Odd troop movements and political machinations in the Senate and throughout Rome were the order of the day; moreover, Antony's network of spies suspected a plot on his life.

The parties finally came to blows near Mutina. Defeated, Antony and his army had to take flight to Gaul, but not before killing Hirtius and Pansa, consuls and parts of Octavius' plan of attack. The Senate — now with Antony safely out of the way, or so they thought — repaid the offense by declaring Antony a rogue and a miscreant and an enemy of the Roman people; celebrations over his expulsion lasted fifty days.

Meanwhile, the Antonians' fare was far from festive: the rawest herbage, water from brackish creeks, and no meat but that of horses that had finally failed to carry them any further. Add to that a particularly cruel winter, an unavoidable crossing of the Alps, and some hotshot by the name of Decimus Brutus leading several legions in pursuit, and the misery was pretty much complete.

Antony had gambled that one of the Roman governors out west would make common cause with him. Either Pollio or Munatius Plancus or Lepidus would surely come through for an old friend? And if Ventidius Bassus and his men could remember their bond and loyalty and make all haste to join their brother in need, why not them? But military comradeship does not count for much in those whose priorities are of a political nature; the governors had already received word from Rome that the Antonians had to be dealt with and did not dare disobey the authority of the state in favor of a once-mighty man fallen from grace.

In the context of this particular chapter of the life of Antony, it is not tangential but crucial to note that wherever you go in the world, SPQR marching camps are all the same, no matter what the terrain, the climate, or the local culture — and this does not even change if you have officially become an outlaw and your men are in flagrant disregard of Senatorial orders. The soldiery has been thoroughly scripted and coded and drilled to repeat the same format: erect the same rows of soldiers' tents and officers' tents, put headquarters and standards and rostrum in the center where they belong, leave room for the ever-same Via Decumana, Via Praetoria, and Via Principalis, and encompass it all with palisades in strictly rectangular format, in turn encompassed by a ditch in strictly rectangular format — to ask your troops to proceed otherwise would only invite confusion. Stultifying but effective.

Yet that very sameness nearly spelt the end for Antony: now deep in Gaul and very close to one of Lepidus' camps, our fugitive at one point felt the need to stretch his legs and go for an extended stroll — and what can we say? It was foggy and Antony was three sheets to the wind and before he knew it he was back in camp, just not his own. Lepidus might have arrested him had he chanced upon Antony first, but the grunts were so bowled over by the sight of the vagabond superstar, mistaking his inebriated act for one of bravery, that they pledged their allegiance to the man at once and en masse. Consequently, Lepidus had no choice but to switch sides as well. This was a massive improvement in support for Antony and enough to negotiate his return to his original standing in Rome and all was well again, for the time being. In sum, proof that even at his worst, Antony is capable of an unintended stroke of genius that lets him escape unscathed.

Which is perhaps why Antony is not taking his current dilemma as seriously as he should.

The Battle of Actium

The day of decision has come! Octavius and Agrippa sail upon the sea and Antony and Cleopatra sail upon the sea! Narrow ships of war of the Octavians have come from Comarus and Leucas to block and corner the enemy! "Everything in its place and a place for everything" says Octavius and the vessels tidily arrange themselves in their squadrons and Agrippa observes that the troops "are very well prepared."

Emerging from the Gulf of Ambracia out to the Ionian waters are those whom fate has ordained that they serve Antony and Cleopatra. The uneven quality of the personnel notwithstanding, their boats are the envy of the cultured part of the world, having won many prestigious design awards, aesthetically daring, magnificent, resplendent, sumptuous. The most choice of historical watercraft.

But dreadful utility! Cleopatra's naval throne pavilion, the very gems of gems of Early Kingdom verse by which her ships were each named-baptized-titled, the limited edition prints of her instructions, the colorful-fancy-atavistic accessories issued to her rowers, the belts with inlaid jewelry given to her songstresses and chanters, and the rarest iconology and epigraphy and art throughout — all is nought against the Octavian (read: Agrippan) skill in sea causes.

Those pesky shiplets are really too maneuverable, harassing Egypt left, right, and center. The battle is not exactly one-sided, as Antonian ramming beaks, arrows, and boarding parties also find their targets; nevertheless, Agrippa is slowly and surely gaining the upper hand, reducing the enemy bit by bit.

In consequence, Antony decides that no stratagem will now lead to complete victory and transfers to a Cleopatran logistical support vessel in the rear. The queen's flagship — thus far sheltered by the Romans fighting on her side — then breaks formation and plows through the contested waters, the rest of her navy following in tight suit. A few Antonian vessels are able to join them; the majority, however, are too involved in action to disengage.

As if all that insult wasn't enough already, Captain Lurius of the Octavians attempts to deny their escape from the carnage and needs to be driven off by even more sacrifice. And to think that Antony once gave that ingrate favorable audience when he was only a soldier, an orphan, a nothing!

Of those left behind, some resist to the bitter end, the odds and Octavius be damned, but most soon put up their oars in surrender. Those of them that will be found to be true military men are to trade their stricken boats for first-line service against Egypt under the command of the liberators when the time is ripe. The others will in due course be sent back to their farms and homesteads in Greece.

Although Octavius is going to stay up through the night to field battle reports and to tie up loose ends, he already is the victor of the world by evening meal.

Antony on the Way Back to Egypt

The sulking triumvir has stubbornly refused to come to see and console his wife on board the *Beloved Reflection of Aquamarine*; instead and most contrarily, he has instructed his ship of current residence to trail behind and to be the last in this caravan of contemptible losers.

Yet again he might have been master of everything under the sun and the moon and the stars and yet again he had blown it. But if Neptune had not crossed him, if his enemies had not been so infuriatingly methodical *and* lucky to boot, if Cleopatra and those Greek layabouts had properly done their part ... and where were Canidius and his massive land army when he needed them?

Those are the thoughts that Antony keeps turning over and over as he sits at the stern of the Egyptian logistical support vessel *Little Duckling in Alluring Profile*, water flask in hand, and watches Greece and the world disappear behind the horizon.

Octavius Frustrated, Plaintive

It just makes Octavius bang his head against the walls again and again. Why does he have to keep dealing with these overgrown children — brats, really — when there is so much else that he wants to do for Rome? The number of aqueduct projects alone that Octavius has to put on hold because of these silly shenanigans is enough to exasperate the most idealistic of men.

Why I Demand a New Investigation of Actium

Eagle against eagle, Roman against Roman,
Our men armed themselves against themselves,
Led on by a strange and mortal god.
–Corneille

I am Apollodorus of Pergamon, master of rhetoric, master of philosophy, master of masters, upright, upstanding, respectable, worthy in all my endeavors. My honor and privilege? Incredible. My voice and speech? Unrivaled. My network? Strong and personal. Furthermore, I am not understating my case when I claim that my insight is my foresight and my foresight is such as other men's hindsight. In short, my track record is *proven* and I know whereof I speak.

And I speak of Actium, my friends! As a Greco-Roman who cares deeply about the well-being of our Mediterranean community I cannot in good conscience remain silent on this crucial matter. We all have friends who sided with Antony, we all have friends who sided with Octavius — *all* mistaken as each and every one of them should have stood by *Rome* against the irritant of *Egypt*. That perversion knew that, being weak, it was also more cunning and thus planned to infect and did indeed infect the stronger and better with its weakness. For reasons of power and out of mistrust of the Senate, Julius Caesar refused to normalize Egypt when he had the opportunity. The result? A "client queendom" that cannot but be a constant *cause of acrimony*, sowing strife and distrust not only among our provinces, but even also betwixt our husbands and wives! Oh, Julius! Oh, Caesar! You helped yourself to prime pussy, but did you help the Egyptian people?

And now, Actium. Apart from Cleopatran feminism, this is perhaps *the* downstream effect of not carrying out social and economic reforms in the Two Lands region when the chance presented itself. Actium, cui bono? Ask yourselves! Loyal soldiers of the Empire, dead. Roman citizens of Greek extraction, dead. Friends and partners of Rome, dead. Whereas *all* the hides of the queen and her retinue weathered one of the worst sea battles in memory *intact*. Whereas the Cleopatran war chest of twenty thousand talents (!) remained *untouched*. Whereas the Egyptian navy suffered *minimal* losses. Such an unlikely outcome does not come about by accident, but *by design*.

Is it out of shame that we deny the truth? We have — by Jupiter! — heard more than enough blow-by-blow accounts of this particular carnage, so why is nobody asking the obvious questions? Canidius and his troops were unbeaten as infantry while Agrippa was invincible at sea, so why did Antony insist on making his men mariners? That is, the few that he did not leave behind *to twiddle their thumbs*? Why did Antony not take up earlier offers of ground war in other theaters? And why did he not in the present emergency request the aid of landlocked King Dicomes who had clearly intimated his sympathy? It speaks to the preternatural *equanimity* of General Canidius that he did not lay hands on both the siren (the word is apt indeed!) and her prey — yet I wish he had done so and saved countless lives by *restoring order* in the east. And it was not just fellow Romans that were lost, but Roman pride as well! The spectacle of the abandoned Antonian foot and horse bargaining away their oaths for sesterces like merchants at the exchange pains me more than even I can describe. May the Empire give them a chance at *redemption*! (Nevertheless, we have to make allowances: with Antony gone and Canidius' whereabouts unknown, they were sheep without a shepherd.)

Is that all I have to say? No, that is not all I have to say! Not by
far! And what I have to say is that I do not blame Antony! I do not!
And I will tell you why. Although I cannot but respect the important work the *Greco-Roman Institute for Egyptian Policy Analysis*
has done throughout the years, I am unable and unwilling to join
them — and many others, I am aware — in their *enmity* towards
Antony. Have they all overlooked what his nemesis has done to her
own country? Which is not even her own country, she *in all likelihood* not being a proper Egyptian? (Her late father — also a pre-
tender — is supposed to have enlisted a Lower Egyptian princess in
her production, yet the details remain murky.) Cleopatra just loves
luxury, they say. Cleopatra is of an artistic persuasion, they say.
Cleopatra *defines* sensuous, they say. Fiddlesticks! What we have
here is *the old ruse* repeated ad nauseam by tyrants and foes of a
united Mediterranean: keep your own people on the brink of starvation, barely able to think straight, let alone in a position to consider
regime change, completely occupied with their own day-to-day *survival*, whereas you incur massive expenditures per your building
projects, your shows, your adventures — which *only the ignorant*
declare impractical, but you yourself have calculated to illustrate
your superior status as an entity far above the likes of them. And
how can a man not be reduced by a woman whose every move and
word and gesture is trained to *subjugate* not merely individuals, but
an entire people? It is upon us Romans to save our oppressed brothers — and, if we can, our brother of brothers! — and to terminate
that bitch *with extreme prejudice.*

The Antonians in Denial

Actium was a victory in disguise! Wise beyond his years, Antony is playing ten-dimensional chess! Octavius could never invade Egypt — the supply lines would become far too long; Octavius cannot reimburse his legions as it is and they have turned mutinous; Italy's farmers have drawn their swords in defense of their property rights as Octavius' subordinates attempt to mitigate the blowback of their ill-considered move; Octavia is too principled not to have switched sides; the people in the homeland are now waking up to the deceit of Octavius. Currently, Antony is biding his time, but when the moment is right, he will swoop in on the Peninsula as if from the heavens to save the day!

An Anonymous Libyan
Court Official Weighs In

Apollodorus of Pergamon, oh my. Well, I guess his latest sexist outburst proves that even foreign policy geeks are men of sorts. And typically miss what every woman of sense has known for ages. Sad, really. All that time spent brooding over maps and statistics and other man-made contrivances. Attending nerdy seminars and conferences. Babbling about transprovincial challenges — man to man. [Laughs.] Citing SPQR talking points. [Laughs.] Imagine that. A manly circle-jerk in honor of the quiet dignity of their very own moral clarity in the face of feminist innuendoes and Egyptian obstructionism. Which reminds me ... you surely haven't told me *every* bit of this season's salacious gossip from Alexandria, have you, darling? Anyway, how *could* they have gotten it all so ass-backwards? Actium was just collateral damage. And Antony and Agrippa and Octavius and all those others? That to a man think themselves masters of the earth? Just pawns. Pawns in an epic bitch fight between Cleopatra and Octavia.

BOOK SEVEN

Timonium

Antony Is Now a Timon

While the free world continues to ponder the problem of Cleopatra, Antony has had emphatically quite enough of both and thus directed the *Little Duckling in Alluring Profile* to make landfall in a solitary spot in the vicinity of a ramshackle defense tower. Here he would forgo the company of men and abstain from partaking in the folly of women. Here he would do as Timon did, in Athens, and quarantine himself from the vanities of this meaningless existence. Here he would not be an Antony who could be bought and distracted by means of trifles like those admittedly very consoling Café Groppi chocolates or any other such momentary joys — no, now he would be a Timon in his Timonium of Pharos and nakedly stare down the wretchedness.

Cleopatra Returns Triumphant

Why go down mourning when you can go down feasting? All of the queen's ships have returned and docked in Alexandria's harbor (Antony's vessel excepted, of course) and have been festively decorated and sundry bands produce what any European with a discerning ear can only describe as a cacophony of sounds and dancers dance a choreography that is so outré it must have been inspired by the postures of precanonical sculptures of the Fifth Dynasty or possibly the Byblites and the young are furnished with brushes and buckets of paint and in an awful anarchy get to redesign the entire pharaonic fleet and Cleopatra — add the depravity of socialism to her catalogue of sins — mocks the long-suffering people of Egypt by freely offering them cakes and drinks which are as to be expected consumed out of all measure by the starving masses and what is this extravaganza if not a stark reminder of the waywardness of matriarchal cultures?

In a joint statement on the issue, longtime Egypt observers Acarnanicus Severus and Ra-Ptahhotep II a) reiterate the above criticisms of fostering vice; b) point out the shocking lack of reverence for those fallen in Greece and that such unconcern is only the foreseeable consequence of monarchist ideology; c) further point out that the monarch in question stymies her subjects' critical thought or any substantive analysis of their predicament on their part by diversionary tactics; d) name and define such diversionary tactics as plying the populace with intoxicants, offering up salutations in the marketplaces and other such pageantry, and generally indulging their natural defects in every way for the sole purpose of seducing them into compliance with her measures; and e) wager that what was once begun out of calculation has become the sincere belief of the woman, that she indeed is the consecrated love of Egypt, that her high station indeed befits her person, that her reign of variance indeed serves her people, all of which meaning that the chances of free and fair elections and a more inclusive government that could reverse the near-perennial trend of declining living standards remain remote if not impossible.

"General Priscus, at Your Service!"

Rome's Campus Martius on a balmy Sunday evening is probably the safest place in the entire Empire and this is precisely where doddering Priscus can be found playing at war. "Attention! All eyes on me!" He is now a front-line combatant in his own simulation and aware of that. So are his household slaves. "Remember: a slip of the tongue is a slip of the ... of the ... of the ... it can be catastrophic! Ca-ta-stro-phic!" For some reason, neither regular troops nor their superiors were to be had for this soirée. "I know you are worried. And you should be worried!" In the heyday of his youth, Priscus once attempted to trap the enemy in the east by marching west; his superiors at first suspected cowardice, but came to the conclusion that poor Priscus had simply lost his bearings. "You are now to rehearse my third formation!" The man regularly brushes up on military manuals written by his own hand. Why busy yourself with the works of lesser minds? "Wait for it!" Priscus is the descendant of capable career officers and also a rather impressive group of noblewomen. Sometimes, though, your personality will get in the way of your genotype. "Trumpeter! Give the signal!" Yet much can still be achieved by having the right name. "Off the field, Cornelius! Off the field!"

Priscus should really be enjoying his retirement instead of making himself such a laughingstock in the vain hope of getting another command by this farcical display. Those servicemen have always been the worst of tittle-tattles (they call it "trading war stories") and there isn't a Roman legion in the world in which "Priscus" hasn't become a byword for senility. It is the consensus of the wise that whatever modicum of reputation he might have had is now lost once and for all and Priscus' Sunday outings will have been the last chapter in the man's pitiful story.

Octavius, however, is of the opinion that even an old fool beyond correction can be put to proper use. In a redemption of sorts, when the time is right.

Cleopatra's Cunning Plan

Ever the practical despot, Cleopatra when at home immediately orders an advance party of boats to sail off, past the Delta, all the way to Pelusium, with instructions to prepare the land (sic!) transport of her galleys to the freedom of the nearby Red Sea, far away from any of those pesky Romans you risk running into everywhere else these days. And that would not be the end of the journey — once through the Strait of Mandeb, so much of Africa and India would welcome the living goddess with open arms, she would be spoilt for choice.

It *is* feasible. They say the narrowest link cannot stretch much more than three hundred furlongs of quite flat terrain; and with all of Egypt ready to cater to every one of Cleopatra's whims, why shouldn't it be possible to drag her fleet this paltry distance?

Antony Does Some More Brooding

The roses have lost their hue, the fruit its flavor.
–Hume

Unctuous supplicants,
long, cold winter nights,
sub-par courtesans,
idiotic peasants,
rain and snow —
I must not complain
or thus only trouble
my spirits further
–Marcus Aurelius, *Meditations*

Put not your trust in commoners, nor in nobility; there is no hope in either.

Armed duty under a flag is the life of man and his day is the day of a soldier.

There are fewer things on earth than are dreamt of in my philosophy.

All grapes are the grapes of Zeuxis.

Cruelty, dishonesty, treachery.

Marcus Aurelius is a jackass.

The only place that is my home is this tower, the only place where I am king is this tower.

I make the world a world without an Antony.

I have not foresworn human society. There is no human society. Brute beasts, that's all there is. Circe did *nothing*.

What is Egypt? One river and a bunch of dunes. What is Rome? Just another empire.

Women are famously useless in any cooperative endeavor, and Egyptians are also famously useless in any cooperative endeavor, but naturally what should have been doubly applied to Cleopatra I refused to do: she was the exception, she was not like all the others, she was way too cool to ever fail me like that, etc. etc.

Egypt's Love Is Not Requited

It is not a shame to absent yourself from your wife and sulk and wallow in self-pity when that is done for a short while, but it is a shame and very unmanly indeed when a husband simply fails to snap out of such behavior.

Envoys of the court in a most diplomatic manner conveyed this point and other pertinent points to the surly Roman in his house of grief. Yet their mild embassies proved fruitless and their soft entreaties went unheard.

The queen is growing weary of having to dwell in solitude when her mate is so nearby. Fool! Does he not understand that there is a world with or without an Antony, but that there is no Antony without the world?

Lessons Learned

Don't stick your dick in crazy don't stick your dick in crazy don't stick your dick in crazy don't stick your dick in crazy don't stick your dick in crazy don't stick your dick in crazy don't stick your dick in crazy don't stick your dick in crazy don't stick your dick in crazy don't stick your dick in crazy don't stick your dick in crazy don't stick your dick in crazy don't stick your dick in crazy don't stick your dick in crazy don't stick your dick in crazy don't stick your dick in crazy don't stick your dick in crazy don't stick your dick in crazy ...

The Octavians Are Back in Rome

Agrippa, asked how he feels post the Actium victory, states that he has never been happier, never been more certain on who he is as a man. Yet "there is still much work to be done," he says and implies that this is the chief reason why he turned down the triumph so graciously offered by Octavius.

Instead, a much quieter seminar cum state dinner is held at the Testudo training range complex, attended by friends and family, by retired military analysts as much as cadets, by Rome's guilds as much as its intelligentsia, by patricians as much as ambassadors.

It is by no means an occasion merely to gloat and bask in victory — although there is admittedly a little bit of that — but a time to be thankful, a time to mend and repair, and a time to take stock. Problems are discussed and possible solutions are proposed. Octavius charms the crowd with his unflinchingly honest assessments as he deconstructs and demystifies feminist propaganda tactics, condemns the solipsism of nations that refuse to fulfill their duties to humanity, observes that Egypt's current turmoil is the inevitable consequence of their having confused innocence with contrary ignorance and sentiment with gross sensuality for far too long, ponders the impossibility of anticipating the actions of a person ruled by impulse, declares Parthia a secondary issue for the time being, shares his hopes of peace not just in the Near East but in all lands, refers questions on transnational threat research to a scholar-official of his entourage, particularly lauds the Nubian delegation, reprimands those that now euphorically think Egyptian freedom a foregone conclusion, and urges caution and humility on everyone.

The evening ends not with dessert, but with a leisurely and companionable run led by some of the homeland's most promising youths.

Enough Is Enough!

Amidst a pride of winged lions, Cleopatra appears as Bastet and
Cleopatra appears as Sekhmet and Cleopatra appears as Sheshmetet
and now Bastet lashes her tail in fury and now Sekhmet lashes
her tail in fury and now Sheshmetet lashes her tail in fury and the
recalcitrant Antony ("Have I not been brought up by a faithful goat-
nymph named Amalthea?! Have I not been nourished on honey
supplied by Cretan bees?! Have I not?!") is quite involuntarily trans-
ported back to the palace where he belongs.

A Gesture of Displeasure Meant
to Be Understood as Such

Cleopatra really should have sent King Malchus of Petra a most
soothing and conciliatory note in reply to his epistolary advances
notwithstanding their inappropriateness and over-the-top argu-
mentation. But to torment such a royal's ardent love with stone-
cold silence is an offense to his honor that cannot remain without
retribution.

And so the man's troops strike at Cleopatra's desert ships in
the desolation of her north-easternmost nome. King Malchus is
proud of his restraint in sparing the lives of the Egyptians who are
only forced to kneel and accept a message written with much cho-
ler: "Cleopatra of Egypt! Why do you spite me so? I offered you my
love, my heart! Numberless, numberless, yes numberless were the
days I awaited your care with anxious solicitude! You were taciturn,
shameless, haughty, impolite — and I, naturally, was despondent,
perplexed, depressed, sorrowful, melancholy, and now angry, mad,
driven to violence and profanity! Fuck you and yours, you fuck
product of a mother monkey! You cock-block, I ship-block! And
I will continue to ship-block! And you suffer the result of being a
Roman whore! Ennobled you are not! Once affectionately yours,

Malchus. P.S. And a dirty lotus-bundle column up the ass of your
principal husband Antony whose principal wife you are not!"

The Resistance

To promote a woman to bear rule, superiority, dominion, or
empire above any realm, nation, or city, is repugnant to nature;
an insult to God, a thing most contrary to his revealed will and
approved ordinance; and finally, it is the subversion of good
order, of all equity and justice.

–Knox

Ra-Ptahhotep III chairs a plenary session on the necessity of we-atti-
tude and we-action in a united Mediterranean (and also drops some
serious knowledge himself) as Ra-Ptahhotep I and Ra-Ptahhotep II
look on approvingly; former Antonians question Cleopatran narratives of the battle of Actium; Agrippa's step-daughter Agrippina
opens up to *SPQR Daily* about her four pregnancies and stresses
the crucial role of plentiful fathering in the face of Egyptian expan-
sionism; in the Forum, a delegation of farmers from Cisalpine Gaul
publicly swear to uphold Mediterranean values, renew their pledges
of fealty to Roman *mores*, and — in spite of recent lapses — vow
to desist from deviant leisure activities going forward; the office
of Croesus reminds the general public that Cleopatran feminism
was never properly peer-reviewed at any point in time and lets it be
known that said feminism has now been disproven to the last tenet
by the professionals of the Croesus Academic Initiative; Antony's
reputation suffers further as embarrassing pencil sketches emerge
from the Afro-Pop dance-off at the Fayium Oasis and are circulated
widely; Roman women from all walks of life enjoy a most somber and
noble colloquy between Octavia and Octavius on the importance of
family, proper child-rearing techniques, and threats to Roman security; Porcus Quintus successfully sues for defamation of character;
the Egypt Committee of the Senate authorizes further countermeasures — HEADSTRONG, CAMELTOE, and NILEFLOOD are all a

go; spurred on by a deteriorating stability situation, SPQR citizens are now learning en masse to spot feminists and pro-Cleopatran front groups — sartorial experts advise and assist; throughout the free world, in places of worship, at sports events, in the plain dwellings of tribal elders as much as in the refined homes of the SPQR administrator class, daring political refugees and dissidents tell the multitudes of a lack of nuance in Egyptian government not seen since the days of Pharaoh Akhenaten's mad (and deservedly brief) one-god rule in Amarna — and these truth-tellers come from a land of sorrows receive nothing but respect and understanding from their new friends.

The tide is turning at last!

Egyptian Nights

A sword is upon us and our cracked throne. We are still sheltered in Nekhbet's outstretched wings, but soon Nekhbet will have to withdraw and fly away. And coiled Wadjet still gives us refuge, but Wadjet, too, cannot be with us much longer, as Wadjet's powers are failing and Wadjet will have to slither away for a cycle of rest.

Then nothing will stop those austere demagogues who hurry-scheme-pursue as if they were a million-parted Onuris. They will come and invade-seize-take and call themselves noted authorities and devoted-lawful-orderly and allot a portion of their grace to our homes and fields. Robust oversight. Robust conviction. Robust death.

In consideration of this impending change of management, it will perhaps not be disagreeable to this court if our royal majesty proposes a fiery finale of excess, indiscipline, and general misconduct that is frowned upon by those that understand themselves to be our betters. Oh, they are going to put an end to it, they are well-versed in that, that is certain, but never will they know such sunny nights as we.

Candles, candles, and more candles! Terracotta lamps! Terracotta lamps from the Winsome Scribe nome! And the consumption of heavenly wine and invaluable lotus to musical accompaniment! We shall affectionately adjust each other's robes and ornaments and trade amulets! Admire each other, drink to each other, love each other! In consequence, how can a female holding an oar be without a fan-bearer to the right? To herd her with his crooked staff without rebuke? As for ourselves, we reserve the right to give you partakers our mouth to kiss, and once drowsy and properly out of it, to quite possibly show you one of our nipples, the left one or the right one, or perhaps quite a bit more. This, our first night of our last nights, is in respect to Hathor, to be followed by more Egyptian gods and goddesses our dearest companions, as long as the stars indulge us.

In Respect to Hapy

How unlike the dull ships that have settled in port is the sacred barque that fancies itself on the Nylus!

The Wheel of Fortune

Antony has of late — and quite understandably so — felt used very unkindly by fortune. Yet many a man before him was rather ungently ousted from the ranks of the kings and commanders of this world and Antony is far from the last to go from unbridled privilege to a fear of having to join those being put in fetters and cangues. It is only a fair equilibrium, as in the long course of history even a bound captive may ascend to rule. Much stranger things have been noted in much shorter annals.

BOOK EIGHT

Endings and Beginnings

One Last Visit to the Library

Cleopatra, this world's greatest lover of learning and the arts, has decided to spend some time with some old friends. To begin with, she runs her fingers over *Like Years of Horus*, a memoir written by one of her royal namesakes, Cleopatra II, in her final decade and studied by Cleopatra in her first; then the attention is briefly turned to the anonymously conceived and rather prim *Schreibstattberichte des auch Thoth genannten und gerufenen Djehuty*, acquired in the Memphite region by the cat servant of Charmian's aunt as part of a package deal, a deal that fortunately also includes the paradoxical-surefooted-sparse *Why Papyrology is Egyptology and Egyptology is Papyrology* and the more than timely and unabashedly political *Some Instances of the Folly which the Ignorance of Men Generates; with Concluding Reflections on the Moral Improvement that a Revolution in Male Manners Might Naturally Be Expected to Produce*, collectively authored and exquisitely scented by the Daughters of Upper Egypt; *Der Lasterkatalog der Römerschufte*, although acquired from an antiquarian in Athens, continues very much in the same vein and gives Cleopatra pause as she remembers reading this particular exposé antecedent to the conspiracy against Julius; she is overcome by gentler and far more soothing emotions as she closely holds and embraces *L'abécédaire magnifique de Ptah, dieu et fils de l'Égypte* — like herself, much too magnifique for those drab-false-thieving dullards bent on confiscating all of her realm's treasures.

To have the tantalizingly titled *Djed-Pillar Potentials* packed up and sent out of Alexandria for mundane analysis at Seven Hills; to know that one of her favorite children's books, *The Good-for-Nothing Sloth: The Wisest of Animals* (not as slim a volume as one might imagine, but the verso pages are blank, the hieroglyphs are needlessly large, and the illustrations predominate) would end up as a trophy at some Roman youth indoctrination center; to understand that Senenmut's *The Mysteries of Side-Chamber V* would be pored over by SPQR verification experts in exactly the same unfeeling manner as

Amenemope's *Onomasticon* would be vetted by their infrastructure analysts; to be certain that Zeidler's *Pfortenbuchstudien* — beyond their comprehension — would not even be given that little amount of respect and would be broken up into pieces to fetch a higher price in the market; and, perhaps worst of all, to be forced to think of having the mesmerizing *Naqada III Period Tchotchkes, More Naqada III Period Tchotchkes, and Even More Naqada III Period Tchotchkes!* carted off to some Roman storage vault — all that is more than a pharaoh can bear.

"Rufio."

"My queen?"

Rufio has never shown Cleopatra anything but love-respect-competence, in the most discreet fashion. An unusual Roman. Which is why she asked him and his men to assist her on this fateful day.

"I have said my goodbyes."

"Yes, of course, my queen."

"I now want to see this site consumed by flames."

Rufio nods and Cleopatra, feeling trust-closure-finality, makes her exit from the scene.

"You heard her, guys. Once you are in position, wait for the signal to fire your barrel-load. First trumpet for loads in area one, second trumpet for loads in area two, etc., as you already know. Once you have completed your task, get yourself to the RV point ASAP. No loitering and no taking anything. Now move out."

Cleopatra, contrary to her words, does not turn around to watch the fireworks, but notes the numerous explosions with satisfaction as she and her retinue make their way back to the palace.

So Much Bigotry, So Much Bias

"Octavius who is dead among the living" and "Octavius who is inimical-barren-undignified to Maat" and "Octavius who is a camel expert" are some of the epithets the Egyptian masses now have for their best benefactor; the Roman people similarly have to endure such idiosyncratic vilification as "you who are all aggression-activity-judgment when you yourself shall be judged, and judged you shall be in the court of the forty-and-two assessor gods and found wanting by Osiris-Thoth-Devourer and suffer oblivion or be stuck in the worst of duats."

Given the debauched state of that society, our men will simply overrun and secure the land within a matter of days. Physical liberation, however, will prove only one tenth of our work. How can we win the hearts and minds of a country that cares for no counsel, that cannot muster more than mean understanding, that is very little disposed to reign in its stormy temper? A future in which Egypt will be our friend and ally rather than a taxing dependent can only come to fruition if Egypt's mistaken education is rectified, if Egypt learns that there is more to life than passing it away in bounding from one empty pleasure to the next, if Egypt arrives at the conclusion that its refusal to stand for Mediterranean values has been nothing but the certain mark of confined views.

Our troops are glorious and steady to their purpose, but this particular victory — and it will be a great victory indeed — is not theirs to achieve. Only a priest of Saturn qualifies, and of those only the most veteran, the most versatile, the most adept must be sent. Only they can discover to Egypt that its orthodoxies far from tally with reality, only they can bring up Egypt to think beyond its own nose, only they can persuade Egypt of the advantages of letting itself be guided by the dictates of reason. To start them on the road to knowledge will be their central goal and enough of a goal it will be.

And finally — finally! — the country will one day have matured to believe — more than believe, *know* — that indifference is not an option and at last transition to an esteemed colleague among nations and begin to make its proper contribution to the world at large. And what a day that will be!

Egyptian Model Not Sustainable, Critics Say

Will you only consider the cherry blossoms in full bloom? Will you only consider the moon on cloudless nights?
–Yoshida Kenkô

Are you not glad, my Antony, to die with a Cleopatra?
–Cleopatra

Apparently, you can take the man out of the Timonium, but you can't take the Timonium out of the man. The catatonic Antony seems to have all but given up on life. Cleopatra, humbled by recent defeats, did not rely solely on her own expertness in poetry, but called to council Egypt's most lucid thinkers and uncommon wits; said council reasoned carefully and judiciously, determined that the *sagesse juste* was to be found in a double question from Yoshida Kenkô, also determined that the calligraphy was to be done by the Alexandrian Applied Semiotics Collective, and thirdly and lastly determined that the commissioned piece would best be delivered by Cleopatra in person at the most opportune time chosen by the soothsayer as he had been known to dabble in horary astrology and suchlike. This she did and tiptoed into her beloved's chambers at the exact moment a hint of daylight was just about to disturb the black of rest over the Sinai and deposited the artwork on his bedside table, together with a handwritten note of her own.

At the time of writing, Antony has yet to respond to the intervention, whether meaningfully or in any other wise.

Arsinoe and Her Narrow Ass

The Office of Mediterranean Security lets it be known that the Spartan commandos that neutralized Princess Arsinoe at Ephesus were dealt with immediately and categorically; moreover, criticism of the minimal protection afforded the lady is deflected by blaming the lacking security arrangement on the Julian administration and also the Senate for not rectifying this matter. Senate aides, speaking on condition of anonymity, either pointed the finger at insufficient political will or arcane bureaucratic regulations that stifle effective leadership.

How Does He Do It?

Ra-Ptahhotep II wins *yet another* Egypt Abroad Man of the Year award. Such presence, such spirit, such perception — this sage would have been honored in any era, in any place!

Trörööö!

Nocturnal Alexandria is as quiet as nocturnal Alexandria can be, the city's lovers and tavern-goers now also done for the night, but what noise do we hear coming from the Canopic Gate? "Stride forward with your left, clap to your left, clap to your left, stride forward with your right, clap to your right, clap to your right, stride forward with your ..." loud-whispered in the Egyptian of the Egyptians dwelling by the Red Sea and venturing out to other shores. And it is a cappella for only a while as the sound of pipes and flutes starts to emanate from somewhere inside the Jewish Quarter and winds and weaves through west- and southbound alleys and streets. Alexandria is roused from its slumber and quite unsettled as dithyrambic singers join the goings-on from yet another direction — Mareotis Way perhaps? Yet though there is much to be heard, there is nothing to be seen! No need to prick up your ears to make out lyrics such as "oh-so-Antonian, oh-so-Antonian, oh-so-presumably Antonian" nor is there any purpose in philosophy as this cannot be but a bacchanal, however ghostly.

On they move, those invisible satyrs and fauns and revelers, past the Gymnasium, over the Paneium, beyond the sanctuary of Isis, sparing the Serapeium, processing to and through the Sunset Gate only to evaporate even more abruptly than they first manifested. Huh! This sudden cease of harps and trumps and voices and the disorder preceding it are taken by one and all to augur the end of Antony, who has always identified as Young Bacchus, and that while Euius and Thriambus will forever be Bacchus, Antony's claim to any title and protection is now forfeit. Oh, he may dress in his dancing habit and carry the vine-branch all he wants, but his god has now bid adieu and taken his tumultuous leave and the great bastion of elation and merrymaking that is Alexandria is now unmoatedly open to the cunning contrivances, intrigues, and plots of Octavius and his ilk.

Freedom Will Be Defended in All Quarters

When Power speaks of Love, Power speaks of Power.
When Love speaks of Power, Love speaks of Love.
–Khamerernebty

Baboon pleading exemption from all labor passive baboon passive baboon passive baboon female baboon lamenting [the lack of navigable rivers(?)] joined by another female baboon lamenting [the lack of navigable rivers(?)] baboon rotated to the right baboon baboon upright baboon weapon-yielding baboon rotated to the right baboon baboon baboon yet another fucking baboon baboon baboon baboon twain of baboons raising clubs twain of baboons upside down baboons!
–Khamerernebty, quite emotionally lapsing into hieroglyphic

Now, as our undaunted troops brave the treacherous sea only to later have to make their way through even more treacherous terrain; now, as they have gone from everyone they love, possibly to never return; now, as they willingly expose themselves to hostility, heat, and perversion — we must most forcefully remind ourselves that those who stay behind also serve. And serve we shall! While we are these days not men of military action, we may presume to *some* influence in the public sphere — ours to use to *push* through superstition and prejudice, through misinformation and ignorance. And valor fights on, though persecuted!

So much has already been said on why we are in this war and so much bears repeating, but let us counter the newest attack on our highest traditions, a screed titled *Eternity is Egypt*, written by a certain Khamerernebty and shipped to our shores by subversives who can no longer call themselves Romans. It is *an unwieldy tome*, an uninterrupted desolation of a text that never seems to end, the typical prolix histrionic outpourings of a female nearing the end of her fertile years, there are far too many pages, not to mention *the sheer number* of words, it just goes on and on, an object too bulky to balance the ricketiest of tables ... This really is the kind of *arduous* read that makes a reviewer want to exchange his stylus for a sword just so that the end comes quicker. Yet the book is its own death: Egyptian platitude follows Egyptian platitude, the hatred for the first men of Rome *only confirms Egypt's pervasive misandrism*, and — though the work's length promises complexity — we are treated to the usual polarizing and unsophisticated *binaries* of Cleopatran feminists: Rome-Egypt and male-female, as if there were no other cultures, as if all men were the same, as if women could ever agree on anything.

Word is that that Khamerernebty is now "in love" with another woman — which only once more proves our point that wherever feminism goes, the dykes cannot be far behind. And the Two Lands region — a topsy-turvy place where animals become gods and gods become animals and where a life beyond counts more than the very real life to be lived in the here and now — regrettably but most understandably is *fertile ground* for such confusion. But it is not confusion as every child knows that only man can be man to woman; it is denial and defiance *against nature* — that, in due time, reasserts itself, no matter how much lavender oil they use, no matter how many scented candles they buy, and no matter how often they gather in groups to prattle on about their lot. "Lovers" become *mere cohabitants* sooner rather than later. Why, then, go to all that trouble? Families are torn apart, husbands are humiliated, and new life is denied entry into this world — for what? Simply put, it is nothing more than *just another case of épater les bourgeois for the sake of épater les bourgeois.* And once the ties are broken, these women have invested themselves so heavily in that new identity that they dare not correct their mistake.

But we are not unmindful that it is all of Egypt that needs rescuing. The man who — by some miracle — still commands a wife has a mate who will not respond to his embraces, who will not look at him when he comes to her, and who will yet have the gall to ask him what cannot be granted. As hard as it is, *we must not bear enmity* towards these wives as they who cannot respect their husbands cannot respect themselves and were led astray by their country's ruling elite.

How, then, to proceed? Not by prescribing the women their duties, but by empowering their men: 1) we raise self-esteem with both *actions* (male-only team-building exercises, assertiveness classes, having them "diary" and share their victories great and small, etc.) and *motivation* (letting no teachable moment go by without valuable feedback, assuming their success in worthwhile endeavors, gifting inexpensive goodies to celebrate achievements, etc.); 2) we *radically* confront and dismantle conscious and subconscious gender bias; 3) for entrepreneurs, we *supernetwork* intergenerational and even international connections in order to create masculine context across industries; 4) we furthermore have the Senate *grant official standing* to male village and neighborhood associations; 5) we let like-minded men sanction the "stragglers" among them who still conflate feminism with femininity (compassionately if possible, severely *if necessary*); 6) lastly and generally, we advocate and "press" maximum public acceptance of masculinity and male empowerment to *create an environment* in which Egypt's men are free: free from oppression, free from discrimination, free from insubordination, free to lead, free to invest, and free to innovate for the good of their country as much as that of all.

As Octavius so succinctly and correctly said, "Men's rights are human rights." That this may become a reality also in Egypt is our greatest wish.

With final thanks and profound acknowledgments to Croesus — father, mentor, and friend

Ra-Ptahhotep II, Acarnanicus Severus, Marcus Promptus, and Porcus Quintus

Antony, in Spite of Having Himself Voluntarily Confined to Quarters, Must Still Consider the Challenge of Another Proud Roman

"Parthia. Oh Parthia. What a clusterfuck. What a total and complete clusterfuck. All Octavia's fault. Egged on by Enobarbus, of course. Too smart for their own good. Stupid smart. Or totally stupid. All those legions just gone. Poof. Clusterfucked. So many men just wasted on some half-assed plan by civilians. And *my* sweat and *my* time. And almost my life, if it hadn't been for that Silius. Good man, that Silius. Even called me 'emperor.' That was nice. Silius. Another legion lost with that man. Sure, that was a lot. But they were just some guys. Nobody of name, really. At least they died for glory, for Rome. You win some, you lose some. Best to be philosophical. Why does this wine taste so familiar? And so bland? Today's selection of bottles seems to be even worse than yesterday's. When it comes to the sauce, that of Alesia remains unbeaten. Powerful, mature, fruity finish, with a hint of venison. Oh Trebonius! Just you and me, commended by Caesar! Now that was a man who knew how to reward his troops!"

Is our Antony capable of anything besides living in the past? This is most emphatically *not* the young SPQR officer near the beginning of his cursus honorum: resourceful, keen, very much in ascent. Have the beds in the East proven to be too soft, the gluttony of the court shown to be too much? Has Cleopatra been too complete in her bewitching of the triumvir? But General Priscus to the rescue! Venerable Priscus, the scourge of African regionalism, *famed* for his frequent lodging in the field, *famed* for his thoughtful presence, *famed* for his learned tutorials. Now the soothsayer has been picked to risk Antony's boozy ire, to tell the pharaoh's love of Priscus' very public proclamations: that it would not just be he who would reclaim Egypt from the errors of feminism, but that it would also be he who would personally fetch Antony, whether the traitor be sleeping off his hangover under the table or between womanish sheets.

Operation Enduring Midas

Globular jars and Sumerian logograms! What are all those whisperings, mutterings, and bare suppositions? Transports from all of Egypt to Alexandria, under cover of night, by birds of every wing? What has the narrow floodplain come to? Does the overflowing Nylus now presage famine?

Why would the caracal cat that is Cleopatra spend the last weeks of her reign prowling around the pharaonic warehouses of her city? Most unseemly, this sudden obsession with glittering gold and other shiny trinkets equally worthless in the world to come. Or is it? If the favor of the gods cannot be invoked with such baubles, then perhaps that of the Romans? A lesser monarch may indeed have harbored delusions of such a kind, but a Cleopatra knows that there is no bargaining with masters of iron.

In actuality, all that abundance is a Trojan horse of sorts, with riches as soldiers. Her Convolutedness wishes that the conquerors shall take that giant booty home to the center of their empire, where the poison will then work through the enemy's veins. Such stupendous wealth cannot fail to give birth to intrigue, to wear down justice, to instigate trouble between fathers and sons, to mix poisons, to have once-productive members of society turn aside after lucre and leave their posts. How can there be sowing-reaping-threshing when greed rules supreme, when every man has become a cobra lying in wait, when neglected youth cannot even name the Five Principles? Let Rome gorge itself on its ill-gotten gains.

Spartan Statement on the Death of Princess Arsinoe

The Equally Noble and Terrible Military Government of Sparta 1) calls the deadly feminist attack on Princess Arsinoe a cowardly deed done by Spartan rogue elements; 2) professes to be shocked by the speed at which said elements — all of whom had passed security and background checks — were radicalized; and 3) offers its most heartfelt condolences both to the Egyptian Government-in-Exile and to the servicemen of Legio Gemina who lost one of their brothers-in-arms in the line of duty, as well as a sincerely valued Nubian.

Quite Blunt, Quite Personal, from One Triumvir to Another

Hey Octavius, you phony little bitch!

You are *nothing* without your troops! Come and face me *like a man*! Hand-to-hand combat is what I dare you to! *This is for real!* I myself will proclaim you victor if you throw me down!

And *you know* that history will deem you a coward and a pansy if you don't do this!

So man up, boy!

Antony

Meta-Egyptology, the Study
of Egyptologists

It is to be observed that in many cases the Frenchman resident
in Egypt is only technically a Frenchman, the Italian may in
reality be only half an Italian in so far as his characteristics are
concerned, and the Austrian is often merely a subject of the
Emperor of Austria for purposes of Consular protection and
nothing more.
–Cromer

I was not visiting Egypt merely as a traveler, to examine its
pyramids and temples and grottoes, and, after satisfying
my curiosity, to quit it for other scenes and other pleasures:
but I was about to throw myself entirely among strangers; to
adopt their language, their customs, and their dress; and, in
associating almost exclusively with the natives, to prosecute
the study of their literature.
–Lane

"If they know anything, it's tactics, but not strategy."

"If Khamerernebty spoke to us, what would she say? That she was
flattered by our interest in her culture? That some of us have taken
this interest beyond obsession? That it would behoove us to address
the future rather than the past? That we are exaggerating the differences between our lives and hers? That all that has been said is
all that could be said? Or, conversely, that our methodologies, our
assumptions, our very minds are still utterly off the mark?"

"These days, the typical Western female's concept of Egyptological
activity is reduced to getting herself rogered by aspiring terrorists
in Sharm el-Sheikh. Or the woman disdains even that and sets out
for the interior, in search of 'A Moor of One's Own.' Sic transit glo-
ria mundi."

"What do you think? Indo-Persian?" — "Definitely Indo-Persian."

"Any mortals who with a pure heart engaged in studies of the Two Lands will be loved-protected-remembered by Horus and their names will be written in everlasting serekhs, no matter how seemingly insignificant their contributions."

"The common people of the world — provided they ever spare a thought for Egyptology — don't understand that Egyptology is not an Egyptian science, the museum-going crowd for the most part is equally ignorant, and even quite a few Egyptologists fail to make the connection.

What kind of Egyptology would we have had if Bernard de Montfaucon had not laid the groundwork with his superb *Antiquité expliquée et representée en figures*? And how could we have begun without Claude Etienne Savary — preromantic, captivating, profound — establishing the first proper literary-linguistic-religious bond with the Arab world? Constantin François de Chasseboeuf, feather-named Volney, in his *Voyage en Égypte et en Syrie* then painted a picture that was not of magical cultural opulence like that of Savary but a rather stark report of a region fallen from grace, with Egypt now being such an unfortunate land that of all the great powers only France would be able to rescue her — depressing, to be sure, but a vigorous call to arms heard from Marseilles to Cherbourg, from the Pyrenees to the Rhine, and above all in Paris, of course, much discussed in the salons and by the various factions vying for preeminence — including that of Bonaparte who years later embarked with a copy of his Volney in his luggage, as did his generals. Only a universal man such as Napoleon was French enough to recognize Egypt as "the most important country" that — once liberated — would once more yield its forgotten treasures to science. To that end, and under the aegis of General Caffarelli, over 150 savants from all branches of knowledge accompanied France to Egypt: mathematicians, poets, designers, zoologists, botanists, engineers, painters, astronomers, geographers, historians, and individuals sui generis — the very crème de la crème, among them such names as Fourier and Geoffroy Saint-Hilaire. So much progress did they make, so much did they discover, so much news did they announce that the natives declared them sorcerers! And it must have been sorcery indeed that yielded up the Rosetta Stone to soldiers under Pierre Bouchard in the summer of 1799! And once again at home, the creation of the landmark of landmarks, suggested by Louis Costaz, but ultimately the brainchild of four hundred men, the *Description de l'Égypte*. Twenty-five years of work produced six volumes on Egyptian antiquities, four volumes of memoirs of the expedition's participants, ten volumes covering modern Egypt including over a thousand pages of musicology but also Suez possibility studies, and finally six volumes spelling out Egypt's natural history. Egypt was returned to the world at last! And, one may say, France returned Egypt to Egypt, too: by way of the Institut français d'archéologie oriental du Caire; by way of the Museum of Egyptian Antiquities, also in Cairo, also founded by a Frenchman, and done by Marcel Dourgnon who put Ferdinand Faivre's wonderful Nekhbet on her fitting pedestal; by way of numerous books and articles illuminating Egypt's glorious past: to name but *Recherches sur le nom égyptien de Thèbes, avec quelques observations sur l'alphabet sémitico-égyptien et sur les singularités orthographiques, Revue retrospective à propos de la publication de la liste royale d'Abydos*, and *Le Calendrier des jours fastes et néfastes de l'année égyptienne: traduction complète du papyrus Sallier IV*, all by François Joseph Chabas, and of course also the *Dictionnaire des noms géographiques contenus dans les Textes Hiéroglyphiques* by Henri Louis Gauthier and *Coins d'Égypte ignorés* by Albert Jean Gayet who also did much for the Musée Guimet — and I haven't even mentioned Benoît de Maillet and Jean-François Champollion!

To be sure, Prussia, Italy, England all had their day in the sun, but the most French of sciences was, is, and always will be that of Egyptology."

"In my opinion — which I take to be the opinion of the department also — Egyptology — and field Egyptology most especially — has invariably been the happy hunting ground of middle daughters, thence propelled by the psychological conundrums particular to their station; very much the same can be said of shortish men, of whom *Le Petit Caporal* would be the most notorious example."

"That most of their major excavation breakthroughs did not come about because of painstaking planning or superior reasoning, but because one of their donkeys suddenly fell through the ground — is that the Egyptologists' dirty secret? Or is it rather their 'romantic' dealings with the local women, their 'above-board' entanglements with antiquities exporters of flexible morality, or their inability to deal with the modern world which got them into this useless pursuit in the first place?"

"Egyptology is the ankh of life, as are its priests."

Progress Report

Ramesside Stelae nome — secured; Lapwing Taking Flight nome — secured; Uneven Promise nome — secured; Injured Thigh nome — secured; Andjeti nome — secured; Pharaoh Confides in Bastet and Bastet Rewards Pharaoh with Love-Guidance-Encouragement nome — secured; Royal Flail and Crook nome — secured; Ass that Brays at Dawn nome — secured; Testifier to True Helmsmanship nome — secured; Behdet nome — secured; New Path Following Abating Sandstorm nome — secured; Three Inconsequential Field Laborers nome — secured.

The speed of liberation has outdone even the most optimistic SPQR projections bumping up the running of framework/sustainment missions as those forces now scramble to join the theater posthaste.

Winning lordship over a territory has never seemed so easy as nowadays, but what kind of satisfaction is there to a war when all you do is win?

Octavius Accepts Antony's Challenge

Antony,

I am ready to do battle in the manner you suggested.

Please follow the setting sun along the shore for twenty klicks from Alexandria. I will only have a minimal complement of personal slaves with me and will assume that you as a Roman will neither exceed that number nor come with any other company. By the time of your arrival, Lepidus as a neutral party will have put up a small infrastructure of tents and will also provide refreshments.

May this meeting prove to be the end of our argument.

Octavius

This Book Cannot Be Without Officer Latournerie, Brilliant-Courageous-Delicate Latournerie in Service to France

Since I arrived in Egypt, this place got to me. Disappointed by everything, I have suffered melancholy and malady: Tintyra has healed me; what I have seen today has repaid me all my tribulations; whatever may be in store for me following this expedition, I will all my life pride myself for having gone, for all the eternal memories that this day has given me.

Octavius Publicly Lauds Agrippa
During a Press Conference on Board
His Flagship *Protective Shield*

First, Octavius cracks a joke that when he as usual told Agrippa "festina lente!" Agrippa must have been in such a hurry that he misheard the second half (do we detect the hand of Acarnanicus Severus here?); following that, Octavius as expected switches from levity to substance and congratulates the man — in absentia, sadly, but bound by duty — on his quick victories. Interestingly enough, Octavius reminds those gathered around him of Agrippa's love of the arts and that a *modicum* of that element when coupled with evenness of mind and careful deliberation helps a commanding officer not only to at least partially understand the Egyptian mind, but also to successfully improvise in mostly data-scarce regions such as those now newly added to Rome.

Spontaneous Grassroots Creativity

And in every one of Egypt's liberated nomes — every one of them! — boys come together to form boy bands and those boy bands perform boy power anthems that transfix the attendant SPQR security personnel as absolutely as the local concert-going teens.

Antony Finally Takes Action

Provoked by the impertinence of Priscus and encouraged by the unusually accommodating Octavius, Antony leaves the comforts of the court and Alexandria in search of renewed honor, in search of renewed freedom, in search of renewed power. He actually finds himself rather enjoying the march along the coast, what with the sun shining and a gentle breeze blowing; some seagulls, too, nice signs of life and good company for the lonely wanderer at the head of a centuria. Twenty klicks, all in all? He now must be there within the hour.

"Sir! They are coming toward us!"

"Centurio? I can't see them — where?"

"Another centuria, ninth dune from the left!"

"Fuck! So many?"

"There are now also several triremes approaching, right in front! Shall we fall back?"

"Fall back?! Fall back?! Where to — Alexandria? They'd overtake us within minutes! No, we'll stand our ground right here, Centurio. Maybe Octavius will hold up his end of the bargain. If not, we'll finish them off — superior numbers mean nothing against superior men. Military history has proven that again and again."

"Sir, yes, sir!"

The commander of the enemy centuria now seems to bid his men halt and makes his way towards Cleopatra's husband.

"General Antony! We meet at last!"

"Priscus! What the fuck are you doing here?"

"Meeting you in personal combat, as per your request."

"As per my request?? With a dunderhead like you?!"

"Will this be a battle of words or a proper battle befitting the heroes of old?"

"I'm here to fight Octavius, not you, you nincompoop!"

Priscus draws his sword. "You offend my name, Antony! Defend yourself or run off to the safe bosom of your wife! Live or die! I swear I will let you escape with my spit on your face if you value your life more than your honor!"

Antony reflects. His soldiers could easily take care of the old fool, but then there might be a very serious confrontation with the enemy camp. And running in such a situation is out of the question, as any Roman troops worth their salt, however loyal, would be too aghast at such sordid meekness not to turn on their commander. Even if not, he would become as much of a laughingstock as Priscus.

"What is it going to be, my General?!"

"Where is Lepidus?"

"Lepidus is in Libya, as you should —"

Antony tries to hit Priscus, who — not exactly surprised — parries the blow. "Is that the hardest you can deliver, Antony?" Priscus, though a man silly enough to have been all but disowned by his formidable relatives, has quite the bodily strength for a crusty old geezer.

To match strength with strength might therefore not be the suitable tactic here, so Antony kicks Priscus in the shin and hits him over the head with his shield.

Octavius' substitute reels, but does not fall and answers Antony's deadly thrust in the same manner.

As both men now bleed out on the ground, Priscus strains his neck to face Antony for the very last time. "Heroes to the end, Antony, heroes to the end." Antony just groans and dies.

The Antonian escort, knowing the futility of their cause, at once surrender to the Octavians whose centurio insists on a "quick and dirty" burial of the two men in addition to the usual relinquishing of weapons.

Octavius himself does not even need to be informed of the outcome. His spies in Alexandria had already relayed Antony's taking of the bait, and further units nearby would — if necessary — have ensured the kill. That no troops needed to be wasted will certainly be welcome news, but the imbalance of power is now such that that may be considered a very minor matter indeed.

The Ranking of Nations

Loud-voiced Rome takes the judge's seat.

"A word," Egypt calls to the strapping boy. "A word, Rome, before your verdict! By what rule will you rate us?"

"By what rule? Why, by the measurable outcomes you have produced for us!"

Thou Shalt Have No Other
Gods Before Us

The Roman Ministry of Things That Are Not Normal has, in a strongly worded statement, dismissed the latest unicorn sightings as "the delusional ravings of Peloponnesian goatherders, who have long been known to be the worst possible kind of fame whores."

Pharaoh Octavius-Caesar-Augustus, He of the Sedge and the Bee, and His Humble Serving-Maid Cleopatra VII

Quarter by quarter all of Alexandria is secured by Roman infantry, as the natives stand by idly, seeming unfocused, dazed, possibly on drugs. The palace perimeter has been doubly secured as technical auxiliaries sketch out the interiors, their progress slowed down by false doors and large bathing complexes; meanwhile, demolitions experts check for improvised explosive devices and also assist army engineers in breaking down walls to allow for SPQR-adequate air ventilation. Although much of the palace must still be deemed unsafe, the message has been sent to the Praetorians that Cleopatra has been located and that the passage to her is sufficiently safe for Octavius to parley with the pharaoh.

Impatient to meet, Octavius marches into the labyrinth of a building, like a Theseus, with his troops serving as his thread. Unfortunately, Cleopatra's part is not seen as that of Ariadne. Then again, the queen also fails to assign the proper role to Egypt's liberator.

"Well, well, well, who's here? The man who can do the math to make all hell break loose. Or should I rather say, the fiend?"

"There is no need to demonize me, Pharaoh. Indeed, such a notion is symptomatic of a mindset that has fouled Egypt for far too long. Superstition, indolence, reflexive antipathy towards Rome — it is time for this country to set aside such childish attitudes and to join the ranks of civilized nations, out of enlightened self-interest, if for nothing else."

"So spoke Seth-Sokar-Apophis."

"I realize that recent developments have given you cause for bitterness. Yet I must say that your flamboyant reputation led me to believe that your conversational skills amounted to more than just ad hominem arguments."

"And you, sir, are like a really fat guy, sitting in a corner naked, playing with his wee wee."

Octavius sighs and shakes his head. "What, then, are you, Pharaoh?"

"I am no pharaoh, no queen, not even a wife anymore. What I am now I know not, but it cannot be more than only the dust under the feet of a really fat guy, sitting in a corner naked, playing with his wee wee."

Octavius had expected some meanness, some depravity, but that a female and an aristocratic female at that could evince such a distressing vulgarity of manners truly perturbs the man, to the point that he forgets himself and starts lecturing her, which had not been his original intent. "I have spent every year that the Fates provided me righting the ship of state, re-establishing much-demanded order, making sure that everyone's basic human needs were met, as fairly as possible. And what have you done? You have committed nothing but the sins of those whom the philosophers have pegged as exoticists: in search of the extraordinary, you scorned what obviously had to be done; pursuing mirage after mirage, you ruined your state; looking for meaning where there is none, you threw out everything tried and true. If all that had been merely your private pleasure ..." Octavius has stumbled in his rhetoric and starts again. "Worst of all, you enveloped Antony in your folly. I do not blame you solely for that as the man had faults of his own. However, he was a capable and dependable enough soldier and administrator before you spun your web. The sheer *chaos* the two of you managed to produce ..." He decides that he has said quite enough and aims to conclude. "The loss of life has been staggering and several provinces, not to mention the homeland, are still in uproar over the taxes we had to levy. So much so that most of our gains will have to be used to pacify our citizenry rather than go towards vital post-conflict reconstruction initiatives."

"As if I were the Marquise de Merteuil to your Madame de Tourvel!"

Octavius turns to his men. "This creature is past reason." He signals them to follow him back out to sanity and this they do, gladly.

A New Era of Peace

And he shall array himself with the land of Egypt, as a shepherd putteth on his garment.
–Jeremiah 43:12

They shut me up in Prose —
–Emily Dickinson

A carpentry detachment of Roman soldiers of the Pegasus III regiment ("with wings to the enemy") has set up a wooden platform-stage in Alexandria's largest park. When Octavius arrives with his Praetorian guards, they assume standard formation between the stage and the expectant crowd, while he briefly confers with two senior staff officers. Nods and salutes. Octavius mounts the stage and begins his speech:

"My friends and brothers,

I am much honored to have the chance to speak to you. Rome has never been interested in occupying Egypt. But your now safely deposed ruler forced our hand. Proving a disruptive element again and again, she engaged in aggressive acts against not only Roman trade ships and Roman patrol vessels, but also against such tribes as the Libu, the Meshwesh, the Kehek, the Sherden, and the Tursha, as well as several kingdoms bound to Rome by the strongest friendship and respect. Most gravely of all, Cleopatra aided and abetted Antony, a man who turned against his own people and whose foolish actions cost innumerable lives. But this dark chapter has now come to an end. I am here to tell you that as of today our seas — and Egypt itself — are free at last. This early morning, the last holdouts of unreason were neutralized. The Egyptian people — under the provisional leadership of the Roman Senate — can from this moment onwards lead productive lives unfettered by the psychological baggage of an admittedly illustrious, but ultimately deeply troubled queen. So now, my friends and brothers, let us together step across the threshold of dysfunction and forward into a new era of peace."

Required Reading?

Neither Cleopatra nor Antony ever got around to reading that sizzler *Roman Sea Superiority: A Probabilistic Geopolitical Perspective*. Come to think of it, they never cracked open *Cincinnatus and Cato as Fathers and Brothers*, either. And *The COUNTER-AGILE: 12 COUNTER-STRATEGIES from Gen. Fabius Cunctator, Explained and Expounded by the Very Same*? Or *ANOTHER 12 Ways of Thwarting the AGILE* by Fabius the Younger? Or if not those, then at least Sulla's *The SPQR Commandments of Statecraft: How to Govern Like a Pro*?

Does one really have to ask?

Would they have won if they had?

Denon Overwhelmed by Beauty

I was too astonished to judge; all my architecture, all my knowledge could not restrain my enchantment. What marvels for the scholar of antiquity!

But the time! I would have halted the sun, every single minute I used to observe and sketch and measure. Now I had only a few hours to reflect what it had cost centuries to conceive, construct, and so beautifully craft, under the direction of the priesthood and done by masters guided by unvarying principles. Every temple is of such equality that they all seem to have been manifested by the same hand; no neglect, no exaggeration on the part of a genius bent on distinguishing himself; oneness and harmony rule throughout.

Roman Shout-Boys

Roman shout-boys run up the dunes and proclaim all over the Two Lands: "Pyramids, you are now Roman pyramids; cats, crocodiles, dung-beetles, you are now Roman cats, crocodiles, dung-beetles; tents, houses, palaces, you are now Roman tents, houses, palaces; scribes, field-laborers, priestesses of Isis, you are now Roman scribes, field-laborers, priestesses of Isis; sands, winds, clouds, you are now Roman sands, winds, clouds ..."

An Auspicious Post-Liberation Measure

In a decree applauded throughout the Mediterranean region, the Roman Senate has recognized the Egyptian tradition of Hathorian undress as a permanent right, only limiting the free exercise thereof to those female citizens who are still under the age of twenty-five.

The clear majority of commentators, including almost all of the proper-serious-respectable commentators, are in agreement that this is a most merciful and tolerant stance that bodes well for Egypt's future as a member state of the Roman Empire.

Acarnanicus Severus Goes Deep

Is it possible that in fighting feminism and that dastardly woman we have only been fighting symptoms? Bear with me here, I know this is a bit of a curveball, a bit out of left field, a bit loopy even, but if you really think it through, what other underlying cause cannot be ruled out besides the sickness of the "science" of Egyptology? Which is itself only the outgrowth of Egypt? And that *that* is the root of all the evil that has befallen us?

Terrorism

Off-duty Romans in Egypt — wearing flip-flops! The horror!

A Question of Manliness

And so Penthesilea and her breed became much more manly than those created by nature as men, but whose sloth and gluttony had turned them into women, helmeted rabbits, even.
–Boccaccio, *On Famous Women*

Friends, Romans, readers of *SPQR Daily*,

as much as I am pleased to address you once more from liberated Egypt, the problem I now have to report on brings me great sorrow — the issue in question of course being the sad state of affairs that is the manhood of Egypt.

Last autumn, when I received advance intelligence on the matter, I was not ready to accept the shocking news sent by some of my most trusted agents. But now the consequences of female rule — and female rule at its worst — can no longer be denied: the men of Egypt are inconceivably, utterly, outrageously womanish. Not only were they unwilling to meet us in battle, in their dress and demeanor these "men" are scarcely distinguishable from their womenfolk. This is why I am personally overseeing a complete overhaul of the Egyptian school system. Per my order, any and all spa weekends have been cancelled, janitors are removing distracting artwork and children at the country's elementary schools are already being taught economics instead of — and that was true madness — Near Eastern women's studies. I am also committed to implementing further measures to ensure that Egypt's boys will grow up to be men worthy of being subjects of our empire. As far away as this new province can seem from Rome, we must make a stand here so as not to let such degeneration spread unchecked. Not to act boldly right here, right now, would invite ruin.

And this brings me to your part, fellow citizens. More than any other of our provinces, Egypt needs male role models — in a word, *fathers*. Until now, the boys of Egypt have been mismanaged, lost in dreams and beauty contests. We must not, we cannot, we will not remain indifferent to the plight of those boys. I call upon you to be fathers.

I am Gaius Octavius Caesar.

Not So! Not So!

Cleopatra was *not* strangled to death by a Roman counter-insurgency advisor!

Preposterous!

Post-Liberation Voices

"The Roman eating of animals is vile-depraved-barbaric! And some of their dealings with other lands are more than questionable. It is my belief, however, that we will be stronger together and that Egypt will — not soon, but soon enough — sway Rome onto the path of righteousness. And I say this as a scribe who has written many epistles on moral betterment."

"Egypt will repeat itself like fucking Abu Simbel! Fuck Rome!"

"We Egyptians — women *and* men — have lived the oh-so-precious *vie trop bien cultivée* long enough. Shoulder to the wheel, I vouch! Nose to the grindstone, I vouch! And I say this not just as an archaeobotany expert, but also as the author of *Plants in Egyptian Horticulture and Archaeology.*"

"Romans go home!"

"I, for one, look forward to Roman macroeconomic management as much as to their regulating the course of the Nile. And I say this as a simple farmer who has lost much harvest, both because of Cleopatran bureaucracy and because of seasonal flooding of my acres."

"What are we now? Phrygians?"

"Egypt gets a seat at the Mediterranean table at last! And I say this as a chef, a philosopher, an entrepreneur, a priest, and an all-around renaissance man."

"Egypt is forsaken-cast down-aggrieved!"

"Is there any general or king Cleopatra didn't sleep with? What did she really *do* outside of that? Sure, she considered herself a myth and a legend and got some people to believe that as well, but what self-centered bitch doesn't? Let's face it: at the end of the day, Cleopatra was just another starfucker in a very long line of starfuckers. And I say this as a Bubastis-based psychotherapist."

"The ba of Egypt will never be conquered!"

"Cleopatra may have been popular, yet that popularity did not come about by way of competent leadership; no, by way of anti-multi-culturalist rhetoric, by way of false dreams, by way of misandry. Furthermore, what kind of value has popularity among a credulous and easily impressed people who believed that that woman's rule was cosmically ordained? And I say this as a storeroom servant, having done honest work every day of my life, ever since I was a toddler."

"Change-Hope-Brotherhood!"

The Egyptian Book of the Dead

No, no, no, no! *The Egyptian Book of the Dead* is not *The Egyptian Book of the Dead*! *The Egyptian Book of the Dead* is *The Book of Coming Forth by Day*! A new life!

To See and to Be Seen

Near their bases, Roman soldiers see the Egyptian children, naked, and the Egyptian youths, near-naked, with little more than their anklets and Oriental makeup on to set them apart from brute beasts. And the Egyptian children, naked, and the Egyptian youths, near-naked, with little more than their anklets and Oriental makeup on to set them apart from brute beasts, see the Roman soldiers, with their helmets with cheek guards on, with their tunics on, with their belts on, with their swords on, with their cloaks on, with their military sandals on, and wonder why.

Confession Time

The truth is, we do not even know what a "pyramid" is anymore.

The Altar of Augustan Peace

Rome forms an important and splendid portion of the history
of the world, and is familiar to all from childhood: our earliest
years are passed amongst her poets, orators, and historians;
in ancient history her name is in every page, in modern it is
conspicuous; the most unlettered know more of Rome than of
any other nation.

–Burford

The four-sided block of stone might seem cold and impersonal, but
the visual message inscribed thereon produces a fine contrast: families and friends in tranquil process, in harmony, in quiet joy, the
man himself merely yet another modest father, yet another modest brother, yet another modest friend, helping hundreds of thousands and being helped by hundreds of thousands in turn. And
hundred-thousand-fold worthy of praise indeed is Augustus: he
who warred and granted mercy; he who stood up to feminism on a
Mediterranean level; he who mended aged water pipelines; he who
pressed forward with gender reform in matriarchal provinces; he
who doubled the delivery of the aqueduct of Marcia; he who penal-
ized inappropriate conduct regardless of rank; he who renovated
eighty-two temples; he who improved medical care and so reversed
falling birth rates; he who left out no temple of note; he who priori-
tized diversity of thought over that of identity; he who repaired the
Via Flaminia from Rome to Ariminum; he who very much mod-
erated extremism in Africa; he who rebuilt the bridges except the
Mulvian and the Minucian; he who scrapped outmoded course syl-
labi so that children would be free to reach their true potential; he
who overhauled veteran affairs; he who inspired every generation by
his attention to detail, by his graciousness, by his being a consum-
mate professional; he who raised awareness concerning the need
for an open and inclusive community of nations; he who provided
uncountable denarii out of his own coffers to victims of earthquakes
and other natural disasters; he who found Rome a city of plots and
left it a city of virtue.

Memories of Egypt

Rooks, pawns, kings and queens —
at the end of the game.
Masks abandoned in the ballroom —
at the end of the night.
A new lightness in the morning —
the awakened difference.

–Anonymous, *Arthur Schopenhauer for Babies* audio-script

A Greek research vessel holding its position off the coast; Enobarbus once more eating lunch all alone; a woman in labor in Hierakonpolis crying out for Meskhenet and Meskhenet easing her daughter's birth; travelers taking in Karnak as if in a dream; Iras and Charmian's first visit with Cleopatra; the building of the temple of Menkaure; a Roman cohort on deep-desert assignment; museum professionals readying unguent cones for homeward transport; the cow goddess Hesat giving her milk to worshippers near the First Cataract; a pair of Kharga Oasis scribes writing their names with throne signs in jest; Octavius, amused by nothing, taking his hasty leave; fisticuffs and debauchery in the new VIP chariot parking lot; nomes in their festival; Livia Drusilla opining on Philae that Egyptian knowledge, though old and great, is of course mostly false; local recruits learning Roman logistics systems; Cleopatra-class stationery for mash notes being introduced on the occasion of her falling in love; birders in the Delta encountering Hatmehyt at Mendes; restoration workers in the Valley of the Queens; a sheepish-looking Antony at a Crédit Agricole ATM in downtown Alexandria, and not much later and not much further, a proud Agrippa personally confiscating an alley of design studios in its entirety; couples walking along the Corniche in the early evening; street vendors, engaging in merchant-to-merchant banter, packing up their wares; beautifully tan children at play in the surf; convivial storytellers relaying their treasures in small cafés across the Pharaonic city; Porcus Quintus at a newly built sports and recreation facility, feasting twice a day and once a night; all of weatherworn Egypt (irregular damage to the surface, various small sections now considered lost to erosion and theft) changing day by day and contradictorily staying the same; mentors mentoring mentors-to-be in philosophy, religion, the arts, the crafts, the sciences, a gentle touch here, a correction there, the whole world drawn in a book ...

POSTSCRIPTUM

Sources and Further Reading

Will mich unter Hirten mischen,
An Oasen mich erfrischen,
Wenn mit Karawanen wandle,
Shawl, Kaffee und Moschus handle;
Jeden Pfad will ich betreten
Von der Wüste zu den Städten.
Will in Bädern und in Schenken,
Heilger Hafis, dein gedenken.

–Goethe, West-östlicher Divan

Quotations, first of all, range from the purely invented such as that from Per-Sekhemkeperre to those that are only true in sentiment — Cato, Cicero, Marcus Aurelius — to those left uncorrupted. The exact origins of the majority of the last category should be easy enough to trace, but let me give particulars concerning the rest: the name Burford stands for the nineteenth-century exhibition-maker Robert Burford, an excerpt of whose *Description of a View of Rome, Ancient and Modern; with the Surrounding Countryside* I simply could not exclude from this tale; equally indispensable from the novel's debates I found the wisdom of Joseph Hoffmann, given the alias of Josephus Septentrionalis in these parts. My French bookshelf consisted of Voltaire's *Dictionnaire philosophique*, Corneille's tragedy *Cinna*, Choderlos de Laclos' *Traité sur l'éducation des femmes* (in which Mirabeau is quoted), and Napoleon's *La campagne d'Égypte et l'avènement 1798-1799*, to be found among his *Correspondance générale*; all translations into English from French, as well as from any other languages, are mine.

Yet more literary banditry of mine ("intertextuality") are the occasional phrases borrowed from Shakespeare or other classics of English literature — those readers eagle-eyed enough to spot them may call themselves true children of Horus.

I also have to acknowledge an artistic debt to entire legions of marvelously daft "intellectuals" who think themselves as knowledgeable-wise-cunning as Thoth-Ptah-Seth and attempt to communicate as such. What would the world be like without their kind? I dare not imagine.

On a slightly more serious note, I wish to recommend the following works and authors: for the most royal queen specifically, Lucy Hughes-Hallett's philosophical *Cleopatra: Queen, Lover, Legend*, Bridget Escolme's Shakespearean *Antony and Cleopatra*, and Patricia Southern's straightforwardly historical *Antony & Cleopatra*; for Egyptology in general, there is so much worthwhile material that I could not possibly list it all, but among the cream of the crop you will definitely find books by Barry Kemp, Brian Fagan, Miriam Lichtheim, John L. Foster, Hilary Wilson, and Richard H. Wilkinson — if none of these names mean anything to you, start with the wonderfully accessible and just plain wonderful *Ancient Egypt: A Very Short Introduction* and the beautifully illustrated Egyptian volume in Wiley's *Dictionaries of Civilizations* series; for the Roman Empire, the eponymous *Very Short Introduction*, Matyszak's *Ancient Rome on Five Denarii a Day*, Beacham's *Spectacle Entertainments of Early Imperial Rome*, Plutarch's *Lives* as translated by Dryden (the second volume especially), Gibbon's *Decline and Fall of the Roman Empire* (take a sabbatical for this one), and Montesquieu's *Considérations sur les causes de la grandeur des Romains et de leur décadence*; for troops and warfare in antiquity, consult the works published by Osprey, all very competently done; for antiquity in general, the wildly entertaining *Classical Bearings* by Peter Green; for Napoleon, Macdonell's witty *Napoleon and His Marshals*; for stylishly written early feminism, you can do no better than Mary Wollstonecraft's *Rights of Woman* and Lady Montagu's *Woman Not Inferior to Man* (but read her travel writing as well); for a modern feminism, combined with a "Global South" point of view, read books by Chandra Mohanty.